TO CONQUER A MOUNTAIN

TO CONQUER A MOUNTAIN

A NOVEL

Jeanie Flierl

CLADACH
Publishing

Published by Cladach Publishing
PO Box 336144 Greeley, CO 80633
http://cladach.com

Cover Illustration and Front Cover Design by:
Jeff Gerke, www.jeffgerke.com

Author Photo: Jamie Herrera Photography

ISBN: 9781945099014

Printed in the United States of America

Dedicated to my husband, Denis, who spent hours and hours brainstorming with me. Thank you for your love, support and encouragement from one writer to another.

PROLOGUE 🍃

With mixed emotions Nora surveyed the bustling kitchen of the Tea and Java du Jour.

For a one hundred and ten year old Victorian house, the kitchen shined, everything state of the art. The commercial dishwasher in the corner waited to ease the cook's job. The eight-burner gas stove—on which two gleaming stainless steel soup pots simmered—would make any chef envious.

The prep tables held everything needed for the day. The aroma of the fresh basil waiting to go into sandwiches filled the kitchen. Next to the basil sat softened cream cheese and sun-dried tomatoes, prepared chicken salad, sliced cucumber and chopped dill—fillings for today's petite sandwiches.

Georgia, the long-time manager of the shop, worked with efficient moves. The tall, Southern transplant knew her way around a kitchen. Over her jeans the red head always wore an apron with pockets. Nora hoped to learn from her, mirroring Georgia's actions the best she could, being much shorter than the willowy Georgia and feeling that, though she was the owner and boss, she was definitely the inferior person in the kitchen.

No time to ruminate. Customers would arrive in thirty minutes.

Together the two women created the last of the

three kinds of sandwiches, first cutting crusts off the artisan bread using long bread knives, then assembling the layers.

With relief in her hazel eyes, Nora stepped back. "Georgia, I couldn't do this without you."

Georgia shook her head, which bounced her red curls. "You'll be a pro in no time."

Nora sighed. "You make it look easy. You don't seem to waste a single step."

"Girl, it's all in the organization." Georgia winked. "Find the most efficient way to prep in the mornings, know what menu works best for each day of the week, and shop for all ingredients the day before."

Nora leaned against the door frame.

Georgia continued, "Monday through Friday we have the same menu each week. Then Saturday is manager's choice."

"So every Monday you have the same choices for soup, salad, scones, sandwiches, and dessert?"

"Yes!" Georgia smiled. "See how easy that makes it."

Nora glanced at the clock again. "But what do you mean by manager's choice?"

"That just means whatever is in season will be featured." Georgia put her arm around Nora's shoulders. "Y'all don't have to learn this in a week. A month from now you'll wonder why you ever worried."

Nora folded and unfolded the tea towel. "You have more faith in me than I have."

Georgia checked on the soup and declared everything ready for the first customers. "Come on, Nora. It's eleven o'clock. Let's sit down and have a cup of tea. While the waitresses do their magic, you can tell me all about Tatum and the online dating thing."

Nora gladly accepted the cup of steaming, fragrant tea. She joined Georgia at the small kitchen table. She shook her head. "Can you believe my timid girl doing something as risky as going online to find a date? And who does she find there? Someone completely different from her!"

Georgia laughed musically, her green eyes sparkling with mischief. Nora couldn't help but feel her heart warmed by Georgia's contagious joy.

"Girl, you think your daughter is timid but I see a strong backbone. To my way of thinking, this online dating shows it. And maybe the apple didn't fall far from the tree. After all, who'd a thunk it? At your age, doing something as risky as buying a new business?"

"Your staying on as manager is the only way I would agree to buy this restaurant."

"I love working here, and I'm just glad you kept me on. Working with you is a pleasure."

Nora smiled back at her new friend, took a sip of the comforting tea and felt herself relax. "Well, I don't doubt Tatum thinks her dad and I are crazy buying a new business at our age. But we couldn't just do nothing in our retirement years."

"I'm sure you and Nathan would never be satisfied to just sit around." Now Georgia glanced at the clock. "Let me make sure the coffee is ready. Then we can talk more. I want to hear about Tatum's young beau."

Nora stared into her cup. *What can I say about the man Tatum might marry? Handsome and extremely fit, for sure, but....* She twisted and untwisted the tea towel in her lap.

When the kitchen door swung open, Nora had a glimpse of the customers waiting in line for a table. Finished with her tea, she went out to look, and even the tables on the wrap-around porch had filled with customers.

She and Georgia sprang into action. Not until two hours later did they take a break and continue their conversation.

🍃 🍃 🍃

Georgia handed Nora another cup of tea. "A nice rush of business! Your lemon raspberry scones were quite a hit. I had five customers buy extra to take home. Y'all should make some of those again soon."

Nora smiled, feeling a glow from the praise. She took a sip of the delicate, crisp-apple and cinnamon tea.

"Now, tell me what you think of Eric."

Cradling her chin in her hand, Nora said, "The obvious answer is he's good looking and athletic. But I think you're asking me about his character. First, he says he's a believer and that his faith is important to him. That's important to her dad and me, too." She unconsciously twisted a piece of hair escaped from her hairnet.

Georgia nodded in agreement then leaned forward.

"What else?" she asked.

"Recreational mountain sports are high on his list of priorities." She paused, and frowned. "That's where I see some potential conflict. Tatum won't relate to his outdoor/mountaineering interests at all. Will there be times when his love of the mountains out-weighs his love for her? Will she be left at home too many days?"

"I understand what you're saying, but you say they've talked about expectations. Hopefully there won't be any big surprises. And, again, we don't want to underestimate Tatum." Georgia raised one eyebrow in a comical fashion that made Nora giggle. Then she turned serious again.

"Maybe Nathan and I have protected our only child too much. Maybe we should have let her make her own decisions more."

"Nora Kessler, you did a great job with Tatum. And if I remember correctly, didn't she go after a different degree in school than what you and Nathan wanted for her?"

Nora chuckled. "Yes, she got her degree in finance instead of social work, much to her dad's chagrin. I guess she has more backbone than I'm giving her credit for. Thanks, Georgia, for sharing your honest thoughts with me. It helps me to see my daughter through different eyes." She rose from the table. "How time has flown! It's almost time for Nathan to pick me up. Thank goodness, I can leave the Tea and Java in capable hands."

They heard a sound at the window and looked up to see Nathan outside waving to them. As Nora went out the door, she called over her shoulder, "See you tomorrow."

A moment later, as Georgia was preparing a fresh pot of coffee, the silence was shattered by the horrific sound of tires squealing and then a crash. She startled, dropped the coffee filter she was filling, and ran to the window to see what had happened and to whom.

BLOG:

May 20

Random Ramblings—My New Life

Welcome to the first blog post of my new life. I, Tatum Kessler, am newly orphaned. I have to learn how to live without my parents, who've always been there for me. I'll be totally honest with my feelings in these posts. This blog won't be published to the whole world, just to the close friends who I know will join me on this journey, trying to make sense of where circumstances have thrown me. #joinmeonmyjourney

1 🍃

"Hey, Nicole."

Tatum typed a message on her iphone. "Garage sales tomorrow? Let me know."

In less than a minute Nicole replied. "Sounds great, roommate. Let's ask Heather too. She loves friendly competition."

"Be ready to go by seven. We'll get coffee first. Not too early for you, is it?"

Nicole texted back, "Ha. Too early for you?"

Tatum sent the same message to Heather. Then, "I'll be at your door at seven."

Heather shot back, "You know we'll be waiting on Nicole."

The three former roommates' ritual of gleaning treasures from other people's cast offs always involved easy teasing. Tatum liked it that way.

Her life had changed so dramatically lately. After having to adjust to living in the Breckenridge house her parents left her, owning a business, and no longer living and working in Denver, she didn't want any more drama.

🍃 🍃 🍃

As she walked up the sidewalk, Tatum glanced at her

phone. Right on time. Heather answered the knock, gave Tatum a comforting hug, and the two girls sat waiting for Nicole's arrival.

"'Punctuality' and 'Nicole' are never used in the same sentence." Heather shook her head, blonde hair swishing.

Tatum, with medium-brown hair, medium tall, giggled.

"You could have just walked in, Tate. You lived here till recently."

"Yeah. Thanks again for letting me out of the lease so I could move to my parent's house and take over at the Tea and Java du Jour." Tatum wrung her hands.

"Bishop Financial just isn't the same without you. We especially miss you in the lunch time rotation for receptionist duty." Heather's eyes twinkled teasingly.

Tatum made a face.

"We all understand why you took a leave of absence."

"I miss all of you, but I have so many loose ends in my life right now. Just need to step back."

"Don't worry, all your clients are well cared for. When you're ready, you can return."

Tatum smiled her appreciation just as Nicole, a brunette, came strutting down the stairs. Always the drama queen!

"I'm only ten minutes late. I'm getting better, don't you think?" Her two friends rolled their eyes and laughed.

"Remember, whoever finds the best deals gets to buy

lunch," said Nicole, deflecting any "late jokes."

Heather's blue eyes flashed. "Let the games begin. After we get coffee, where should we go?"

Tatum had done her homework. "A subdivision in Parker is having a neighborhood garage sale. We can park the car, hit four or five driveways within sight of each other, then move on."

To save time, they decided on drive-through coffee. With latte in hand, Nicole pushed her hair behind her ear. She glanced at Tatum in the rearview mirror. "What's it like living as a lady of leisure in the mountains?"

"I despise change, especially change I can't control. I know nothing about owning a business like the Tea and Java du Jour. Thank heaven, Georgia is managing the daily routine. I depend on that Southern lady."

"Sounds exciting to me."

"I'm so out of my element! Running a business is a giant step from helping people with financial planning." Tatum sighed. "The house is amazing, though. It's located just over Hoosier Pass, a three-bedroom, three-bath home on two acres. At ten-thousand feet elevation, I have incredible views of Mount Lincoln and Mount Bross."

"Wow. If you ever get the urge to hike those fourteeners, let me know," Nicole said.

Tatum shuddered. "Absolutely not! I'm perfectly content to admire their beauty from afar. I don't think I'll ever get tired of gazing at the scenery outside my window, though."

"What do you do all day in your mountain town?" asked Heather. "I'm rather envious."

"When I'm not at the tea shop, I'm slowly packing away my parents' stuff; but it brings back such memories, it'll take me forever." Tatum swallowed the lump in her throat then switched to a less emotional subject. "Oh, I'm now the proud owner of a cat named Spartacus. He's definitely a fighter, not a lover, but we're gradually becoming friends."

"I didn't think you liked cats. Just shows how well you're handling all this," said Heather.

"I don't know. There are so many questions. Who's going to walk me down the aisle when the time comes? Who's going to baby sit my children? Who's going to answer my questions about family? I don't think I can do this alone."

Heather turned in her seat to look at Tatum. She had tears in her eyes. "Tate, all those questions are legitimate, but you don't need the answers all at once."

"We don't have many answers, but Heather and I both have shoulders you can lean on any time," said Nicole. "Speaking of time, we have to put this conversation on hold, because here we are. Let the best girl win."

The morning passed quickly. The hunt for treasures in the midst of junk was just what Tatum needed to get her mind off her troubles.

"Tate, you won that round. I saw that metal bird house at the same time you did, but you got there first. Two dollars! What a steal. But wait until the next house." Nicole marched up the next driveway. "Watch how it's done, girls."

Nicole found a cute basket containing everything needed for a perfect picnic for two. As she bartered to get this treasure for less than marked, Tatum slipped in and snatched the basket. She gave the woman's husband the amount marked, then waited at the end of the driveway.

"What? How did you do that?" Nicole asked, wide-eyed. "You don't even like competition, and here you are winning. Let's put our treasures in the car and drive to the next street."

At lunchtime, the three friends sat at an outdoor café table and tallied up their acquisitions.

Nicole put on a pout when Tatum and Heather scored better than she did. That meant she had to buy lunch. She laughed and said, "We need to do this more often. It's not the same without you, Tate. Thanks for coming. But before you get away, tell us: is this serious boyfriend of yours as good as he looks on paper?"

"Oh, I was upset with you guys. You were relentlessness about the online dating thing. But now I'm glad. Eric's even better than his profile! Hope this doesn't sound too cliché, but he's tall, dark and handsome. And his eyes are really as blue as his picture."

Heather lifted her eyebrows and Nicole pretended to swoon.

Tatum made a face. "And guess what? No, you'll never guess.... I've agreed to go hiking with him! Can you believe that? I'll tell you all about it next week."

2 🍃

The day dawned picture perfect, the bluebird-colored sky holding only a hint of clouds. The rising sun would quickly warm the crisp, cool air. Parking near the trailhead, Eric was in his element. His sapphire eyes twinkled.

"Tatum, turn around and you'll see why I wanted to leave so early."

Tatum looked. Clouds behind the ridge glowed pink and orange. "No painter's pallet could match those colors."

As they started up the trail, Tatum's senses came alive. "Ahh. The air smells fresh. And the sound of the stream thundering down the mountainside—I can almost feel it." She stopped walking. "We won't have to cross that, will we?"

Eric grinned at her. "We cross at a bridge. There's an old mine up here. I want to take a picture of you in front of the sign that says 'Trespassers Will Be Shot.'"

"What? You're not serious, are you?"

Eric laughed."The look on your face is priceless. I'm serious about the sign, but no one will be shooting at us."

Tatum felt only slightly relieved. "We're not going to the top of that mountain, are we?" She pointed to the rocky peak looming over them to the southwest.

"We're on the back doorstep of that fourteener, Mount Quandary. I've climbed that one four times, twice in the summer and twice in the winter. Someday you can climb it with me, I hope."

"Uh, no hikes like that any time soon. Let's see if I can get through this one first."

They trekked on up the steep road that had been used by miners. Wildflowers bloomed prolifically on both sides of the road, their yellows and purples contrasting beautifully with the browns and grays of the soil and rocks. They came to the wide board bridge just as Eric had said. With the spring runoff flowing at its peak, they had to shout to be heard.

"Where does all that water come from? Is it only snow melt?"

"Yes. Just wait till you see the waterfalls."

They passed a dilapidated cabin with thick logs pushed over like tinker toys in a playroom. "Wow, Eric. How old do you think it is?"

"My guess is at least one hundred fifty years old. Can you imagine living in that cabin summer and winter?"

Tatum shook her head.

"The gold miners must have been a hardy lot."

They continued up the trail, rounded a huge boulder, and entered the pine forest. Diffused light came through the canopy of trees. The dry, floral scent of the sunlit meadow gave way to the more earthy smells of decomposing pine needles, wet dirt, and decaying wood. A thick growth of trees blocked the sounds of the cascading water pouring through the rocky gorge. The hush sent tingles up her arms. Tree roots crisscrossed the trail, forming steps. The damp ground muted their footfalls.

With awe Tatum whispered, "Feels like a cathedral. I never knew what I was missing."

"Wait till you experience the water crashing through the gorge, and see the rock walls surrounding the lake. The beauty of nature—reading about it in a book doesn't compare to the actual experience."

The trail broke out of the forest into a sunny, wild-flower-dotted meadow. The warm, light breeze carried grassy, floral scents in all directions.

Tatum stopped and pulled out her phone to take pictures of the Indian Paint Brush and Alpine Wall-flowers. Then she spotted yellow Butter and Eggs. Quick tears stung her eyes. "One of my mom's favorites."

Eric nodded and looked away.

It wasn't the first time Tatum sensed his discomfort with sudden emotion.

They walked in silence for a while until they reached the talus field, then Eric eased into his instructor mode. "It's sometimes called a scree field. But *scree* means smaller rocks, not these larger ones. You go first, because if you try to step on the same rocks I take, you'll be frustrated pretty quickly. Almost none of these rocks are loose, so just take your time. Pick your route, and I'll be right behind you."

They crossed slowly but easily. When they reached the falls, they sat on a rock in the sunshine. A fine spray of mist cooled them as they drank from the water bottles and ate trail mix. They had to speak louder to be heard over the fast moving liquid descent. Tatum felt energized. Eric had opened to her a whole new world.

She stood and pulled Eric to his feet. "Let's go!"

Although the trail to the lake proved somewhat more difficult, they took their time and she found the destination well worth the journey. The crystal clear water reflected the amphitheater-like rock walls.

"You were right, Eric. This is heavenly." Again she twirled around, this time ending up facing west. "Hey, is that a mountain goat at the end of the lake? So cool." She looked upward. "But those clouds look like they're growing."

"That's the only uncontrolled danger in mountain climbing. We just have to get off the mountain before the afternoon storms come. There's plenty of time; but let's head down." Tatum could have spent all day exploring around the lake, but the white fluffy clouds were turning dark.

After a twenty-minute descent, Tatum stopped to rest. "This is harder and scarier to me than going up. But it doesn't feel like the heights I imagined."

They had just enough time to make the quick detour to get the picture near the old mine, which did, indeed read *Trespassers Will Be Shot*. They sprinted the last two minutes to the car, with lightning flashing and thunder rumbling. The downpour had come.

"That was awesome. I'm totally won over. I'll gladly go hiking again."

"We'll do another moderate hike. Maybe then you'll consider hiking a fourteener. Do you think you might? I know you can do it."

Tatum laughed. "When should we go?"

Eric gave her a hug, then started the car. "Let's go in August. We met on December fifth. We'll tackle Bierstadt on August fifth. Now let's find something to eat in Breckenridge. I'm starving!"

🍃 🍃 🍃

As they started with chips and salsa in their favorite Mexican restaurant, Tatum laughingly asked, "Do you remember the first time we met? We had talked on the phone but it was our first face to face. I was afraid I'd find out you had used someone else's picture in the online dating profile."

"Ha. I guess I was a little worried about the same possibility." He chuckled.

Tatum looked into his eyes. "Tell me exactly what you thought when you first saw me. And no joking around. Be serious."

Eric broke their gaze and stared at his water glass with a far-away look in his eyes. "I didn't go to the online dating site to find a fun girlfriend, I went on there to look for a potential, godly wife. So my first thought when I saw you open the door of the coffee shop was, 'Lord, is this the one you want me to share the rest of my life with?'" He placed his hand on the table as if reaching toward her.

"Eric, that is so sweet." She leaned over the table and

placed her hand over his larger one. "I have to admit my thoughts were only about me messing up that important meeting. You were just like your profile picture, which was a relief, but you seemed so perfect, I figured I was out of my league." She pulled her hand back with a wry grin.

Eric chuckled, dipped a chip in salsa, then popped it into his mouth. "Well, by now, you know I'm not perfect. You, on the other hand, are more than I could ever have hoped for. You have all the attributes I wish I had. You're patient, kind, thoughtful, loving. You especially give grace, something I need to learn. Should I go on?"

"No, that's enough." She chuckled and waved her hand in front of her face. "And to think we both joined the Christian dating site on a dare. My roommates' shenanigans made me do it. Who did you say dared you?" She reached for a chip, enjoying the crisp saltiness. She decided against the hot salsa, though.

"My good climbing buddy, Alex. He was relentless; I did it to get him off my back. I was upset at first that he kept pushing, but now I'm thankful. I'd never have met you otherwise."

Tatum took a drink of water. "I love that you challenge me to be more than I am. If you'll be patient with me, I'll probably even climb the fourteener with you. But I still have a fear of heights." She shuddered a little and squeezed her arms as if cold. "Tell me more about this mountain you want me to climb with you."

Eric eased into his element, talking about the mountains he loved and the challenges they presented. "I've climbed Bierstadt six times, I think. It's the fourteener closest to Denver, so that's where I take friends who want to climb their first fourteen-thousand foot peak. I wouldn't exactly call it a walk in the park, but Bierstadt is the easiest one to climb, and I know you can do it."

"It sounds scary but maybe I'll give it a try." Now that she was off the mountain, her fearful imaginings again outweighed her actual experience. She decided to change the subject.

"On your profile you said you have a brother. Tell me about him."

"If I don't mention him often, it's because Walker is the black sheep of the family." A pained look crossed Eric's face. He paused but looked like he had more to say, so Tatum waited.

"In fact, he was such a disappointment to my parents that I tried to make up for it by doing whatever my father wanted me to do. I became an attorney like dad, but I drew the line at joining his practice."

"I wonder what I'd have done differently if I wasn't an only child. I always wanted a sibling."

"Mine isn't the kind you would want. Walker's been in and out of jail for petty offenses—and to add insult to injury, he even brags about it. Makes family gatherings awkward. I almost wish I had been an only child."

"It has its up sides." Tatum wasn't sure she wanted to go there but surprised herself by continuing. "My parents spoiled me in many ways, I'll admit. But when it came to issues of character they were super strict. I don't think I've told you yet about my three speeding tickets in one year when I was sixteen. They didn't ground me; but my freedom was certainly restricted when I lost my license. They just reminded me about consequences of my choices. But when they caught me lying about where I'd been, they took my car away for two weeks." She winced.

Eric chuckled sympathetically but looked wistful. "I sure wish Walker had learned that lesson." Then he straightened in his chair and changed the subject. "I haven't seen your house in Alma yet. Since we're in Breck, what do you think about taking me to see it?"

"Sure. Let's go!—after we eat, that is. Here comes our lunch, and it looks delicious. That hike famished me."

🍃 🍃 🍃

The rain slowed their ride over Hoosier Pass, but by the time they drove into Tatum's driveway, the skies had cleared.

"This has to be the most amazing view of Mount Lincoln and Mount Bross I've ever seen, except for actually climbing them. Wow. I don't think I could just look at these all day without wanting to be out there!"

"I don't ever get tired of the view, but I've never had the desire to be out there—before. Now you've given me a whole new perspective."

She showed him the rest of the house and he commented politely, but he kept glancing toward the picture window with the westward mountain view.

"Why don't we go to the Tea and Java du Jour and

see if we can catch Georgia. I know you've met her, but we've really not spent much time with her. She means more and more to me since my mom died. She'd never forgive me if she found out we were in Breckenridge and didn't stop to say hi."

Thirty minutes later, they walked in the back door of the restaurant. Georgia looked up from vegetable chopping, surprised delight on her face. She wiped her hands on her ever-present apron, gave Tatum a hug and exclaimed, "Girl, y'all make my heart glad. Thanks for stopping in." She offered a hand to Eric. "So good to see you again, Eric. What brings you to Breck today?"

Before they could answer, she sat down at the small table and, with an air of gratitude and expectation, gestured toward the other two chairs.

Eric sat. "Tate and I went on a hike and I introduced her to one of my other loves—Mt. Bierstadt." He winked at Tatum.

Georgia's eyebrows arched. "Tatum!"

"I know. Can you believe it? Eric is good for me. He stretches me in areas I've avoided all my life."

Eric looked pleased. "I'll be sure to take a picture of her on the summit, to prove just how brave she is."

"Georgia, we can't stay long. But I couldn't be in Breckenridge and not get a hug from my Southern momma."

"I'm so glad y'all came by. And I appreciate the excuse for a break."

In the car on the way home, Eric made an observation. "I don't think she likes me very much."

"Why would you say that? Georgia likes everybody. Maybe she's feeling protective of me. I'm sure as she gets to know you, she'll love you just like she loves me."

The ride back to Denver was quiet. Tatum dozed. The mountain air and exertion took more out of her than she would have believed just yesterday.

BLOG:

June 4

Random Ramblings—Mountain Experience

I did it! I went hiking with Eric and loved it! All my senses came alive: colors more vibrant, smells more pleasant, sounds more distinct, the air more fresh. The heights that loomed in my imagination, didn't materialize. I think one more foray into the mountains for practice, and I'll be ready for Mount Bierstadt. #bringiton

Heather: *Good for you!*

Nicole: *Just saw this post from two days ago. I must say, you're amazing!*

3 🍃

Eric and Tatum were enjoying lunch at their favorite food truck location in the Highlands. They ate quickly in anticipation of ice cream for dessert.

"Tate, some of my friends decided to stay at Francie's cabin this weekend. Would you go with me?"

"Will Francie mind an extra person?"

Eric laughed. "There's no Francie. The cabin is part of the thirty-one huts in the Tenth Mountain Division Hut Association."

"Hut? Sounds primitive..."

Again he laughed. "Francie's is an amazing log cabin that sleeps twenty, just a few miles from Breckenridge. You pass the turn off twice a day when you work at the Tea and Java. It's only a mile hike from where we'll park the cars. The only primitive part is no electricity."

"And that's fun?" She frowned.

"It has solar-powered lighting and lanterns." Eric crossed his arms with feigned reproach. "Don't say no until you've heard this."

Tatum stubbornly mimicked his crossed arms but remained silent.

"There'll be eight of us—four couples—make that five if Alex and his fiancée come." He waited.

She didn't reply—just frowned disapprovingly.

"One couple offered to cook gourmet meals for us."

Tatum uncrossed her arms.

"We'll be staying two nights and take short hikes each day. They won't be any harder than our last one." He looked at Tatum expectantly.

She finally laughed. "If it's like our last hike, I'll go."

Eric hugged her with joy and kissed her lightly.

The high country at the end of June had dressed in her wardrobe of wildflowers. The one-mile hike to the cabin only took a half hour. The trail was actually a very steep four wheel drive road. A jeep passed as they started out and they had to get off the narrow road to let it by.

"What pleasant views of the creek. I think I prefer the powerful sounds of the raging stream, though."

Eric nodded. "Each area has its own beauty. That's why every visit to the mountains is so refreshing."

The steep, tree-lined avenue offered nary a switch to break up the ascent. The breeze coming through the spruce pines felt nothing like the sanctuary she remembered. Was she going to compare every hike to the first one? They rounded a bend and there stood a two-story log cabin. Tatum gawked. "Eric, *this* is the cabin? Who woulda thunk? Clear up here."

Eric looked pleased. "Isn't it awesome? These huts make the wilderness accessible. And this one makes it downright comfortable."

"How could anyone build it, up here in the middle of nowhere?" She tried to imagine hiking in with all the materials to build this impressive structure.

"This road is a summer four-wheel-drive road. So it's not too difficult." Eric smiled. "This hut's the nicest and least primitive. Any other questions?" Eric laughed at her but sounded pleased.

"Yes, as a matter of fact. You promise the hike tomorrow will be easy and nothing can happen?"

"Nothing bad will happen. Come on, I'll show you inside." Eric grabbed her hand and they climbed the stairs to the wrap-around deck. Tatum stopped to gaze at the emerald, wildflower-dotted meadow bordering the tall gray peaks.

Inside, Tatum exclaimed, "Looks like we won't be roughing it at all!"

"Solar power and wood-burning heat is as rough as it gets!"

Tatum explored the open interior: a living room/ kitchen area that could hold ten people comfortably, an easy-clean wood floor, a huge picnic table, and a wood-burning stove.

"The firewood supply is included in the rent we pay. So is the propane for the kitchen stove." Eric was obviously enjoying himself.

She surveyed the kitchen more closely. "Open shelves. Perfect for this cabin. Plenty of counter space. But no refrigerator? Or faucet at the sink? Aha. The primitive part. I see why coolers with ice and large containers of water are necessary."

"Yes, Seth and Heather, our designated cooks, came up in a vehicle so they could bring the ice and water."

He winked. "This time we didn't want to haul it all on our backs." Eric laughed at the look on Tatum's face. "Tate, I never have to guess what you're thinking."

She smiled into his eyes and squeezed his hand, glad they both could give a little.

The others arrived, with greetings all around.

Eric whispered, "Alex and his fiancée won't be here this time. He's part of a mountain rescue team and he got called out. Too bad. We could have been regaled with Alex's rescue stories. Now we'll have to endure Jonathan's jokes, instead."

As it turned out, Jonathan embraced his role as the group's entertainer. His girlfriend, Christie, just rolled her eyes when he said, "I'm sure glad Ty, our resident EMT, and his girlfriend Bailey could join us. Ty will help with any food poisoning or broken legs." He noticed Tatum's look of concern and added, "Just kidding."

Andrew and Jamie completed the group as couple number four. Jamie was never without her camera. She even took a picture of the pot of beer cheese soup, which quickly disappeared, along with the Reuben sandwiches on thick slices of homemade, rye bread. After munching on the veggie tray, the group consumed blackberry cobbler for dessert.

"Tate." Eric stood at the door. "Come out on the deck and see the sunset. They're almost as good as the sunrises here." Eric took her hand and they found a bench to sit on. Tatum stared in awe. Again the sky was painted with a divine pallet of oranges and blues in an inimitable array. As the sun set, the mountain ridges turned to black silhouettes.

"I can see why you're drawn to the mountains, Eric. I've been missing out." They sat in comfortable silence holding hands while darkness fell and stars gradually appeared against the dark sky like splashes of diamonds on black velvet.

Eric finally stood and and pulled Tatum up next to him. "We better turn in. See you in the morning." He gave her a gentle hug and light kiss that left Tatum full of joy and expectancy.

🍃 🍃 🍃

The aroma of breakfast pulled everyone into the kitchen.

"What's with this rarefied air? I've never eaten that many pancakes before. And the coffee tastes amazing." She popped the last blueberry in her mouth and swallowed the last gulp of coffee. Then she held her hands over her stomach.

Eric's mind was on the day's hike. "Yeah, I always eat more up here. That's OK. We'll need the energy on our excursion. Oh, and by the way, I'll carry all our essentials in my pack. You'll just need your hat, gloves, sunglasses, and extra jacket. I'll bring the rest."

"All that, for just a day hike?" Was this turning into more than she'd anticipated?

"We always prepare for worse-case scenario. Better to have it and not need it than the other way around." He opened his pack and ticked off a verbal list.

"Navigation, illumination, first aid supplies, fire starter, repair kit and tools, nutrition, hydration and emergency shelter."

"You sound like a thorough lawyer. Seriously, though, I'm glad you're so prepared."

🍃 🍃 🍃

Two hours later, Tatum stepped off the trail to take an up-close photo of wildflowers. Her foot landed in a hole, she was caught off balance, and down she went.

"Eric!"

He turned, saw the situation, and called up the trail for Ty. "We might have an issue here!" he shouted.

Ty came running back. Kneeling next to Tatum, he touched her ankle.

She winced and glared at Eric, to which he responded with a look of surprise.

"Only a sprain," said Ty. "You'll be limping for a few days. Let me wrap it with an ace bandage."

Eric reached for Tatum's hand, but she pulled it away. "You said everything would be all right, no problems." She gritted her teeth as Ty wrapped the ankle.

"Tatum, these things just happen. It's no one's fault," Eric said with a bewildered and perturbed look.

Tatum felt guilty for blaming him.

Ty came to Eric's defense. "Tate, this could have happened to anyone. We'll help you get back to the hut and put ice on your ankle."

Get back *how*, she wondered.

But Eric had her climb on his back. She had no

choice but to hold on tight to his shoulders and endure the embarrassment.

Back at the cabin, her attitude was almost as cold as the ice on her ankle. Eric took the easy way out and left her in the hands of Seth and Heather, who hovered over her solicitously.

"Tatum, here's a cup of peach tea. Want anything else?"

She sighed. Now that Eric had gone, she felt more willingness to adjust her attitude.

"I'm sorry, I'm acting like a child," she told Seth and Heather. "It wasn't Eric's fault that I got hurt. I just expected everything to go perfect."

Heather squeezed her hand. "Don't worry, Tatum. I'm sure Eric understands. It could happen to anyone."

The hikers came back before the afternoon rains set in. Eric sat hesitantly next to Tatum. She grabbed his hand. "I'm sorry, Eric, for blaming you for my dumb mistake. Forgive me?"

Eric's shoulders relaxed and his eyes softened a little. "Well, there was nothing dumb about it. Things happen."

"I still love the beauty of these mountains. I'm not going to let this stop me from hiking with you again. But I guess I'll have to sit out tomorrow's hike." She looked up at Ty. "Do you think my ankle will be better in three weeks? Eric's planning to take me up Bierstadt."

"I think you'll be good as new in three weeks. Just keep ice on it to relieve the swelling, and let Eric pamper you." Ty snickered. Eric's friends knew he was not the pampering kind.

The Mexican-themed evening meal was good enough to have come off a food truck: fish tacos with shredded cabbage and a special white sauce, chips and homemade salsa, guacamole, and cinnamon churros.

The board games came out, courtesy of Francie's cabin, and Pictionary was a big hit; girls against guys. The logical-minded guys couldn't guess the girls' creative (to say it nicely) drawings.

The next morning a sumptuous breakfast again greeted Tatum and the hikers: focaccia breakfast sandwiches with eggs and bacon.

"Get the recipe, Tate," said Eric. "We'll have to try to duplicate this."

"Everything tastes good at this high altitude," said Seth.

The day went quickly and, although Tatum had to sit on the deck and just look at the mountains, the weekend was declared a success by all. Tatum rode back down to the parking lot with Seth and Heather in their truck.

4 🍃

"I have to pinch myself to make sure this isn't a dream. Am I really going to climb a fourteener?" Tatum said to Eric, who was at the wheel as they drove up the twisty road to the top of Guanella Pass.

"I'm glad you didn't say nightmare." Eric chuckled.

"The thought did come to me." Tatum laughed to hide her nervousness but she knew it didn't work.

"As far as I can control anything, nothing bad will happen." Eric drove on in silence.

They reached the top of Guanella Pass before sunrise.

"Tate, look. There's a cow moose and her calf." Just twenty feet ahead of them, in the pre-dawn light, two gangly animals ambled across as if they owned the road.

"Awesome. I've never seen a moose up close. The baby's so cute. Is it called a *calf*?"

"Yes. However cute it may be, though, we don't want to meet moose on the trail. That mama will ignore cars. But if hikers come close, she's super-protective of her baby and could even attack. I'd much rather see the bull, although I can't say he's especially friendly, either."

"I didn't even know they lived at this altitude."

"Oh, yeah. We could also see marmots or pikas. And mountain goats."

They followed several other cars into the parking lot.

"Great." Sarcasm gave an edge to Eric's voice. "It will be us and forty friends climbing today." Then his eyes brightened as if he remembered something that cheered him. "But we'll make the best of it!" He hoisted his meticulously-filled backpack and fit his arms through the straps. "Let's go."

Behind the majestic peak of Mt. Bierstadt the eastern sky began to glow with subtle pinks and oranges. The high meadow still lay in darkness. Tatum followed Eric onto the trail, which surprisingly sloped downward. She made a mental note to save some energy for getting back up to the car. Ten or fifteen minutes later Tatum remembered something.

"Oh, Eric. I left my water bottle on the hood of the car." Tatum held her breath as Eric looked at his watch and then back at her. He kept his face neutral, but was that a hint of displeasure she detected in the set of his mouth?

"You stay here. I'll run back and get it." Eric set his pack down next to her beside the trail. "No use taking more time than necessary."

He came jogging back in a surprisingly short time. Soon they were walking down the path side by side.

"Tate, this first part will take us through the annoying willows. The wooden boardwalk has made it much easier than it used to be, though. Then we'll cross Gomer Creek, and then the real work begins."

"Will my feet get wet crossing the creek?" That wouldn't be a good start to a hike.

"No, I know a spot just around the bend that's

much easier since the spring runoff has eased. Then we continue up the switchbacks and after that, only three miles to the summit."

"*Only* three miles. You make it sound so delightful. I hope you'll let me stop for a breather now and then. I already feel the altitude."

"Don't worry, we'll take rest stops. And don't forget to stay hydrated."

The sky brightened fast as the rising sun crested the peaks, and the eastern sky became cloudless sapphire blue. To the west, only a few small clouds appeared.

"Eric, the pictures I've seen don't do justice to this place," Tatum said breathlessly. "I think I need to take a break and enjoy the view. Could we rest a minute? This is becoming work already."

They stepped off the trail and drank from their water bottles. Eric glanced at his watch. "Mount Bierstadt was named after Albert Bierstadt, a Nineteenth-Century painter of the Colorado Rockies, and I don't mean the baseball team!" Eric wasn't one to make jokes, but the statement struck Tatum as funny. She was chuckling as they started on the trail again.

Above timberline, the green of the willows and the high, flower-specked meadow gave way to browns and grays.

"There, did you hear that whistling sound? That's a marmot. Ha! There are two of them and they seem to be playing patty cake. See them?"

She followed the direction Eric was pointing. Two furry brown animals looked at them as though the humans were disturbing their play. Tatum reached for her phone but wasn't quick enough to record the cuteness, as Eric led her onward and upward.

She concentrated on putting one foot in front of the other, hoping they were making good progress; but when she glanced up, the summit didn't look any closer. The hikers ahead of them looked as small as ants. When Eric called for a water stop, he seemed preoccupied. Tatum guessed he was thinking of standing on the summit.

"Look how far we've come."

"Looks like the parking lot is full of toy cars. You were right about lots of hikers today."

"Hear that chirp, like a house sparrow? That's the pika." They tried but couldn't spot it.

"At least the trail doesn't give me too much of a sense of height. Not yet, anyway."

Eric said matter-of-factly, "The last boulder field we have to climb may be hardest. We'll have to use our hands to scramble. But you can do it. I'll be right behind you."

"Can we get some selfies to prove to my friends that I really did this?" Anything to delay the inevitable. They got the pictures, which she couldn't wait to share with her friends, then they were back on the trail.

It was ten-thirty a.m. and the summit was close, but they still had the boulder field, the steepest part, to scramble up.

"Eric, do you think maybe this is far enough?"

"You can do it. Twenty more minutes. Just one rock

at a time. See that cairn over there?"

Tatum felt a little grumpy. "I don't even know what a cairn is."

"They are trail markers that others have built to show you the best way up," Eric said, making an effort to remain patient with this beginner. "Just take your time and pick your route. One boulder, then the next. I'm right behind you."

In her fear and hesitation, the next half hour felt like an hour, but they reached the summit. She plopped down on a boulder and her mouth formed a soundless 'O.' What a magnificent, panoramic view—on top of the world! "Awesome," she finally said. "You were right."

Eric sat next to her. "Drink some water and then I have a surprise for you." His face didn't give away any clues.

Curious, she drank fast, then smiled at him.

To her surprise, he got down on one knee, reached into a pocket and pulled out a small box. He opened it. On the royal-blue velvet lining rested a sparkling, one-carat solitaire diamond. "Tatum Kessler, will you marry me? I wanted this to be our mountain top experience."

The thin air had slowed Tatum's thinking processes, but what he had just said finally registered. She threw her arms around Eric. "Yes, Eric Martin, I will marry you." He kissed her intently and she was in no hurry for him to stop.

Other hikers standing nearby on the summit clapped and whistled. Tatum had forgotten they weren't alone on their mountaintop. She looked around shyly, hardly realizing what a huge smile she had on her face. Wow. They even had "friends" to make it all the more special.

The ring fit perfectly. How did he know? For her, the sight of that ring on her finger even overshadowed the spectacular view.

They lingered to consume energy bars, more water, and to bask in the moment. "Tate, I want Alex as my best man. I've had more time to think about this than you have." He winked at her affectionately. "Have any idea who you'd want to stand up with you?"

"Hmmm. I'm not sure. Now that my dream of getting married is a reality, I'll have a wedding to plan."

Eric pointed out and told her the names of the peaks visible in all directions. He had climbed them all, and seemed to have an intimate knowledge of each one. "Tate, you can now say you've climbed a fourteener. It's an exclusive club. When should we climb another one together? How about Grays and Torrys?" He pointed to the east.

She wasn't going to commit to anything just yet. She still had to get back down this mountain.

Eric made a joke to lighten the prospects. "I've heard it said that ascending is optional, descending is mandatory."

Tatum frowned. That one didn't sound funny to her.

"You can sit on a rock, lower your feet to the one below and take your time."

Going down proved much slower, with the dizzying twenty-foot drop off on either side. Eric was patient.

He kept an eye on the sky, however. The small,

far-away clouds had grown dark and threatening. Just past the boulder field, he urged, "Tate, we're going to have to pick up the pace."

Like an exclamation mark to his sentence, just above their heads a bolt of lightning split the dark sky and practically blinded Tatum.

Knocked off her feet, she landed painfully on her hip. Her hair stood on end. In the electrified air, as if in a dream, she had a vague awareness of Eric hitting the ground like a heavy rag doll.

5 🍃

Momentum carried Eric off the trail. He plunged twenty feet downward. A large rock stopped his descent. The sound of his head hitting the rock made Tatum want to vomit. There, below the trail, he sprawled at an awkward angle.

Forgetting about heights and her hurting hip, Tatum scrambled down to his sprawled body. His shoes had blown off. And she couldn't see him breathing! She felt his chest, his wrist.

"Help! Someone help me!" Tatum screamed up the mountain. This wasn't supposed to happen. Could his heart have stopped? Her CPR training kicked in and she started the chest compressions. Other climbers nearby rushed toward them to see what they could do. One hiker touched her shoulder.

"I'm a doctor. Let me take over for you." He began working to resuscitate Eric.

Tatum reached for her cell phone. It was dead! She hadn't plugged it in last night. Taking pictures had used up what charge she had left. She jammed it back in her pocket. She reached for Eric's backpack, hoping the lightning hadn't destroyed his cell phone. *Oh, God. Please.*

It rested unharmed in its special compartment. A signal! She dialed 9-1-1.

"9-1-1, what is your emergency?"

"Help! He was hit by lightning!"

"What is your location?"

"Mount Bierstadt. My fiancé was hit by lightning!"

"Is he breathing?"

"No. A doctor and another guy are giving him CPR!"

"I'm contacting Mountain Rescue Team as we speak. What is your name?"

"Tatum. Oh, please hurry."

"What is your phone number in case we're disconnected?"

"I don't know. This isn't my phone."

"That's all right. Are you hurt?"

"No. What is taking so long?"

"Mountain Rescue will be there in thirty minutes. Are you near the top of the mountain?"

"Yes, just below the boulders."

"I will stay on the line with you, if you'd like. Tell me what happened."

""We were starting down the trail past the boulder field when lightning struck—right above us. It hit Eric!"

What is Eric's last name?"

"Martin."

"What is happening now?"

"They're still giving him CPR."

"Is it raining?"

"Yes, pretty hard. Are you sure the rescue people are coming?"

"Yes, they should be there shortly."

"As long as they're coming, you don't have to stay on the line with me. I need to go and help if I can."

"Let the doctor do it. He's trained."

"OK. Thanks. Bye."

Eric's still body was in the hands of people she didn't know. One man, wearing a red Chiefs cap, who said he could physically feel the lightning from somewhere up the trail, was counting chest compressions, giving the doctor a break from the strenuous work, as the doctor knelt at Eric's side feeling for a pulse. The men counted together: "Twenty-eight, twenty-nine, thirty." The compressions stopped and the doctor blew two breaths into Eric's mouth and nose. Then the compressions started again.

Tatum felt sick.

They were literally pumping his heart for him, pushing the blood to his brain, hoping to sustain him until he could be revived.

"Mountain Rescue Team is coming," she told the doctor.

"That's good. They're located in Evergreen, not far. They're available day and night, 24/7. And they're highly trained professional rescue mountaineers."

This information gave Tatum some small comfort. All she could do was sit next to her prone, unconscious fiancé and wait. As if in a dream, she heard herself praying, *Oh, God. How could you let this happen? Where are you, God? Were you busy somewhere else? Oh, God. Oh, God.*

The doctor moved back into place to relieve the man in the red cap. "Twenty-nine, thirty." Two more breaths. The man collapsed on the ground, exhausted, while the doctor took over the compressions.

"Was it my fault for forgetting my water bottle?" Tatum whispered. Her confused thoughts alternated between anger, guilt and denial. She hunched over Eric, trying to keep the rain from his face. She was chilled through and through, and not only from the cold rain. "Eric," she whispered. "You said you had everything under control and there was very little risk. You said nothing bad would happen. Please wake up. Let me know you're all right."

As Tatum spoke, someone came running up the trail towards them, strapped with a radio and carrying an emergency bag. This efficient stranger knelt to assess the injuries. Somehow his calm demeanor eased Tatum's racing mind a little. He checked twice for a pulse then pulled an apparatus from his bag. The doctor stepped back to let the rescuer do his work. Tatum heard a whirring sound, and words were exchanged about jolting Eric's heart. The rescuer rubbed two paddles together, and placed them on Eric's chest, as the doctor pulled Tatum back from the scene. "Clear" was called out and Eric's body jolted into a convulsion. The doctor checked for a pulse and shook his head and the whole process was repeated. This time when the doctor checked, the words made Tatum let out a breath she didn't know she'd been holding.

"There it is," he said, "weak but we're beating." The

man with the paddles double checked then yelled down the path.

"We've got a beat—let's move," and suddenly they were engulfed in a mass of methodical, quick-thinking activity, all revolving around Eric. One team carried a six-foot metal basket used as a stretcher. Two men followed with what looked like a dune buggy wheel that they attached underneath the basket with adept swiftness. Tatum didn't count them, but there must have been fifteen rescuers that had responded to the call.

Once, six-foot, two-inch Eric was secure in the stretcher, the team leader prepared for evacuation by assigning six volunteers to handle the first run. Eric's weight and the force of gravity wanted to propel the litter downward; the six rescuers had to hold it back from taking off without them.

A second group of six runners positioned themselves part-way down the hill out of sight while the starting team surrounded the litter and took off running, the dune buggy wheel bouncing easily over the rough terrain. Their main concern was to get Eric down the mountain. They never stopped. To switch runners, the second team came alongside and tapped the others out without missing a beat. The exchange was made seamlessly like a running ballet. Tatum hurried behind them, barely able to match their pace, doing all she could to keep her eyes on Eric. She forgot her fear of heights in her concern for Eric.

Flight for Life had been called to transport Eric to the hospital. The rain had continued, as well as the lightning, making it an easy choice for the pilot to decide to abort the landing altogether. An ambulance would take Eric to St. Anthony's Hospital.

Besides four extra volunteers, Sheriff Rick Santiago from Summit County responded to the call for assistance and was jogging toward Mountain Rescue as they came out of the willows and ascended the final up-hill leg of the trail toward the parking lot. He asked Tatum if he could help her in any way. His calm demeanor was lost on her.

"I have to ride with Eric to the hospital. I can't talk right now." She pressed her fist to her mouth. The Sheriff responded in a firm voice.

"You won't be able to ride along in the ambulance," he said. "Let me take you to the hospital in the patrol car. He's in good hands and the only thing we can do now is pray."

He opened the door for Tatum. Not resisting, she sank exhausted into the passenger seat of the patrol car. She was soaked and tired, the adrenaline used up. The sheriff tried to reassure her as they followed the ambulance with Eric in it to Georgetown and then on to Denver.

"They will be taking your fiancé to the new St. Anthony's Hospital," he explained with deliberate care, "because they have excellent level-one trauma care. Their new campus is near Sixth and Simms. We'll all be there before you know it." He handed her a bottle of water, and she took it gratefully.

"Let me tell you a little about myself," Sheriff Rick

said. "I've been an under sheriff in Breckenridge for three years and recently was elected sheriff when our top guy retired. I love my job because of the interaction with people. I go to Grace Church in Breckenridge."

"That's where I've seen you before." That's why he had looked familiar. She remembered his medium height, brown eyes from her parents' church.

"By the way, my condolences on the death of your parents. Everyone loved them. Because of my work schedule I'm not as faithful as I'd like to be. I also know Georgia Winter, your parents' store manager, because I used to be in a small accountability group with her husband, Chris, before he passed away. Did you know him?"

"No, I only got to know Georgia well when my parents bought the Tea and Java du Jour and kept her as manager. I think her husband died some years earlier. I should call her. At least I have Georgia's phone number memorized. My phone battery is dead and I was so afraid the lightning had done something to Eric's phone in his backpack, but it wasn't affected."

Georgia answered her phone right away. "Hello, Georgia speaking."

"Georgia, this is Tatum. I'm using Eric's phone. I'm with Sheriff Rick Santiago in his squad car on the way to Denver. There's been a terrible accident." Tatum took a big breath, willing away the sob that threatened to escape. "Eric was struck by lightning this morning as we were climbing down Mount Bierstadt. He is being taken to St. Anthony's Hospital in an ambulance, and the sheriff is taking me down in his squad car. Please pray! I'll keep in touch." This time the sob escaped.

"God be with you, honey!"

The squad car reached the hospital parking lot. Sheriff Santiago turned off the engine. He reached over and placed a gentle hand on Tatum's arm. "Can I pray for you before you go in?" he asked. Tatum could only nod. She kept her face to the door so Rick couldn't see the tears coursing down her cheeks.

"Lord," he began, "you know all about Eric inside the hospital and Tatum in this car. Would you guide the doctors as they figure out the best treatment for Eric's injuries, and Lord, would you comfort Tatum as she waits? Thank you, Father. Amen.... Tatum, go on in now, and I'll catch up with you later."

Hours later Tatum sat in the hospital room staring at Eric's form, still except for the rise and fall of his chest as he breathed. She was too numb to decide her next step. She only knew she'd sit here and silently support her fiancé. In her mind, her whole future lay in that bed. She couldn't even entertain the thoughts of "what if." Eric had to wake up. She tried to pray but all she could think was, *Oh God, Oh God.*

What had her pastor said? "We can trust Him. We may not understand it, but he is working, even in this. He will walk through this with you. He will never leave you nor forsake you."

6 🍃

Tatum made the call to Eric's parents as soon as she felt a little more under control emotionally. She had only met them once; and their reception had been rather cold. She dialed the number from Eric's phone. His father answered.

"Hi, Eric. You called at an inopportune time. We're just leaving for the airport. Taking a much-needed vacation to Aruba."

Tatum cringed at his challenging, irritated tone, but she pressed on.

"I'm sorry, Mr. Martin. This is Tatum. There's been an accident. Eric is in the hospital. His prognosis is uncertain."

There was silence for a space of five seconds.

"Tell me what happened." His voice was sharp.

She explained the circumstances as best she could.

Silence again. Then a harsh sigh. "Guess we'll have to change our plans and come to Colorado. You calling from Denver?"

She imagined an angry look on Gordon Martin's face to match his tone. She gave him the address of St. Anthony's Hospital. He promised to call back with their flight information and time of arrival.

Tatum remained next to Eric, watching his chest move up and down with each labored breath. She breathed with him, willing him to continue. She cleared her throat and spoke into the stillness.

"I'm going to call a few of your friends from your phone and let them know about the accident. Oh, I hope I can just leave a message and not have to talk to anyone."

She hoped he'd approve. She found the names in Eric's phone and left short messages for Alex and Ty.

🍃 🍃 🍃

The sounds of the hospital instruments rang through the silent room. She spoke over the noise.

"Eric, I've read that sometimes unconscious people remember what was said around them after they wake up. So I'm hoping you can hear me."

She realized she had been slumping in the chair and now sat up straighter. She stared at her engagement ring, absentmindedly twirling it on her finger.

"I love you. What will I do if you... All our plans, our future.... Your passion for the mountains. You have to get better so you can keep teaching me to climb." Her emotions lifted and plummeted like a roller coaster; up, down, slow, fast, fast, slow, up, down.

"A long time ago I made a list of all the qualities I wanted in a husband. First on the list was that he had to be a follower of Jesus. The rest of the list was superficial in comparison." She stared at Eric, waiting for a response.

None came.

She sighed.

"The first Christian dating site I went on was not very user friendly. They even decided your matches for you. I wasn't comfortable with the computer choosing a potential mate for me. After a few phone conversations with those matches, I realized the men chosen for me were too much like me. I remember thinking, 'Does this have to be so hard?'"

Still no response from Eric.

"The next site offered a 'free trial.' The only problem was I could see the men who wanted to communicate with me, but I couldn't communicate back unless I paid my money. So much for free! This was more work than I wanted, but my friends' dare came back to mind, so I kept plugging away. Did you know any of this before now?"

She paused to recall the sequence of events.

"I thought this new site would be the answer. It matched me up with some men, but one was too intense, another too shallow. I hesitated to meet any of them. I knew after a fifteen-minute phone conversation that a match on paper didn't mean a match in real life."

She gently touched Eric's hand.

"Then your match came up. I was tentative and a little fearful, but willing to give it a try. Nicole and Heather were positively giddy, thinking about the potential! They had failed to find a good match for themselves; but for some reason, they believed I'd do better.

"Bless your heart for not rushing things. Emailing back and forth and talking on the phone with you calmed some of my fears. Then when I finally agreed to meet you in a coffee shop, of course I was a klutz and spilled my coffee all over the table and myself! Not a great first impression. You just laughed and got me a bunch of napkins and another latte."

The memory gave Tatum something to chuckle about. That felt good.

"I didn't realize at the time, but as I reflect on the weeks since meeting you, Eric, and all our conversations and time together, I was falling head over heels in love with you. What was there not to love?

'Please, Lord,' I'd pray. 'Help this to be the real thing. He's perfect!' I often used the word perfect in speaking or thinking of you. I do love you, Eric."

7 🍃

It took Gordon and Anne twelve hours to arrive at Eric's bedside. Gordon was an older version of Eric, tall and attractive. His eyes were the same color blue as his son's, but harder, much harder.

Eric still had not gained consciousness. Tatum cringed when Gordon immediately started making demands of the nursing staff.

The nurses called in the doctor.

"Mr. Martin." The young doctor put an arm around Eric's father's shoulders and gently but firmly pulled him away from his son's bedside. "We are doing everything humanly possible for your son. Short of a miracle, he may not make it. I suggest if you know the Miracle Worker, you should pray and let us do the rest."

Anne Martin stood back quietly with Tatum, evidently accustomed to her husband's rants. She gazed sadly at her son, her dark brown eyes deepening in color. She was dressed fashionably and looked perfectly put together even after a four-hour plane ride and a forty-five minute taxi ride; but the strain in her features revealed her emotional stress.

Tatum took her hand and squeezed it. Anne squeezed back but didn't look at her. Not until Gordon had stormed out of the room did she speak.

"Eric told us he was going to propose." She forced

a bit of a smile. "You have to know, Gordon is not very accepting of Eric's decision.

Gordon has tried to control everything Eric does, even though it's been years since they lived in the same house. Eric went to the university his father chose and to the law school of his father's choice. Eric seemed to want to please his father. Then he refused to practice law with him and moved out here. Even though Eric is thirty four, he usually has respected his father's wishes. Gordon usually gets what Gordon wants.

So please understand. It's not that he doesn't like you; he doesn't like anything about Eric's move to Denver."

As the older woman spoke, Tatum saw Eric in a new light. He really was a lot like his father. He was nicer about it; but he did seem to need to control everything in his perfect world.

She looked at the inert form of her fiancé and shoved back the little doubts. They faced more important issues at the moment.

Anne stood next to the bed, stroking her son's forehead.

Tatum resolved it in her mind that these people would be allies, if for no other reason than the fact that they also loved this man.

Anne and Tatum found chairs and sat quietly, each lost in her own thoughts. Finally, Anne spoke up.

"Eric told me you lost your parents in a car accident a while ago. Is that something you can talk about?"

"I think about it every day. I guess talking about it

out loud won't hurt." Tears stung her eyes as she spoke. "It's been hard. Sometimes it's overwhelming. But with God's grace I'm coping, day to day."

Although bringing up the memories was difficult, Tatum felt grateful to Eric's mother for her interest, especially on a day filled with such heartache for her. So Tatum went ahead and told Anne about losing her parents and the resulting changes in her life.

When she finished, Anne reached over and gave her a hug. That felt good. But Tatum moved the conversation to something less personal. "Eric said he has a younger brother."

"Yes, his incorrigible younger brother." She laughed bitterly. "I'm afraid Walker got the worst of my spoiling." A flicker of regret crossed her face, but she tossed her head as if to shake it off. She patted Tatum's hand. "You know, I couldn't ask for a nicer wife for my son, and daughter-in-law for us. Thank you for loving Eric."

Tatum smiled through her tears and felt grateful Anne was there.

8 🍃

The monitor attached to Eric beeped. Two nurses rushed in, one pushing Tatum and Anne out the door as the other attended to Eric.

A doctor hurried down the hall with Eric's father on his heels. However, before Gordon could enter the room, the door shut firmly.

The three of them—Tatum and Eric's parents—were directed to a small waiting room where the two women sat side by side on the sofa watching Gordon pace back and forth, anger seeming to simmer just below the surface.

He isn't in control, thought Tatum.

He occasionally glared at the two women as he paced, as if they were the reason for his discomfort. His chin was held high and his breathing was louder than before.

Anne ignored him, but Tatum felt intimidated. She shook her head and made the decision to do the same as Anne. *It doesn't matter. The important thing is Eric. Please, Lord, give the doctor wisdom and work a miracle in that room.*

The thirty minutes seemed like an eternity until the doctor finally appeared. By the look on his face, even before he spoke, Tatum knew.

"I am so sorry." The doctor shook his head. "Eric's

heart stopped and we couldn't get it started again. We did everything we could. His heart arrhythmia played a part in why his heart wouldn't respond. We can let you see him one last time before we take him downstairs. Take all the time you need."

Anne was crying. Gordon was silent and pale.

Tatum sat in a daze. *Not Eric. Not my perfect Eric, my rock, my everything.* How could he be gone?

She stood, feeling cold to the core. She squeezed her eyes closed, hid her face in her hands. Her world would be forever different. Again....

Anne's arm came around her and she turned toward her. The women clung to each other, weeping.

Anne released Tatum, straightened her back, and said to her husband, "Gordon, let Tatum go alone, first to see Eric. We can go after her."

Gordon looked startled at his wife's words. But he complied, stepping away from the door and turning his back on the two women.

"Go ahead, Tatum." Anne's voice was gentle. "Take the time you need. We'll go in when you're done."

Shoulders drooping, Tatum left the waiting room. The nurse opened the door to Eric's room. She went to the bedside and stood gazing into the tranquil, immobile face.

"Eric, I know you're with the Lord now. And if I know you, you're looking around for mountains to climb in heaven." Her voice caught, her chin quivered.

"Lord, how could you let this happen? You are almighty. What were you thinking? I need Eric. We were planning our future. He had one more fourteener to climb. We were going to have children."

She gazed one last time and with an aching chest, kissed his forehead, which was cool to her lips.

"Goodbye, Eric. I love you."

She turned and walked slowly out of the room. To her mind came the too-fresh memory of saying goodbye to her parents. She was exhausted.

The funeral, three days later, planned and orchestrated by Gordon, was as hard as her parents' funeral had been months earlier. At least Gordon allowed a service here in Denver; though the casket would be shipped back to New York to be buried in the family plot.

Tatum wore a simple black dress and stayed in the background as much as possible. Georgia was by her side as they walked in. "I can't do this, Georgia. Please let me leave. No one will miss me."

"I know. I've been where you are. But with me on one side and God on the other, you will get through this." Tatum nodded reluctantly, straightened her shoulders, and took a seat next to Georgia.

Seeing her roommates, Heather and Nicole, was a comfort. She caught their eye and nodded to them. Hymns were played softly as people made their way to the pews. Tatum sat, looking at her hands. She wasn't related to Eric yet, and Gordon didn't ask for any input from her. She was only the fiancée, after all.

The funeral director rose to speak. "We're here today

to honor..." He looked at his notes in his folder. "Eric Martin, and his parents..." Again he consulted his notes. "...Gordon and Anne Martin."

Tatum huffed in disbelief.

Georgia reached for her hand and squeezed it.

She kept still but clenched her jaw, anger easier to deal with than sorrow. Then it seemed her mind and heart shut down. She listened through a fog as scriptures were read and friends of Eric's were invited to offer eulogies. Some were acquaintances from his law office. Then his climbing buddies spoke of Eric's perfect planning and perfect climbs. It vaguely registered on her conscience that Eric's friend, Alex, who he had chosen as his best man, was one of those who spoke.

Pastor Jim shared in a more personal and sincere tone than did Gordon's choice for the officiating minister. Tatum's lower lip quivered; but she held herself together. Over and over thought, *I never had a chance to say goodbye to any of them.*

As the casket went down the aisle for the ride in the hearse to the plane, a recording of bagpipes played "Amazing Grace." It was the only thing she would have done the same if she had been in charge of the service.

Georgia reached over and gave her hand another squeeze. "I know this is hard, but I think Nora would be proud of you."

Her mother's name brought a tear to her eye but also helped her steel herself. Only the reception was left to endure.

Eric's brother, Walker, came for the funeral along

with his girlfriend, Brandi—definitely a matched pair. Walker was everything that Eric had mentioned and more. Tatum could hardly believe they were brothers, and it wasn't just their looks. Walker was shorter by at least four inches. He had nondescript hazel eyes and a face scarred by juvenile acne. His hair was a straight mousy brown, so unlike Eric's dark waves. The cologne wafting from his person was overpowering enough to make her want to take a step back. He wore a conservative, stylish black suit with a red and orange tie.

He walked with a cocky strut. The look in his eye revealed a sense of superiority, at least a desire to think of himself that way.

Brandi carried herself in a similar way. Her bleached-blonde hair clashed with her darker complexion. Her makeup might be appropriate for the stage, and her red and orange dress might match Walker's tie, but for a funeral? They didn't seem to mind the attention they attracted, though.

Walker greeted her with a wink. "Hey, Tate, glad to meetcha."

She cringed. Only close friends had earned the right to call her by her nickname.

"This is my woman, Brandi." His voice was smoky harsh and attention-getting. "Can you believe I wasn't even mentioned as the brother?" He shook his head in mock disgust, then seemed to shake it off.

As Tatum shook Walker's limp hand, and then Brandi's, something in the woman's posture sent a shiver down her spine. Brandi's hooded eyes held a gleam of disdain; but why? It mirrored the look in Walker's eye.

They were mercifully interrupted by Georgia, but Walker hovered in the background while people offered their condolences to Tatum.

When Walker approached Tatum again, he was alone.

"I can see why my big brother was attracted to you! But he always got the pretty ones." Walker hovered inappropriately close, the smell of cigarettes on his breath.

"I'm glad to finally meet you, Walker," she said hesitantly. "Eric told me a lot about you." She had to bite her tongue to refrain from telling him exactly what Eric had said. Walker preened slightly, missing the sarcasm.

"How about you and me going out before I leave town and you can tell me all about my big brother." Walker flashed a toothy grin. "Brandi won't mind. I'll send her to a spa or leave her in Black Hawk for the day. Eric and I haven't spent too much time together in the last ten years and you can fill me in. I'm always up for a party and ..." He looked around. "This one doesn't meet my expectations!"

Tatum shuddered again and searched for a nice way to tell Eric's brother to get lost. Then Pastor Jim, being among the last to leave, approached her.

"Tatum, I'm so sorry for your loss. How are you holding up?"

His look of concern nearly undid her resolve not to cry.

"If there's anything my wife and I can do, won't you

let us know? She sends her condolences also. We'll be praying for you." He gave her the pastoral hug and left.

Walker had faded into the background again but as soon as Pastor Jim left, he was back. Brandi was still nowhere near.

"I'm really serious about a time to get together," Walker breathed into Tatum's face. She struggled to face him and not turn away. "I really want to know about my big brother, and maybe we can become good friends." He raised his eyebrows suggestively.

"I'm sorry, Walker, but I'm not very good company now. I'd really rather not." She stopped when she saw the look of disappointment on Walker's face. However, related to Eric or not, the last thing she wanted to do was be seen with this man. "I don't have the energy to carry on a conversation."

"Aw, come on Tate. Humor me. I just lost a brother, myself, and could use some comfort."

Tatum's mouth dropped open at his selfish attitude. Walker didn't notice.

But Georgia must have noticed because she was at Tatum's side like a mamma bear with a cub in danger.

"Walker, this is Georgia Winter, my good friend and the manager of the Tea and Java du Jour, which I own."

Georgia stepped between Walker and Tatum and held out her hand.

Walker looked surprised but returned the handshake. "Ms. Winter, tell Tate she should go out with me to show brotherly love. I want to learn more about the brother I barely knew."

Does he know he's whining? Tatum wondered.

"That seems like a reasonable request," said Georgia. "Why don't you meet Tatum up in Breckenridge for lunch? We're leaving now. I can see she's ready to drop, so I'm going to take her home. How is tomorrow noon, at the Breckenridge Brewery? You can plug it into your GPS and get exact directions. She'll see you then."

"At least let me pick you up in the BMW I rented." Walker wasn't going to let Georgia have the last word.

"Tatum will meet you there at twelve o'clock. Goodbye, Walker. It was nice to meet you." Georgia put her arm around Tatum's shoulders and guided her out of the building. When they were out of Walker's hearing, Tatum hugged Georgia.

"Thanks for making the decision for me... I think. I don't want to spend any time with that man, but he *is* Eric's brother. He seems about as trustworthy as the proverbial car salesman. To think he might have been my brother-in-law." Tatum shuddered. Then, as she settled into Georgia's car for the ride back to Breckenridge, she sat back with eyes closed.

"Am I glad that's over! The funeral would've been hard enough to bear without that exchange with Walker. Do I have to meet him tomorrow?"

Georgia chuckled grimly. "I understand. But you can do it. In fact, with the little I know about Walker, you won't have to say much tomorrow."

During the strained, silent ride back to Breck, Tatum kept her eyes closed, not wanting to see the Georgetown exit, trying to shove down the memory of a sudden lightning strike. It came to her then that Eric's vehicle was still in the parking lot at the Bierstadt trailhead. Well, let Gordon make a decision about the car in the next couple days. I hope it gives him more than a little aggravation.

🍂 🍂 🍂

Noon the next day Tatum arrived with reluctance at the restaurant. She found Walker at a table, already consuming his second beer. The anything-but-subtle cologne greeted her. She pasted a weak smile on her face and hoped it wouldn't come unglued. He seemed to feed on the noise and confusion and never even noticed her reticence in being there.

"Let me tell you about myself," he jump started the conversation. "Eric was the goody two-shoes of the family. He did everything right just to show me up. If my father said 'jump,' I asked 'why,' but Eric asked 'how high.'" Walker finished off his beer and signaled the bartender for another.

"The only fair thing that happened to both of us was the trust fund set up by our grandfather. We each got the same amount. If Eric has no will, and since he wasn't married yet, his share will go to me according to the terms of the trust. At least my grandfather didn't play favorites." His New York accent became more pronounced.

This was the first Tatum had heard about a trust fund.

Walker wasn't stopping. "As kids, we always had to

go to church with Father and Mother. The church was small, but the people there were big-time judgmental! I couldn't do anything right in their eyes. I guess it stuck with Eric. It sure didn't with me! But that was just another way Eric tried to show me up. As we got to be teenagers, he went to church with them every Sunday morning. Not me! I much prefered my Sunday morning sleep." He gazed at her over his beer. "Saturday was a party night for me!"

Walker was no doubt adept at stretching the truth; but Tatum couldn't help wondering why Eric had withheld these things from her. She didn't think Eric would lie, but.... What else would she discover? Fearing a dark secret, she decided not to go there.

"Earth to Tate." Walker broke into her reverie. "Where you been? The waitress wants to know what you want to order."

"Oh, sorry, I'm really not hungry. I'll have a dinner salad." Tatum was sure Walker would have lunch and then dessert, extending this rather painful exchange.

Actually there was no exchange. It was just Walker talking nonstop. And he didn't disappoint. Even as he ate, he kept up the subject of the trust fund.

"Our grandfather's will states that the money he left us wasn't accessible until we were twenty five. I invested a small amount just to please dear old dad and have been enjoying the good life with the rest. I've traveled— mostly to Las Vegas. I bought a Cadillac Escalade. But the money's running out fast, so I'm glad I'll get Eric's portion." He stopped short then, perhaps realizing how that sounded. "Don't get me wrong. I'm not glad he died. But I might as well be honest about the money."

What a jerk! Tatum almost choked on her salad. "The only thing you can say about your brother's death is that you'll get the trust fund money? That's really sad." Tatum crossed her arms, glad to have said that.

Walker looked uncomfortable. He hung his head and apologized.

"Tate, let me make it up to you for sounding so greedy. Since Denver is more than half way to Vegas from New York, I'm headed there next. Why don't you come with me? I'll treat you to a really good time. I can send Brandi back to New York."

"Ah, no thanks." Tatum bit her lip. *Hell will freeze over before I'll do that!* "I'm really not up to going anywhere. But have a good time."

"I'll keep in touch, Tate." Walker was clearly undaunted.

The bill arrived and surprisingly, Walker picked it up and paid with his credit card. "You were almost my sister-in-law and that's almost family. Believe it or not, family's important to me. You'd really like New York. I could show you a good time there."

They left the restaurant and again Tatum was surprised—this time by the gentle hug Walker gave her. Then he got into his rented BMW, squealing the tires as he pulled out of the parking lot.

BLOG:

July 10

Random Ramblings—Disaster

On Friday, July 5th, I got engaged and within an hour my life turned into disaster…again. On Mount Bierstadt a lightning bolt hit Eric. He said there would be no problems, that he had everything under control. Well, he was wrong.

We conquered the mountain; but lightning conquered Eric.

Although he was resuscitated on the mountain, two days later his heart stopped beating, and it felt like my heart did too.

Here I am, abandoned again.

Our future was zapped by that bolt of lightning. I loved him so much and I was looking forward to growing old with him. Now what?

The funeral, orchestrated by Eric's father (I had no input whatsoever), was only slightly more bearable than amputation without anesthetic. As with my parents' death in the car accident, I never got a chance to say good-bye. I have a collection of unused good-byes. Do you need one? Or two? They're free for the asking. I have no use for them. #lifeforeverdifferent

Heather: *Dear friend, let me know if I can do anything. Praying for you.*

Nicole: *I'm here for you, Tate.*

9

Tatum was spending time with Georgia at her Breck-enridge condo. It felt good having no agenda. They enjoyed a taco salad lunch together. Georgia, while gracious and warm as always, seemed mentally preoccupied. The salad eaten, the women sipped cups of herbal tea in companionable silence. Then Georgia rose from the table, excused herself and wiped her hands on her apron.

"Tatum, I have something to share with you. Let me finish in the kitchen, then join you in the living room."

Tatum relaxed her body in an over-stuffed chair; but her mind churned. *Now what?*

A quick clattering of dishes and running of water in the kitchen and Georgia came in with a preoccupied look and eased gracefully onto a chair opposite Tatum. "You've been on my mind and heart constantly these days, Tatum. I know you're hurting after all that's happened, all these losses. I won't tell you to just get over it. We all grieve in different ways and according to different timelines. But I want you to know I understand."

"Thank you. What would I do without you?"

"But you don't know how much I empathize. I want to tell you a story—"

"Will I need tissues with this story?" She glanced at the tissue box on the coffee table. "I don't really want any more tears."

Georgia patted the box of tissues. "It's here if we need it." She smiled, but her eyes kept a faraway look. "Where do I start?" Her hands were clenched into fists on her lap. "You know my husband died of cancer five years ago. But I've never told you how we met, how I came to Breckenridge, and why I stay here." She sat up a little straighter and crossed her legs. She stared at the box on the coffee table.

"Twenty-five years ago I was an avowed single. I just wanted to go on mission trips. I was fulfilling my dream very nicely and had seen many countries and had many great experiences. Then twenty years ago I went with an organization to help with an orphanage in Mexico for three weeks." She lifted her gaze to meet Tatum's eyes and smiled. "That's where I met you and your parents for the first time. But most importantly, that's when I met Chris."

"I remember that trip, but I guess I didn't notice about Chris." Tatum chuckled. "I was kinda young."

Georgia acknowledged the comment with a slight smile.

"There was an instant attraction, though we both tried to deny it." Georgia sighed wistfully. "When we got back to the states, he was called to pastor the church here in Breck. I went back to my parents' house in Georgia and found a job to finance my next mission trip. We carried on a long distance relationship for a short time, and then he asked me to marry him and be a pastor's wife. That certainly didn't fit into my plans. But after much wrestling in prayer, I gave up my own vision—for a much better one.

"Oh, Georgia, was it hard to come to Colorado?"

"The hardest thing for this Southern girl was living in a cold place. But after a time, I adapted. I love it now. I'm now a mountain girl—"

"With a big helping of Southern charm. Quite a combination!"

"Yeah, I guess the Southern accent won't ever go away, even if I try. I don't mind being unique; this town has its share of transplants."

"I'd never thought about what an adjustment that was for you. I guess I just thought everything in your life was the way you planned it."

"Adjustment is a mild word for it. It was more like a struggle—or battle. Chris and I tried for ten years to have kids. I could get pregnant, but I could never carry the pregnancy past fourteen weeks. Oh, how I yelled at God. He brought me through every disappointment, though. Then when Chris found out about the cancer, I went back to yelling at God. Surely He had a better plan than that!"

Tears welled uninvited in Tatum's eyes.

Georgia took her hand. "I can't say I understand why God allowed cancer to conquer Chris, but I do know God is trustworthy. I stayed in Breck because it seemed God kept bringing people into my life who needed me. When one person changed, grew, and moved on, He'd bring another. Now, He has me ministering to you."

"Georgia..." Tatum squeezed the older woman's hand, as one tear escaped down her cheek. "I don't think I'm strong enough to adopt your paradigm." She reached for a tissue, dabbed her eyes and cheeks. "A double dose of loss and grief just isn't fair. The death of my parents almost overwhelmed me. Then Eric coming into my life went a long way in healing those wounds. But the parent void is still there. And now I'm back at step one of the grieving process."

Tatum twisted the tissue in her hands and swallowed the lump in her throat. "The loss of Eric has just added to the emptiness. I don't think I'll ever get over it. Everywhere I turn I'm reminded of what I don't have anymore. Every time I go to the Tea and Java du Jour I'm aware that it's mine because my parents are gone. When I look at the high mountain peaks, I can't help but think how Eric loved those mountains and the times I spent there with him." She squeezed her eyes tight then opened them again. She released the breath she'd been holding. "God has turned the vision I had for my life upside down. I don't see how my new life could possibly be better—"

Tatum stopped herself. *I sound like I'm whining.* She shrugged. "I appreciate you sharing your experience with me, though, Georgia."

"God doesn't have to answer the whys in our lives. But He might surprise you. Be patient and see what he has in store."

Back at her Alma house, she made her way to the great room. The inspirational views of the snowcapped peaks usually helped her think. Today the mountains were shrouded in fog like a veil; and it seemed her future was shrouded too. A bolt of fresh grief hit without warning. She sank on the couch with her head in her hands.

"Mom and Dad, how can I live without you? I still have so many questions I need answers to. Georgia's a big help but she doesn't know answers to my questions about family. What does my future hold? And now Eric's not here. It was so romantic when he asked me to marry him on top of Mount Bierstadt, and two days later he was gone." She fingered her engagement ring. Too many memories. She slipped it off and fought the urge to throw it across the room.

"Now what?" She put her head on the sofa pillow and closed her eyes. She hoped a small nap would help her escape from the decisions she needed to make.

When she woke and looked out the window, the fog was gone and blue skies had reappeared. She stepped out the patio door to sit on the deck. A hummingbird flew close. The Ruby-throated male flew straight up into the air and then dive bombed straight down, its wings making a trilling sound the whole time. The females were more subdued, or maybe just smarter! While the males played their games, the females would drink at the feeder uninterrupted. As she watched, a brave, or maybe disoriented, little bird flew into the house through the open sliding-glass door. It flew around in confusion then perched on an inside window sill. Tatum tiptoed into the house and picked up a baseball cap she'd left lying on the couch, using it to scoop up the tiny, terrified bird. Good thing her cat Spartacus was only playful and not hungry! The hummer was too tired to fly, and since it couldn't use its feet to walk, only perch, she easily captured it and set it gently outside. When she looked a few minutes later, it was gone.

Then Tatum noticed Rufous, her favorite humming-bird, named for his orange coloring. The self-designated clown and policeman of the feeder crowd always arrived in August. The other hummingbirds seem to know that Rufous would chase them away from the feeder; so they developed decoys and tag teams. As the Rufous chased a set of birds away, another team of birds took over the feeding spots. This would go on for hours at a time.

Tatum often wondered where the hummingbirds went at dusk when the shadows softened. They were so well camouflaged, their colors blending into the browns and greens of the pine trees. Unless she saw them land, she could never spot them on the branches.

Tatum reached up and took down the feeder to keep in the house overnight, taking the precaution so as not to attract bears. In the morning she'd put it out again, and the hummingbirds would be back to begin their day of drinking, chasing, and playing. She thought sadly that she'd soon have to take down the feeder for the winter, to make sure the tiny birds didn't stay around but headed south until springtime, when they always returned with shrill trills to announce their arrival.

Oh, to have no cares in the world.

BLOG:

July 12
Random Ramblings—Lightning Bolt

They say time heals all wounds. I wonder who 'they' are? And anyway, I don't believe them. I think it's a lie. Will I ever come to the place where, when I think about Eric and the lightning, I don't feel the hurt take my breath away? My world was knocked off its axis. Nothing is the same.

The storm clouds came so quickly, then left. Now my storm clouds seem permanent. Eric died two days later and my future died with him. It will now be forever called The Accident.

It may look like I'm coping better than I did after the death of my parents. But that doesn't mean I'm grieving less. My world shattered into pieces too small to ever put together again. For me, it's easier to deal with this alone. These wounds run too deep.

Will I survive? Oh God, I don't think I can do this.

I'm thankful for Georgia who puts no demands on me right now. #whenwillwoundsheal?

July 20
Random Ramblings—Georgia and the South

What would I do without Georgia? For all her gentle charm, she's a force to be reckoned with! She's the shoulder to cry on (oh, how I've done that in this past year), the strong arms to hold me up (literally and figuratively), the humor to make me laugh in spite of myself (she's funny without trying), the challenge to make me think (sometimes I don't want to be challenged, but thanks anyway, Georgia.)

Since I have a western/northern ear, her Southern accent and sayings make me stop and ask, "What did she just say?"

For instance:

- "Have your picture made."
- "We might should."
- "All y'all." (The plural of y'all!)
- "Fixin' to."
- "Bless her heart." (You can say anything derogatory about someone and it makes it OK if you finish your statement with, "Bless her heart!") So a true Southerner might say something like, "We're fixin' to have our picture made and mama thought we might should see if all y'all wanted to join us, bless her heart."

I love her. I couldn't do without Georgia. She's been through more than she lets on, and I know she understands. Thanks, Georgia! #mysouthernmama

Heather: *When you're ready, Nicole and I are here. We love you, friend.*

10 🍃

Sheriff Rick Santiago waited three weeks before completing his report of the mutual aid given by Summit County the day of the lightning strike. He came to the Tea and Java du Jour during the afternoon slow period so he and Tatum would be uninterrupted as they sat at a table.

After giving Georgia a friendly greeting, Rick turned to Tatum. "I have almost all I need; but a few questions remain. Do you mind?"

Tatum couldn't say no. He was obviously trying to be as gentle as he could. She steeled herself to hold back tears. This was the first time she had talked about the events of that day.

"Summit County was only there to help," said Sheriff Rick. "So I can make this quick. From what I saw, Mountain Rescue Team was professional as always."

Tatum looked at her hands a moment, then, "I felt reassured when I saw them. I can't remember how quickly they got to us, but the first two people were running as they approached. In a detached way, it registered on my mind that that was pretty awesome. Who can run up a mountain?"

"Yea, some of our team are ultra runners; they make it look easy. Can you tell me anything else?"

"As more mountain rescue got there, the two men

that were doing CPR on Eric stepped aside, and I never got to thank them for rushing over when it first happened." Tatum stopped to think. "And I couldn't believe how quickly they got Eric off the mountain. They went as fast as they could on the slippery trail."

"Mountain Rescue knows Mount Bierstadt well. Not only do they train on the mountain, they get quite a few hiker-injury calls. That's a popular hike." Rick waited expectantly for Tatum to continue.

"By then I think there were eight or ten people. Maybe more. It's kind of a blur, getting off the mountain. One of the team helped me down, since it was slick from the rain."

Tatum wished they could change the subject. She was thankful to see him close his notebook.

"How do you like living in Breckenridge and being involved with the tea shop?"

"I'm glad Georgia handles the daily decisions. I come to work but just live day to day. I'm told it gets better."

"Have you done anything just for fun since the accident?" He looked concerned.

"Fun? No." Tatum looked away.

"Come with me to the Jazz Festival and Farmer's Market in Vail this weekend. You need a change of scenery, and the food and music are always good. Actually it's every weekend for twelve weeks, but I don't have to work this Sunday. What do you say?"

Georgia passed by the table just then and overheard Rick's statement.

"Y'all need to do that, Tate. We're not open on Sundays, so you can't use work as an excuse. I insist you go with Rick to Vail."

Tatum might have been able to say no to Rick, but not Georgia.

"All right; I'll go. But you can't make me have a good time. I'm just going because it's no use arguing with you." She tried to act mad, but seeing Rick's and Georgia's grins, she couldn't help grinning herself. And it felt good! Suddenly, Sunday couldn't come quickly enough.

BLOG:

August 16

Relevant Ramblings: Before the Fact

I usually wait to post about an event until after I've experienced it, but I want to get these feelings down on paper and then see if they're justified or unfounded. I'm going to the farmer's market/music festival with Sheriff Rick in Vail on Sunday. He insists it's not a date. But how do you go to an event with a guy and not think of it as a date? Will I compare him to Eric? Can I even bring up Eric's name? Will other people think we're an item? Will I feel uncomfortable? Should I pay for my part of the day so it doesn't feel like a date? Oh, all these questions! I'll have to wait and see. #somethingtolookforwardto

Nicole: *I'm glad you have something to look forward to. I want to know every detail—soon.*

11 🍃

Sunday morning Tatum took more time to get ready than she had in weeks. After three discarded outfits, she almost gave up. *This shouldn't be so hard.* She had to keep reminding herself Rick was just being nice. This wasn't a date. She finally went back to the first outfit she had thrown on the bed. It would do.

"Actually, I look pretty good!" She laughed. Spartacus, used to her silent moods, came into the bedroom to see what the noise was about. She laughed again at the look on his face. She was thankful to have somewhere to go and someone to go with, and she was determined not to think of Eric today. Nothing would dampen her mood.

When Rick picked Tatum up at nine-thirty a.m. on Sunday, she was more than a little nervous. On the drive from Breckenridge to Vail she talked about anything that came to her mind so Rick wouldn't have a chance to ask personal questions. She usually wasn't talkative with relative strangers, but in her uneasiness she filled in the silence.

"I don't know anything about jazz. Well, to be honest, I don't know a lot about any kind of music. Of course I know the Beatles and the Rolling Stones, but I wouldn't know any jazz artists. Oh, what about Kenny G? Is he considered jazz? The more I'm talking, the more you're probably thinking I'm not happy about going to a jazz festival. I really am. I just don't know anything about jazz."

"Sorry," she added sheepishly, feeling embarrassed. "I don't usually talk just to be talking." She was relieved to see they had gotten off I-70 at the Vail exit and were driving into the parking area.

Rick appeared to take it all in stride. He politely assisted her out of the car.

They joined the sea of eager people walking from the parking lot to the tents in this picturesque setting in the beautiful Vail valley. All her senses awakened. Baskets of flowers hanging from light poles added splashes of color to the scene. Delightful scents wafted on the air. She could almost taste them, even before a morsel entered her mouth. The fresh mountain breeze on her face energized her. The sounds of dogs happily barking and people joyously chatting made this market more than a place to sell goods, but an event of the highest caliber. And what a wonderful venue to people watch.

"Come this way, Tatum." Rick touched her arm to guide her to the right. "We'll first taste all the samples the vendors are offering, before we choose what we want to eat."

"How do you choose? Everything looks and smells heavenly."

Rick grinned. "I know my favorites. But one needs to sample them all."

They strolled from booth to booth, inspecting the

artist's photography, paintings, and sculptures. The homemade-craft booths held unique items. They finally reached the food samples. After sampling a few, Tatum said, "Rick, they're all scrumptious. Why don't I just have what you're having. Then I don't have to choose."

"OK. Let's get lunch then sit in the shade. The music will start by noon, and we'll listen as we eat. Then we'll find dessert."

The day flew by as Tatum and Rick enjoyed wandering around, munching on goodies, and listening to music. She liked what she heard. Rick knew the names of artists and songs.

They were in no hurry.

"I can't believe how good that chicken Caesar salad in the crepe turned out. I'm going to have to tell Georgia about it and see if she can duplicate it." They sat in the cool mountain air listening to the horns and saxophones ringing through the valley.

Rick stood. "Let's find dessert—something sweet to hit the spot."

After the perfect cupcakes, they listened to various musical ensembles and browsed more arts and crafts booths. Even the short downpour was fun.

On the way to the car, Tatum exclaimed, "That was awesome, Rick. Thanks for inviting me. I'll have to tell Georgia she was right. I needed this."

Rick just smiled.

BLOG:

August 18

Random Ramblings—A Fun Day/Memories/Musings

All my fears were unfounded! I had fun today with Rick, and it felt good to laugh. He put no pressure on me with anything. Now I feel silly for worrying.

I did compare Rick to Eric a little. Rick is so much more laid back and easy going than Eric ever was. Memories of Eric are fading a little; I feel as if I'm betraying him. Rick brought his name up in easy reference, so I relaxed about that. If Rick asks me to go to another farmer's market (not that I'm hoping. OK, I'm hoping a little!), I'll say yes. I hope I don't answer too quickly! #notasbadasIthought

Heather: *I could have told you that! Glad you had a good time.*

More musings...

After I wrote that my memories of Eric were fading, I realized I have to put my memories of him onto paper. I remember his eyes, but not his smile. I remember his hands, but not his touch. I remember his muscular arms, but not his hugs. I remember his voice, but not his words of love. I remember an attitude of legalism, but not an attitude of mercy. I remember his perfection, but not his compassion. I remember using the word perfect a lot when speaking about Eric. But what may look perfect rarely is. Consider roses (they have thorns); clear mountain streams (they carry giardia); or babies (they cry and poop).

Now the only perfection I can think of is that he was a perfectionist. He not only demanded perfection of himself, he demanded it of others as well. Everything around him had to be exact. Why he was attracted to me, I'll never understand—I'm far from perfect. Did he see me as a project he could mold? My perfect world died with The Accident. #perfectnomore

Even more musings...

Somehow, being out with Rick, made me realize I've become dependent on those around me for my spiritual, emotional, and even physical well being. All my inner turmoil is because of the external challenges I have no control over. I've heard it said that change is inevitable but growth is optional. Part of me wants to throw a tantrum because of all the change in my life. It's testing what I've held true spiritually and emotionally. I don't have the luxury of depending on others for the answers. I'll need to find them on my own. Another part of me (it's a small part, but maybe it will grow) wants to see what God will bring into my life now that everything I held dear has been taken away.

The only thing I know: God's love hasn't changed.

Thanks for listening to my ramblings. #learningtogrow #nomoresurprisesplease

12 🍃

"Tatum, can you come here when you're through?" Georgia broke into Tatum's thoughts. "There's someone here y'all need to talk to." •

Tatum turned from her work shaping pastry to see Georgia standing in the doorway that led from the tea shop into the kitchen. Just behind Georgia stood a tall young woman. Tatum looked into the young woman's eyes and almost gasped. Eric's eyes! Dark blue, they peered back at her. But no, it couldn't be. Anyway, those eyes didn't have the hard edge that Eric's had. This young woman's eyes were soft and inquisitive.

Why was she seeing Eric everywhere—in a crowded mall, at the gas station, and now at the Tea and Java du Jour. *Will it always be this way?*

Over Georgia's shoulder the striking young woman watched Tatum with amusement.

"Tatum, this is Erica," Georgia said. "She came to Breckenridge looking for information about her father. How she knew to come to the Tea and Java du Jour, I can only guess. Must've been God's hand working."

"What's her father's name? Do I know him?"

Georgia stared intently into Tatum's face. "Her father was Eric Martin."

Tatum's knees turned to jelly. She sat down. *Eric had a daughter? My Eric? When was he going to tell me?*

The beautiful, dark-haired young woman who, except for the eyes, appeared of Hispanic heritage, came around from behind Georgia and offered her hand. "I'm Erica. Georgia says you knew my father."

I was engaged to him, but I don't think I really knew him. She accepted the handshake, aware of Georgia watching her. She glanced at Georgia and back at Erica. *What other surprises will surface? I don't know if I want to find out. And why is Georgia smiling?*

"'Bless your hearts. Have a seat here at the table with Erica. She has a story to tell you. Let me get y'all a cup of tea." Georgia got the teapot and cups as the two younger women arranged themselves at the small table. She brought them lavender tea.

Tatum took the steaming cup gratefully. *Ahh, she knows I need calming.* "Thanks, Georgia." Then she gave reluctant attention to the stranger.

"My name is Erica Reyes. Nineteen years ago my mom, Soledad, and Eric had a short relationship."

Tatum tried to detach from the words, imagining she was looking into Eric's eyes. *I wonder if Eric held this girl as a baby.*

"My mom loved him fiercely. But Eric's family pressured him, and at sixteen he chose to walk away from my pregnant mom. But now, since I'm named in his will, I guess he cared—at least a little, at least—"

"But why did you come to Breckenridge? Eric lived in Denver," Tatum asked. "Eric's brother mentioned to me something about the will. What did it say?" She heard herself and winced at her own demanding tone.

"Let me start at the beginning," Erica demurred. "I'll get to that part; but you need to hear the whole story." She sipped the fragrant tea.

Tatum assessed her. She was fairly tall. Dark hair from her mother's side. Eric's eyes for sure. Heavy, dark lashes. Striking. Dressed fashionably in impossibly-skinny jeans and a swingy rayon blouse, a patterned scarf wrapped loosely around her slim neck. Carried herself with graceful poise.

Tatum waited, tense. *Inhale the lavender. Breathe.*

Finally Erica began. "My mom went to the same high school as Eric. One day she was taking sh--, er, I mean garbage, from a bunch of jocks. Eric intervened. A friendship started. They didn't acknowledge the friendship in school but they'd meet on the sly and hang out. I'm a result of that friendship." The thick eyelashes lowered. "Eric turned his back on my mom." Surprisingly, she didn't sound bitter.

"In our culture, a girl having a baby on her own is acceptable." Erica seemed to anticipate questions. "But abortion is not. So my mom became a single teen parent. But she kind of went off the deep end, and she left. So my grandparents raised me. The lawyer told me Eric's father pressured him into the decision to turn his back on us. But he said that, even though he wouldn't acknowledge he was the father, he wanted to make sure the child would eventually be taken care of. I was named beneficiary of his trust fund and the insurance policy." Erica paused. "But I'll have to wait until I'm twenty-five to see most of the money." She met Tatum's gaze. "You mentioned Eric's brother, Walker. I've heard through the lawyer that he's really upset about all this."

Tatum's thoughts went to her meeting with Walker. *Knowing Walker, he's not just upset but livid that he's not getting any of the trust fund. That's what I saw at the funeral and what he hinted at when I met him for lunch. That scum! I'm glad Walker didn't get the money.*

"The reason I'm here in Breckenridge is to meet you and hear what my father was like. His lawyer who contacted me gave me your name and phone number and it was just dumb luck that I stopped in here before calling you." Georgia, walking through the kitchen again, overheard the last statement and patted Erica's hand.

"Oh, no, honey. Nothing is just a coincidence. Everything can turn into a God incident."

"God isn't interested in me." She shook her head, a puzzled look on her face.

Tatum knew what was coming next. *She can no more keep quiet about Jesus than she can not breathe.*

"I do declare! Then you don't know my Jesus."

Erica's puzzled expression intensified.

"What does Jesus have to do with this?" she asked. "All I know about him is he's the one on the cross at the front of *la iglesia de mi abuela.*"

Ah, she's bilingual.

"I'm fixin' to close up," said Georgia. "We might should continue this conversation at my house! In fact, why don't y'all plan on staying the night. I have room and I reckon we can stay up as late as y'all would like."

"Oh, I'll get a hotel room," Erica said.

89

"Nonsense," said Georgia. "You don't know the cost of lodging in a resort town. Besides, you're family."

Reluctantly, both Erica and Tatum agreed. While Georgia closed up, the two girls—one Eric's fiancée and the other his daughter—assessed each other as they engaged in small talk. Now that the shock had eased, Tatum could view Erica with more realism. She was beautiful but without conceit.

Lord, what are you doing? I was feeling like I could forget, for a little while each day, that my life was turned upside down. Eric, perfect Eric, who had so much condemnation of anyone who slept around, had yielded to temptation himself. His deception is what hurts the most. A sob almost escaped, uninvited, definitely unwanted.

Erica excused herself to find the restroom. Tatum turned to Georgia. "What in the world? This is just too much."

Georgia chuckled. "Really, Tatum, there is no such thing as 'too much.' God is still almighty and all-loving. Honey, one day you will look back on this time in your life that seems so bad now, and you'll see how God brought good out of it all."

"I don't want to wait for hindsight." snapped Tatum.

"Then where would trust come in, honey?"

For the short ride to the condo, Georgia took Erica in her car. Tatum followed in hers.

Erica commented how dark it was in the mountains, then the rest of the short drive was silent.

Georgia prayed silently for the two women thrown together because of one man.

Erica silently wondered what she would learn about a father who must have cared for her a little.

Meanwhile, in her silent car, Tatum was trying to process yet another strange turn of events.

At the condo, as Georgia put the inevitable tea kettle on the stove to boil, the girls sat down at the round, cloth-covered table. Erica seemed uneasy, but the tea did help the conversation. This time chamomile. Not only did the tea give them something to do with their hands, it definitely provided a balm on a cool night, soothing both physically and emotionally.

The tastefully-decorated condo reflected Georgia's Southern heritage. Most decorating in this town was mountain-lodge inspired, with darker colors and lots of wood, but Georgia would have none of it. The white front door they entered through bespoke of what lay inside: soft sage green and taupe accent colors; richly-upholstered living room furniture.

Tatum noticed Erica staring as if this wasn't what she was used to seeing in a home.

Erica finally focused her attention to the ladies at the table with her. "How did you meet Eric?" she asked Tatum. "I have so many questions, but that's a place to start."

In spite of the pain Tatum knew would surface with

reliving all this, she was actually beginning to like this young girl sitting across the table from her who was so unlike Eric, yet whose dark blue eyes watching her intently now, were Eric's. She sighed.

"Eric and I met through an online dating service. It sounds strange but that's what happened."

"That doesn't sound so strange. I have friends who do that regularly."

Tatum raised her eyebrows but continued. "Two of my friends dared me to go on a site and see what I could find. Let me tell you, I found that not all dating sites are created equal. I visited a number of them before I came to the site where I met your father. Of all the matches, I picked Eric. Because of all the areas of compatibility I thought we could have the perfect relationship, in spite of our age difference. After all, we were both born again Christians and—"

"Isn't everyone in this country Christian?—Except of course, the atheists, the Jews, and the Muslims?"

"I'll explain that later. Let me continue. We both liked the outdoors, but Eric took it to a whole other level. He was an expert mountain climber, and he had climbed almost all fifty-four fourteeners in the state."

Again puzzlement crossed Erica's face.

Tatum explained, "Colorado has fifty-four peaks that are fourteen-thousand feet above sea level in elevation."

"Is that high?" asked Erica.

"Yes. More than two-and-a-half miles above sea level." Tatum let that sink in, then continued. "It's very prestigious to be able to say you've climbed all those mountains, and Eric was almost there, having only one more to go. We were climbing Mount Bierstadt, my very first fourteener when The Accident happened." Her voice began to quaver. She sipped tea until she could continue.

"Our first date was in a coffee shop in Denver. We had emailed each other and talked on the phone, but hadn't yet met. Here was this handsome guy, with the most amazing blue eyes I'd ever seen—just like yours. He had on khakis, a blue polo shirt that seemed to match his eyes, and a leather jacket. Over the next seven weeks, emailing, talking, and going out to dinner, I fell head over heels in love with him. His spiritual walk was what impressed me the most."

Erica's eyebrows knit together.

I don't have to wonder what Erica's thinking. It's written on her face. "Is that confusing? We can come back to that, too—"

Georgia interrupted with the offer of more tea. Both declined and glanced at the clock.

Georgia suggested they get some rest then resume in the morning and, with yawns, the girls agreed. Georgia showed them each to a guest room.

Tatum lay awake in the large bed and stared at the ceiling. Too many surprises. She didn't feel like praying just now. But she was pretty sure Georgia was not only lifting her up to the God of the universe, but was also lifting up Eric's daughter.

Tatum vowed to ask Erica in the morning about *her*

93

story. As she drifted to sleep, she saw those dark blue eyes. Erica's eyes. Or were they Eric's eyes?

🍃 🍃 🍃

Next morning she woke to the smell of bacon and eggs. And coffee. She threw on the pink chenille robe Georgia had left on the chair next to the bed and appeared in the hallway as Erica did the same from her room. They shared a smile when they realized they were in identical robes and slippers! They headed toward the tantalizing smells.

Georgia greeted them each with a hug. "How many pieces of bacon and how many biscuits do all y'all want with your eggs?" Georgia sat down with them. After saying grace for the meal, they ate in silence for a time.

Between bites, Erica asked Tatum how she came to know Georgia. In true 'few-words Tatum' style, she answered, "Georgia is my second mom and the manager of the tea shop, which I inherited from my parents."

Erica continued the questions. "Georgia, I know a Southern accent when I hear one, so you must not be from Colorado."

Their host smiled. "You're right, I grew up in Georgia. I came to Breckenridge when I got married. My husband has since passed away, but I stayed."

Then Georgia beat Tatum to the question. "Erica, tell us about your life."

Erica finished her last bite of bacon, took a sip of coffee, then began. "My mom was living in my grandparents' house, of course, when I was born and when I was two and a half she took off. I guess she felt too confined in her social life, with a two year old. She would show up maybe twice a year, usually holidays. My grandparents, Maria and Diego Reyes, raised me. They did the best they could; but I really did whatever I wanted, whenever I wanted."

"Did you finish high school?" asked Tatum.

Erica grinned. "I didn't apply myself very much in school, but I could bluff pretty good, and I graduated."

Georgia asked, "Did you have a job during high school?"

"When I turned fourteen I got a job because I lied about my age. I always looked and acted older than I was." She pulled her shoulders back and lifted her chin.

"How old are you, Erica?"

"I'm eighteen. I usually tell people I'm twenty-one, though. And I have a fake ID to prove it!"

"I got a job in a trendy boutique where the clientele flashed around lots of money. I got good at add-on sales, and the owner turned a blind eye to my age. I bought lots of nice clothes with my discount."

"Yes, if your outfit yesterday was any indication, I'd say you dress quite fashionably," Georgia said.

Erica smiled at the compliment. "I was impressed with all the money I saw being spent. One man, especially, seemed to have unlimited cash to buy the girls he came in with whatever they wanted. He noticed my interest and when I turned sixteen he took me under his wing and began grooming me to be one of his girls."

She stopped, then visibly shook herself and continued.

"I don't want to go into detail about my summer with Julio, but he treated me special. When he asked the other girls to teach me the ropes, I was smart enough to know what I would become if I stayed with him, so I broke off that relationship. Part of me loved the drugs, the money, the attention; but another part of me knew the lifestyle that came along with the exciting things could kill me."

Tatum expected Georgia to jump into the conversation with a "Thank heaven." But she only asked if the girls wanted more coffee. Erica declined, but Tatum accepted another refill. She sipped the rich liquid absentmindedly.

Her thoughts were spinning. *What if Eric hadn't died? What if he could be sitting here listening to Erica's story? What if Erica had stayed in the lifestyle of money, drugs, and who knows what else? What if Erica hadn't walked into the Tea and Java du Jour and encountered Georgia?*

Georgia returned to the table.

Erica continued her story. "My uncle Antonio, who is older than my mom, lived at my grandparents' house off and on. He was part of a gang. As I grew up, we'd have gang members at our house for dinner all the time. They looked scary with all their tats, but I felt protected having them around. They treated Tonio's little niece with affection and seemed to look out for me as I grew up and made my way around the neighborhood.

"When I called out Tonio on something, he would

say to me 'Erica, *mi corazon*, do what I say, not what I do!' I'm not sure why he called me that; but I loved it." She put her hand palm up on the table and pulled up her sleeve to show Tatum and Georgia the small red heart tattoo on the inside of her wrist. "That's why I got this." A wistful look settled on her face.

"*Mi Tio* Tonio was the closest thing I had to a father. *Mis abuelos* were easy to manipulate, but Tonio saw through my lies. When he was around, he gave me advice and discipline. Whenever I would ask about my father, *mis abuelos* would quickly change the subject. But Tonio would say, 'Where do think you got your beautiful blue eyes?'" She paused in thought. "I've missed Antonio since he moved out of state."

Tatum tried to process it all. "What are your plans?" she asked.

"Now that so many possibilities have opened up, I'm really overwhelmed. Part of my reason for coming here to learn more about a father I've known nothing about, is to explore my options."

Georgia's eyes twinkled. "Honey, since you have retail experience, while you decide about your next step, would you like to work the cash register at the Tea and Java du Jour? Tatum, we are looking for a cashier, and it seems like one just appeared!"

Tatum shrugged her shoulders but nodded.

"Erica, what do you think? Would you like to stay in Breckenridge and work here?" asked Georgia. "You could stay in my guest room and pay a small amount for room and board."

Tatum considered this silently. *Can I continue to look at those eyes and not long for Eric? What are you doing, Lord?*

"Since nothing is waiting for me back in New York, and I don't have a clue what my next step is, it seems logical to take you up on the offer. I like to work with people; and since I've never been in Colorado before, it might be exciting to get to know the mountains. What do you think, Tatum?"

Tatum wanted to stamp her foot and give a retort. *What choice do I have?!* Instead she said (though without much warmth), "That sounds good. But I need to get home and see what kind of trouble Spartacus has gotten into." To Erica she explained, "That's my parents' cat I inherited." Then as an afterthought, not knowing why she said it, "Would you like to come with me, Erica?"

Erica said she would. She excused herself and went to the bedroom to change.

Though Georgia's back was turned, Tatum was sure her older friend was smiling. Well, Tatum didn't feel like smiling. Things were constantly being decided for her and around her, and she hated it!

"This won't be nearly as bad as you think. I'll be lifting y'all up in prayer," said Georgia.

When Georgia said she'd pray, she meant it, but this time Tatum didn't know whether she was glad or not.

13 🍃

"Wow! How do you get anything done? All I'd be doing is looking out the window at the view! The only time I've ever seen anything like this was in movies." Erica stared, slack jawed, at the scene out the great room windows of Tatum's house.

"That's the Placer Valley below, with the river meandering through it."

"The river couldn't be more picturesque if an artist painted it on paper and pasted it in that valley."

"The view changes with the seasons. In spring, light green leaves open on trees and bushes, even while brilliant white is still clinging to the high peaks. Then, as grasses and willows along the river mature, the summer greens grow darker."

Erica's eyes wandered—with wonderment—over the valley and up the mountains.

"But my favorite season is fall, when patches of yellow aspen splash across the valley. I love the gold touches among the dark evergreens. They look almost like bursts of flame." As soon as she said it, Tatum thought, *Hmmm, maybe flames in the forest isn't such a wonderful metaphor.*

"Winter is almost as awe inspiring. The two fourteeners gather snow and stand like white sentries, so impressive in their grand stateliness."

Tatum chuckled. "I didn't know I was so poetic!"

"Well, it's awesome."

"Never grows old. I can't walk into this room without stopping to admire the view. I'd give all this up in a heartbeat, though, to have my parents back. This will always feel like my parents' house, not my house. I can understand how the opportunities you have in your future are exciting as well as scary."

"This is so different from anything I've ever known. And it's not only the scenery. New York City was all hustle and bustle—excitement 24/7. Here, on the other hand, it's so…laid back." Another pause and she switched the subject. "Tell me about your parents. You sound like a normal family, something I don't know much about. Do you have brothers or sisters?" As Erica spoke she never took her eyes off the snow-dusted peaks and the blue sky.

Does she know her eyes are the same color as today's sky? Tatum studied her new acquaintance. Then she replied, "I don't know how normal my family was. My parents were Nathan and Nora. I was their only child, so you and I have that in common. They were very involved in our church and took me there from the time I was two weeks old. My dad's job as an engineer gave him a lot of vacation time, and we usually traveled somewhere to do mission work."

Erica looked away from the window with an expression that told Tatum she'd never before heard of doing such a thing.

"When I was fourteen, I went with them for three

months to help in an orphanage in Mexico. My school counted it as days learning if I would write a paper about my experience. That trip was where we met Georgia. I had to catch up on math over the next summer, but it was worth it. Traveling and missions were something that Eric and I had in common." She couldn't yet bring herself to call Eric this girl's dad.

"Tatum, will you tell me more about my father? It seems strange to call someone that. I knew nothing before today."

Yeah, I guess I can do that for her.

"I can tell you that Eric was very good at everything he did. He was near the head of his class in high school, college, and law school. And he was an excellent athlete. I would even call him an extreme athlete. He didn't do anything halfway. I think 'perfect' was Eric's middle name." *Too perfect.*

"He loved to be in the mountains. I think he only practiced law to finance his mountain climbing. He was so patient with me and my fear of heights. All his stress seemed to vanish when he stepped foot on the mountain. He loved to point out the areas of interest I knew nothing about. Eric was," Tatum chose the words carefully, "knowledgeable and generous with what he knew."

"What about his brother, Walker?"

"Well, he's a piece of work! I don't know how two people, coming from the same family can be so different. It seems Walker's only care in the world is, 'Where's the next party?'"

"Sorry, but I think my father wasn't all that perfect.

Otherwise, I wouldn't be here. So maybe Eric and Walker were really not all that different?"

"Maybe you're right. I guess I wanted to paint a good picture of Eric."

"You don't need to protect me. I can handle anything. I grew up on the streets of New York. I could also remind you that Eric abandoned me and my mom." Tatum was taken aback by the sharpness of Erica's words.

"You have to realize, Erica, that the less-perfect side of Eric is kind of new to me. I've only known for two days that he had a daughter. Please forgive me. I'll try to be more honest in the future."

Now it was Erica's turn to look surprised. But she covered it up by saying, "Since I'm going to be here for a while, you'll be glad to know you never have to guess what I'm thinking. I'll let you know straight up."

"That's good to know. Now, are you hungry? I'll make us some lunch."

Tatum, who needed some space from all this bluntness, hurried into the kitchen. She left Erica gazing at the view, as if she was trying to memorize it.

BLOG:

August 29

Random Ramblings—Surprise!

Just when I think all is going smoothly—BAM! I

just met Eric's eighteen year old daughter. Yes, you read that right. Perfect Eric had a daughter and I wonder when he was planning to tell me.

Georgia offered her a job (which I reluctantly agreed to) and she accepted. So I guess I'll be getting to know her better.

Didn't I tag my last post "#nomoresurprises"?

After the shock wore off, I discovered she's a delightful girl. Apparently she's now also wealthy. The only part that doesn't sit well with me is that this is another thing he withheld from me. Would you be surprised? And how would you feel? #surprisedandhurt

Heather: *Girl, we need to talk in person!*

Nicole: *WHAT??????*

September 10
Random Ramblings—Erica

There's no mistaking her sapphire-blue eyes. And that east-coast accent and bluntness! She called me out on painting a perfect picture of her father. I have to admit, it's true. She'll be a constant reminder of how much I didn't know about Eric. Maybe I can just let Georgia deal with her.

Now that I think of it, though, she *is* something tangible left of Eric. She's innocent of his apparent deception. I need to separate my thoughts and feelings about Eric from my attitude toward his daughter.

But, oh Lord, help me. #eyeslikeherdad

14 🌿

Monday at the Tea and Java du Jour, Tatum was finishing up with the lunch crowd when Georgia approached with a furrowed brow.

"Tatum, I have something for you." She was making an effort to smile. She reached into her apron pocket, retrieving an envelope. "I have no idea what this is about, but Eric mailed this to me just before you were engaged. He said I should ask no questions, but if anything happened to him and if someone named Erica showed up, I was to give you this. So here it is. I guess because of the danger of his mountain climbing it's possible he realized he needed to cover his bases—or because of his lawyer mind. Whatever his reasons, maybe you'll find some answers here."

Tatum took a step backward, anger flaring inside her. "You kept this secret from me until now? How could you? I thought you cared about me more than that. You had a secret with Eric that could have hurt me. He was wrong to make you choose, but you should have told him to man up and talk to me."

Georgia hung her head. "It seemed the right thing to do at the time."

That answer just threw oil on her fire. "Eric and I would have started our marriage without openness and honesty. And you would have been part of that. How could you think that would be a good thing?"

Georgia's head came up and her green eyes flashed. "I may have done the wrong thing by keeping this secret, but don't you question my reasoning and integrity. I did it to protect you. We don't even know what's in the envelope."

"No matter what's in it, you should have told Eric nothing good comes from secrets. What if he hadn't died? If this has something to do with Erica, when do you think it would have been the right time for Eric to tell me about her? You could have refused to be a part of the secret." She paused but wasn't quite done. "How can I trust you again?" Now she was done.

Georgia sighed and her shoulders slumped. "You're right. I handled this the wrong way. Will you forgive me? You've taught me a valuable lesson I won't soon forget. But you have to find out what's in this letter." She held out the envelope.

After an uncomfortable moment, Tatum reached for the letter, not sure she wanted any more surprises. But maybe some of her questions would be answered. Questions like "why" and "how dare you" and "what were you thinking?"

The letter seemed to burn her hand as she fled the shop. Her anger spent, she gave in to curiosity. What did it say? She got in her car but just sat there. Her hands shook as she finally tore open the seal. Her fingers were cold. The sight of Eric's neat handwriting brought tears to her eyes. She swallowed and began to read.

Dear Tatum,

If you're reading this, I never got to tell you the truth in person. I've been living a lie, withholding the fact that I have a daughter. I would have told you after we were married. I guess I was afraid it would be a deal breaker for you. I guess at heart I was a coward. Oh, not on the mountain—never a coward there, but in my personal life. I gave you such a hard time about fearing risk, and yet...

My behavior was hypocritical, and I knew it, but I couldn't risk the truth coming out about my past and the girl who would have been your stepdaughter. Now you've met her. Georgia was sworn to secrecy. Please don't blame her. I take all the blame.

But now that you've met Erica, I have to ask you to do something that may not be easy. Will you love her like you loved me? Although I've never met her, I've kept apprised of her life as she grew up.

Will you forgive me? You've always had much more grace than I've ever had, so I have hope that you will.

I was looking forward to growing old with you. You are the best thing that ever happened to me.

I love you, Tatum.

Eric

Tatum was stunned. Her mouth felt dry and her throat painfully tight. She dropped the letter in her lap and rubbed the back of her neck. Her thoughts were spinning, refusing to land. She couldn't absorb this new information. A moan escaped without warning. She clamped her hand over her mouth to keep any other sound—like a scream— from leaking out.

Through gritted teeth she spat, "How dare you ask me to love a girl you didn't even have the courage to meet? You took the easy way out with your daughter and you took the easy way out with me. I can't forgive you for either of those. And I don't see how Erica could either. It will be difficult, but I'll love her all right—in spite of you!"

Not ready to face Georgia just yet, she drove home.

BLOG:

September 13
Relevant Ramblings—Apology Letter

In the midst of my confusion and pain, Georgia gave me a letter from Eric. He told her to only give it to me if Erica showed up. Well, the girl showed up. And I'm angry. Georgia got a piece of my mind. She should have shown more allegiance to me. She will have to build trust again with me. But on top of the sorrow of losing both my parents and then my fiancé, how on earth does God expect me to handle this deception? It's too much. How do I process all this? #lifeisthepits

September 16
Relevant Ramblings—Mad at God

Did I just write that? Oh, well. I've had too many

losses. Losing either my parents or Eric was unthinkable. Why both? Now there's Eric's deception. And
Georgia keeping this from me until now. Couldn't
God have prevented it all? When my parents died, I
remember saying God and I weren't on speaking terms
anymore. It's true again. #madatGod

September 17
Random Ramblings—Is God Fair?

No, He absolutely is not. #Hesnotfair!

September 20
Random Ramblings—Is God Fair, revisited

Isn't it just like God to meet me right where I am?
I just read this:

> *Do you think God is fair? He must not be. I've never
> done anything to deserve the love and mercy He gives
> me each day. If He were fair, I'd be condemned. (author
> unknown)*

In Lamentations chapter three, the author is com-
plaining that his life stinks. Then he says, "Yet this I
call to mind and therefore I have hope: Because of
the Lord's great love we are not consumed, for his
compassion never fails. They are new every morning;
great is your faithfulness." #Heisfaithful

Heather *I see some healing. I'm so glad.*

15 🍃

The next day Tatum called Georgia and asked if she could meet her at Georgia's condo early, before the tea shop opened. Georgia agreed.

The front door opened before Tatum knocked. Georgia had been watching for her. "Come in, dear heart. Thanks for coming. I spent a miserable night wrestling with my actions and with God."

Tatum went purposefully to Georgia and gave her a hug. Georgia's eyes filled with tears. "Thank you, Tatum." The usually more talkative Georgia stopped.

The usually less talkative Tatum spoke up. "I don't want there to be anything between us. Georgia, you're all I have. What I said yesterday was because I was hurt about all the deception I'm discovering. I know you were just trying to protect me."

They made their way to the kitchen table.

"I'm so sorry. If I could do it over, I'd do it differently." Georgia paused and then seemed to think of something. "Will you tell me what was in the letter?"

"Here, read it."

Georgia took the letter and read it once and then re-read it. "Tell me what you're thinking, Tate."

"I'm thinking the Eric I knew was a lie. I'm angry, hurt, I feel deceived, and I'm wondering if there were any clues I missed because I thought Eric was so perfect."

"Honey, it's not your fault. Eric was a master at making himself look good. The blame lands squarely on him. The next question is, what are you going to do with Erica?"

"She's not at fault here. I've chosen to love and accept her, in spite of Eric. Or maybe to spite him." She smiled and then her smile faded. "Eric valued truth in others so much. But apparently he lived a life that was much less than truthful. I wonder if he was miserable?"

"I have to think he was. Maybe that was why he controlled everything in his world. But we could sit here speculating all day and never know. Let's use our energy on what we can control." This was practical Georgia speaking.

"I agree. I love you, Georgia. Now let's get to work!"

"Tell me more about this 'relationship with God' thing."

Erica and Tatum were relaxing on Sunday afternoon at Tatum's house. Erica again gazed intently at the views.

"Isn't God somewhere in heaven, too busy doing whatever He does to really care much about what goes on day to day down here? And how can you have a relationship with someone you can't even see? Why would He want to have a relationship with someone like me, anyway?"

"Whoa." Tatum laughed. "That's a load of questions!

First I'll ask you a question. You didn't have a dad while you were growing up, but if you could imagine a dad who really loves you, wouldn't you want to spend time with him?"

"It's hard for me to imagine a dad like that. Thinking of a father reminds me of someone who abandoned me."

"Fortunately our heavenly Father is not like that, and He reaches down to start a relationship with us. It started in the Garden of Eden with the first man and woman God made."

Erica gave a *hrrumph*. "You don't really believe that myth, do you?"

Tatum smiled. "Yes, I do." She breathed a quick prayer and continued. "God created a perfect world but Adam and Eve sinned, and fellowship with God was broken. In order to be children of a perfect God, we can't be sinful. God provided a way through his Son, Jesus, that takes away that sin. Jesus paid the price so we don't have to. God loved us so much He let His Son die on the cross, like you saw in your grandmother's church. But Jesus didn't stay dead. He rose from the dead and we have a living Savior and someone who loves us and wants to have a relationship with us. He offers us a free gift. But we must accept His gift."

Erica was quiet for a time, then spoke slowly. "I've never heard any of this before."

Tatum smiled. "Jesus said, 'I am the way, the truth, and the life. No one comes to the Father except through me.' It's in the Bible."

"I thought the Bible was an ancient book full of myths and stories. I've never heard anyone say it was true. You really believe this?"

"Yes!"

"But if God is so true and big and powerful, why didn't he prevent my father from getting killed by lightning?"

"I don't know the answer to that question yet myself. I don't know about you, but the events of this past month are almost more than I can wrap my head around."

Erica agreed emphatically and seemed relieved that the conversation didn't continue in that vein.

"Let's talk about something I'm familiar with, like fashion and accessories." Erica was now in her element. "Let's go shopping and I'll help you look stunning in the perfect outfit!"

Tatum laughed. This beautiful girl might be fun to have around! She got up to make them a quick lunch while Erica folded her legs under her on the couch and gazed out the window at the beauty of the mountains.

BLOG:

September 22

Relevant Ramblings—First Questions

Erica and I had our first spiritual-journey talk. After a few easy questions came this one: If God is so loving and powerful, why did he let Eric get hit by lightning? OK, Erica, way to jump in with both feet and not beat around the bush! #Thehardquestion

September 24
Relevant Ramblings—An unexpected answer

I wasn't expecting God to answer my prayer about deepening my relationship with Him the way he did. Erica is asking some deep questions. I have to understand what I believe in order to tell her. The ground rules are that she can ask anything. And if I don't know the answer, I will research it and answer the next week. That gives me time to think before I speak—which sometimes frustrates her. I might have to explain that God had a design in creating some people as introverts—that's me, and some people extroverts—that's definitely her! We start next Thursday. I'll keep you posted! #deepquestionsdeepanswers

September 25
Relevant Ramblings—Introvert/Extrovert

This is going to be a simplistic explanation but, since I brought it up in my last post, I thought I'd explain what I mean. Introverts and extroverts differ in how they process information. Introverts get their energy internally and extroverts gain energy from being with other people. An introvert gets energy from ideas, emotions, and impressions. We introverts like to concentrate. An extrovert gets energy from people, activities, and objects. They like to interact. The "E" wants to talk through a difficult situation, and the "I" wants to think it through—in solitude. An "E" tends to act, reflect, and act again, whereas the "I" tends to reflect, act, and reflect again. To rebuild energy, the "E" needs breaks from time spent in reflection, and the "I" needs quiet time alone, away from activity. Fortunately, there is no right or wrong. Unfortunately, in relationships, generally an "E" is attracted to an "I." "E"s and "I"s are evenly split between male and female. See how easily conflict can arise?

By the way, did you know Albert Einstein, Bill Gates, Rosa Parks, and Mother Teresa were/are all introverts? Just a little trivia! #intovertextrovert #onesnotbetterthantheother

Nicole: *I'm certainly the "E." You and Heather are certainly the "I." It's interesting!*

16 🍃

Erica was spending the whole weekend with Tatum in the Alma house.

"Hey, Tate. I've been thinking about this question for some time now," Erica said over her coffee cup. "Hope you can answer it."

"Oh, no! Every time I hear that, I know I'm in for a challenge. OK, hit me with it." Tatum gripped her coffee cup tighter.

"When someone starts their journey with Jesus, why do some people get healed of their addictions immediately and others struggle big time trying to overcome those addictions? Georgia introduced me to Tom; and in our conversations he admitted that, although he's a Christian, he still struggles with alcohol addiction."

"I've asked that same question!" Tatum admitted. "Here's the answer I got from Georgia, and I respect her opinions and answers because she always has scriptures to back them up." Tatum stopped to gather her thoughts. "I think the difference is, whatever glorifies God the most. If the miracle of instant healing when someone comes to Christ will show His power and faithfulness best, that will happen. But I think we learn the most through the journey."

Erica nodded her head slowly.

"How could our testimony to someone else struggling with addiction be helpful if we had never wrestled in that way? There's a verse in Second Corinthians that says we get comfort from God so we can comfort others with the same comfort. That says to me that as we overcome whatever we struggle with, God is there; and as we learn from that, we can help others more than we could if we were just instantly healed. I'm glad I'm not the one to decide who gets the healing and who gets the journey to the healing."

"I like that, Tate. The journey to the healing."

BLOG:

September 27

Relevant Ramblings—Erica's Questions

What an enjoyable weekend in Alma with Erica. She is maturing and I love being around her. She is still a searcher, spiritually, but she asks great questions. Whether she knows it or not, God is pursuing her. I hope she doesn't have to come to the end of her rope before she opens her heart to God, but maybe that's how it works. I pray the Lord will help me speak truth into Erica's life. It's kind of exciting and shows how, in God's economy, nothing is wasted, even tragedy. Or maybe, especially tragedy. #bringonthequestions

September 30
Relevant Ramblings—Erica?

This will be short, but I wanted to get my thoughts down even if I don't have answers. How can I show Erica that her heavenly Father loves her when her earthly father had nothing to do with her while he was alive? I guess it's my job to tell her and God's job to help her understand. That takes the burden off me. More to come. #GodcandoitIdonthaveto

17 🍃

Now that Erica was working at the Tea and Java du Jour, she looked at the shop through new eyes. Walking up the sidewalk, Erica took more notice of the old, two-story Victorian house. On the sides were dormers with two windows each. The wrap-around porch made summer lunches a charming experience. White paint brightened the posts supporting the porch. And the requisite three colors? White, sage green, and darker green. Erica thought a bolder color combination would make the building even more of a standout.

Inside, the Victorian theme continued with antique, white-lace curtains and chandeliers over each of the six tables in the two rooms. The largest table, which held six guests, had the most elegant chandelier, the centerpiece of the room, with warm, buttermilk-and-green fluted glass shades. Erica glanced around and noticed two matching sconces on either side of the large ornate china hutch. The four other chandeliers, though less decorative, were equally as beautiful with their creamy-beige glass held by tarnished brass. The one by the window featured a color palette of burnt oranges with subtle hints of green and creamy beige in Tiffany style metalwork. Erica's excitement grew as she pictured this chandelier as her color inspiration for the outside. It was really much like putting fashion colors together.

She went back outside to stare at the house. She knew what colors she wanted! She couldn't wait to tell Tatum.

Back inside she continued her survey. The large antique china hutch held still more dishes, in various patterns. She had never seen much china and the delicate pieces and exquisite patterns enchanted her. Just as she had thought in Georgia's house, she now whispered under her breath, "People really live like this?" Her grandmother's dishes, though antiques, were far less ornate. Grandma's dishes weren't stored in a hutch, but were piled in a cupboard and were brought out for special occasions: heavy, colorful pottery painted with red, yellow and blue flowers. The matching platters, large serving bowls, and heavy pitchers and mugs were beautiful, but nothing like these delicate pieces.

She opened each drawer of the china hutch to discover sets of silverware, cloth napkins and tablecloths. She wondered fleetingly who did the laundry and where were the washer and dryer.

On the wall opposite the china hutch stood an equally large but less ornate, open hutch which held tea items for sale. There were several cups and matching saucers, teapots, cozies, demitasse spoon sets, cream and sugar sets. With her retail experience, she saw these as the add-on items she could sell to interested customers. There was also a cold case for fresh-baked goods, clotted cream, and lemon curd. The day before, Tatum had shown her the empty second floor of the old house. Her mind went to the empty rooms, imagining what they might become if the rooms were given a chance.

"Hey, Tate," Erica said, pulling herself from her reverie. "When you have a minute, could you come upstairs with me? I want to ask you about a couple ideas I have." Tatum gently placed the china plate she had taken out of the dishwasher on the stack of clean plates.

"Sure," she answered as she hung a dish towel that had been thrown over her shoulder on a hook at the end of the counter. "What do you have in mind?"

They climbed the sweeping stairs. At the top was a large room with a smaller room to the left—duplicates of the downstairs two rooms, with hardwood floors and in fairly good condition. The walls were a dull beige (*A coat of paint will brighten the whole appearance,* thought Erica). The dormers held two good sized windows each, which let in the morning sunshine from the east and the afternoon light from the west. Erica walked around the room clicking her pen as she made mental notes of what she envisioned.

Tatum waited for what her new, young friend had to say.

"What would you think about this room being used for selling little-girl stuff? The room right off this one could have scaled-down tables and chairs for little girl tea parties and we could start advertising birthday party themes like princess parties and teddy bear teas."

"I love the idea. Princesses and dress-up come to mind."

"And maybe pirate-themed parties for little boys. We can't leave them out." Erica was just getting started.

"Then the little girls and their moms would have to go past the merchandise and if I know anything about women and shopping, this could become a profit center. The little girls would like to have tea sets and princess accessories to take home and recreate the wonderful experience they had here at the Tea and Java. I can see lots of impulse buying! What do you think?"

"I think those are great ideas. Georgia could do the decorating, I could serve the girls their tea and treats, and you could do the selling!" Erica's enthusiasm was contagious.

"If we moved all our retail items up here, it would free up space downstairs for another table for customers. We'll sell only the baked goods downstairs and have all the other things up here. It wouldn't take too much effort to paint and decorate up here. You're brilliant, Erica. Let's go share this with Georgia and see what she has to say!"

Tatum marveled again that this business was hers, and there was enough money for expansion and renovation. She wanted to get Georgia's approval but knew her opinion would be positive. Tatum pictured taking Erica into Denver to purchase furniture for the upstairs renovation. She would finally be doing something proactive for the Tea and Java du Jour. It would give her more of a sense of ownership; and, besides, she needed something to look forward to.

The girls found Georgia sitting in the kitchen with a cup of tea in her hand. They joined her, and Erica couldn't get the words out fast enough. "Georgia, Tatum and I came up with a great idea for the upstairs. It would really expand our profits with children's parties and retail sales."

Tatum laughed. "This is all Erica's idea, actually; but I think it's a good one! I don't think the cost of changing the upstairs to accommodate what we want to do would be exorbitant."

Erica jumped in. "Also, I've come up with a color scheme for the outside that will really make this house stand out. What would you think about changing the colors to cream, bronze and burnt orange? I got my inspiration from that light fixture over there." She pointed to the chandelier near the window. "I'll go to the hardware store and get paint chips so you can see how those colors will compliment each other. What do you think?"

"Well, I'll be! We needed Erica's new eyes to see potential that we never thought about! I think the ideas are superb!"

Erica interrupted in excitement. "And what if we changed out these white tablecloths to a creamy off-white? It would be in keeping with our warm color palette. The lace curtains are already off-white."

Georgia turned in a circle slowly, imagining the colors. "Why don't y'all come to my house after work tonight and we'll start putting it all on paper. Then we can decide on a budget for the project!"

Oh, yeah, budget. That's wise. I'm so glad I have Georgia to help with decisions. Tatum glanced at Erica and guessed by the smug look on her face that she was thinking she'd talked Georgia into something. She didn't know Georgia well enough yet or she would have never thought that. You didn't talk Georgia into anything—she talked you into things!

At Georgia's house that evening, after the small talk around the table, Georgia brought the conversation around to the matter at hand.

"Let's pray before we start," she said reaching for the hands of the other two women. "We don't want to make a big change like this at the shop without God's blessing because it would all be for naught. Erica, have you ever heard of the prophet Isaiah in the Old Testament?"

"No," Erica took a sip of her coffee before reluctantly taking Georgia's hand, "but I'm sure you'll tell me! I don't understand why a big God who has lots of important things to do in this world, would even care about small details like running a tea shop."

"Oh honey, you'd be surprised what God cares about. Isaiah wrote a book that's included in the Bible. In Isaiah's book he said, 'Unless the Lord builds the house, the laborers labor in vain.'" Erica gave Georgia an incredulous look. As Georgia prayed, Tatum wondered how Erica was handling all of this. Anything spiritual was all new to her and praying about everything probably seemed weird. Tatum prayed her own prayer silently. "Lord, use this all to draw Erica to yourself."

18 🍃

Tatum and Erica were excited for their shopping trip to Denver. They decided to remodel the upstairs for the kids' tea parties first. Together they had come up with a budget, something Erica had never done before, and they left early to make the most out of the day.

The drive down the mountain was filled with talk about everything under the sun. Erica started the discussion. "This is what I was thinking. For the themed children's tea parties, I've come up with three different ones. The first one is princess parties, with tiaras to take home and other princess stuff to buy."

Tatum jumped in. Her excitement showed in her huge smile. "We could have flavored hot tea and small sandwiches with a small dessert cake to finish it off. And add-ons for purchase are a great idea."

"Every little girl would want a little tea set to re-create the experience at home. Let's look for those today."

Brainstorming stimulated Tatum's creative juices. "I see the teddy bear teas as something maybe little boys wouldn't mind. Those teas don't have to be so fancy. The children would bring their own teddy bear along; but what could we sell to them?"

"Maybe outfits for those teddy bears, kind of like the build-a-bear places have. With action-themed outfits that would appeal to boys."

"Oh, that's good. And I can imagine the dress-up teas, with a hat on each chair for the girls to wear, which they could also purchase. Would the little girls come dressed up, or should we have things for them to put on?"

Erica was all over that. "Anything we can supply them, which they can also choose to buy, is more potential profit for us. I never played dress-up much as a little girl, but I know about trying to talk someone into buying me something I thought I couldn't live without!"

They discussed what they could look for related to the tea room expansion and the decorations that could lend themselves to children.

"Tatum, did you know that the color of a room will help people want to buy more?" Erica looked smug, like she knew something Tatum didn't know. "I was researching this on the web and found out in our situation, with fixed prices, a calm blue works best."

"I would have never thought to look that up. That's great research! Then it's blue for the sales room. What about the dining room?"

"A soft yellow is my choice, but what do you think?"

Tatum thought a moment and then agreed.

As Tatum drove, Erica called Georgia and told her their ideas, and she agreed wholeheartedly.

When small talk seemed stalled, Erica asked Tatum more about The Accident. Tatum took a deep breath and explained a little about the rescue on Mount Bierstadt.

"It's hard for me to let myself remember that day. It started out so nice. I was excited to be on my first climb. Of course, this was nothing new for Eric. He seemed happy for me to be sharing in his love of the mountains. And his proposal at fourteen-thousand feet was amazing. That altitude was where he was most happy. But the one thing I keep thinking about is, as we started the hike, I forgot my water bottle on the hood of the car; and part-way up, I remembered. He went all the way back to get it for me. I can't help but wonder if it was my fault he was in the right spot at the wrong time to be hit by the lightning bolt?"

"Oh, Tatum. You can't blame yourself." Erica spoke with confidence. "It was just a freak thing."

"Maybe so." Tatum shook herself. She decided to talk instead about something less painful. "Mountain Rescue Team was amazing. They responded immediately. And they absolutely know what they're doing. They're all volunteers who just love to help people who are having a bad day in the mountains. I'd sure like to get a chance to talk with one of them again.... Hey, I have an idea! I have a card that one of the team members handed me." She searched in her purse. "Here it is. Maybe we could call this guy and ask if he'd meet with us, to help us understand it all better."

The girls pulled off the highway in Idaho Springs. Tatum called Jerry Manelli of Mountain Rescue, who said he'd be happy to meet with them, and he had this evening free. They decided on a dinner meeting for the three of them at Tuscany Tavern that evening.

Meanwhile, during their day of shopping, they had success in finding just the right tables, chairs, and even some china place settings. The only decision left was the table-setting color scheme.

"You know, Tatum, if we stick with white for the tablecloths, we can use different colors of china and table decorations, depending on our party theme."

Tatum jumped all over that one. "You are so right, but little kids spill on tablecloths.... I have an idea. Let's get antique-white linen tablecloths for the main dining room and use the white ones upstairs. Then we can get thick plastic to cover all the tables so they wipe off easily."

"Oh, I wasn't thinking about that. You are so right. So our color will be in the china." Erica stopped and looked around. "Look at these children's sets. I think we scored, not only to serve on but to buy for resale. All the colors in the flowers—yellow, pink and blue—will give us a lot of choices in other decorations. I never had anything like this growing up. I could have had doll tea parties. I didn't play with dolls much, though."

Tatum was fascinated by the running dialogue with Erica throughout the day. She never had to guess what Erica was thinking. She was learning more about this almost stepdaughter.

"Look, Tate! Here's the perfect display case for us. And it's on sale! What do you think?"

"I think, with the charming little china sets and this case to display it in, we'll be set! Let's see if it fits in my vehicle. Then we need to get to Evergreen for dinner."

Tatum and Erica arrived at the Italian restaurant ten minutes early, ordered an appetizer of fried calamari and diet cokes, and chatted about their day.

Tatum enjoyed Erica's shopping savvy. She almost felt she had a little sister now. She could hardly wrap her head around the fact that if she and Eric had married, this fun, vivacious girl might have become her stepdaughter. But then she may never have sat here with Erica if The Accident hadn't happened. Could this be some good coming out of a difficult situation?

A little after six thirty, Jerry Manelli came rushing to their table. He wore his red jacket with RESCUE in bold letters on the back. He had on hiking boots and rain-gear pants. He apologized repeatedly for his tardiness. "I was on a mission that I thought for sure would take a short time, but we ran into some unforeseen circumstances, and I didn't have cell service to let you know I'd be late. Thus the rescue attire. Good to see you again, Tatum." To Erica he offered his hand. "Hi. I'm Jerry." In spite of his rush, he smiled warmly.

Erica returned his handshake and smile.

"This is Erica. Her father was Eric, whom you rescued off Bierstadt," said Tatum. "I'm sure you go on lots of rescues and don't necessarily remember them all."

Jerry thanked her for the reminder. He explained he was a retired police officer who thrived on the unexpected nature of police work and, now, as a volunteer on the rescue team.

"You probably have seen every kind of rescue there could be," Erica said.

"Yes, I've pretty much seen it all during my six years on the team."

The waitress came to take their order. Jerry said, "May I suggest the cioppino."

"What in the world is that?" asked Erica with a small frown on her face. "Is it edible?"

"It's a seafood stew in a clam based, herb and tomato sauce. It's delicious."

"I'll try it," said Tatum.

"I guess I will too, but you two will have to eat mine if I don't like it." Evidently Erica's adventurous spirit drew the line at new foods.

"And all three of us will have affogato for dessert." Jerry grinned at the girls. "Don't ask. You'll like it."

The waitress went to put the order in. Erica asked the first question.

"What kind of problems do people call you about? And what do you charge?" She wasn't familiar with mountain recreation, much less having to be rescued.

"We are all highly trained, experienced mountaineers who volunteer to find lost hikers, missing snowmobilers, wandering children, and climbers stuck on mountain ledges. We serve three counties but will aid any rescue organization anywhere in the state as well as the country. None of the members are compensated for their time, personal equipment, or transportation expenses. We all love the mountains and want others to have safe experiences there. We do this for free; otherwise, financial concerns might postpone calls for help and cost a life."

"Are all of you nuts?" Erica blurted.

Jerry laughed. "Yes, I think we're all a little nuts! We're all free spirits who just want to help. And, I confess, we sometimes flaunt our sense of independence. It doesn't faze us to risk our lives for total strangers, and I've heard victims more than once say our upbeat attitude and energy gave them a sense of hope." He smiled with a far-away look in his eyes. "We don't depend on tax dollars, so we do fundraising throughout the year. We get the most up-to-date equipment we can afford."

"Sounds exciting! Can anyone join?" Erica was now leaning forward with her questions.

"Anyone can apply. But there is a very rigorous training period, and only a few are chosen to fill limited openings."

"Tell us about a typical mission," Tatum said.

Throughout dinner, Jerry kept them on the edge of their seats with story after story about different rescues.

"Do all your missions turn out so well?" Erica asked.

"Unfortunately, no." He frowned. "Sometimes we go in for body recovery, many times in avalanche situations. Even when hikers or skiers wear beacons, we can't always reach them in time."

"How come people get lost?" Erica asked. "Can't they turn around and head back on the same trail they hiked in on?"

"If they're lucky, they can," Jerry said. "But what if it gets foggy and all the landmarks they thought they would remember are obscured? Or what if they can't remember if they took the left fork or the right fork on the trail? And sometimes they take a shortcut that seems quicker and get 'cliffed' out, meaning they can't go up or down."

"What is someone supposed to do if that happens?" Tatum found her interest piqued also.

"Discovering you're lost in the back country, or cliffed out, can be pretty scary, but remaining calm and staying put will make all the difference. It's more difficult to find a moving target. And they can make noise. A whistle is the best for attracting attention, but yelling for help will suffice. Streams and howling wind can mask a calling voice, so we tell people to keep trying. A lost person's persistence can make rescue possible!"

"Can't you just use your cell phone and call for help?" Erica asked the obvious.

"Great question, Erica! Yes you can, if you've got a signal, but when you're lost it's impossible to tell 9-1-1 where you are. And what if your battery dies? Your phone-mapping app may be incomplete, or some trails even nonexistent, so it's not a good idea to rely on them."

"Well, I don't plan on ever getting lost!" Erica said.

When Tatum realized they'd spent ninety minutes listening to Jerry, she spoke up. "This has been really interesting. Thanks so much for telling us about rescuing and for answering all our questions. You're the best! Now we better go soon."

They finished their affogato, which turned out to be

ice cream drowned in a shot of hot espresso, only lingered a short time, paid the bill, and left to head back to Breckenridge.

BLOG:

September 30
Relevant Ramblings—Tea Room Expansion

We are expanding the Tea and Java du Jour. Erica helped us see a vision for the upstairs and the profitability of catering to families. As soon as the upstairs is painted, the decorating done, and lighting hung, we'll start. We'll be expanding our choices as we think of them. We'll be selling all things child sized, things that the kids will insist on having and the moms can't say no to! We'll have to wait and see what other creative business ideas are going through Erica's mind. #fresheyesfreshvision

Nicole: *Heather told me to tell you that we want to see this tea shop. Expect us soon!*

19

Javier hung up the phone. The call had been short and rather brusque. The caller wanted someone in Colorado kidnapped and gotten rid of. The voice was disguised, but he thought he knew who it was. He or she wanted to be four times removed from the deed. He would be paid but not have to do anything except make a phone call.

OK, he could do that. He briefly wondered what this was all about, but the thought held no guilt whatsoever. That feeling had left him years ago.

He guessed money was the motive. It was usually about money. He knew some thugs in Denver who could find two money-hungry compatriots to do the job. Easy money for him. He scrolled through his contacts, stopped at a certain one, and smiled.

Erica switched to hostess mode as two nice-looking Hispanic guys came into the tea shop. They looked completely out of their element. One was taller than the other, but neither was taller than Erica. They swaggered in, as if they knew they could turn heads in a room full of women.

"*Buenos dias*, gentlemen." Erica spoke in her

brightest voice. "How are you, and welcome! May I show you to a table?"

The two returned the greeting in Spanish then switched to English just as Erica had. They took seats at the empty table and each accepted a menu. They looked around as if they hadn't seen a tea shop before.

Erica, good at reading the body language of her customers, stayed at the table. "May I suggest today's special? It's very good and very popular. It includes a pot of tea and scones with four different accompaniments. I will then bring out a three-tiered plate with Black Forest quiche, a variety of tea sandwiches, and two kinds of dessert. I also have coffee, if tea isn't your thing." They looked relieved and agreed the special and the coffee would be great.

These guys dressed in black jeans and black hoodies would have looked sinister if not for the colored T-shirts under the hoodies. They were certainly good looking, but Erica had never seen them before. When she brought their order, one of the two struck up a conversation.

"From your accent you must not be from around here," said the taller of the two. "My name is Jose and my friend is Manuel. Where are you from?"

"I'm from New York, but most people who work here in town are from someplace else. My name is Erica." She had her name tag on, so she wasn't telling them anything they couldn't discover.

There was a nearly imperceptible exchange between the two men.

It was enough to make her guard go up. Were they

more than two customers enjoying sandwiches, coffee, and scones?

"Where are you two from?" she asked as she filled their water glasses.

"Denver," said Manuel. "We're in the relocation business." The two men bumped fists clumsily.

"No more questions, then. Enjoy." She started to walk away.

Manuel stopped her. "We want to go out tonight," he said, giving her an insider look. "Do you have a recommendation of a bar where we can have a good time?"

"The locals usually hang out at Breckenridge Brewery. It's not far from here and pretty easy to find."

Jose said, "How about meeting us there tonight? Manuel's sister was going to come with us, but something came up at the last minute. It would be more fun with someone from Breckenridge."

"Oh, I don't know. I usually don't accept invitations from strangers."

"Manuel may be strange, but I'm really not! Aw, come on."

Manuel affected an offended look.

Erica laughed at their antics. "Maybe I'll see you there. I was planning on going out tonight."

"That sounds great! When do you get off work? We'll probably be there already, so look for us!"

Erica continued waiting on other tables. The only further interaction with the two men was when Erica gave them the check. They paid with cash, left a big tip, and told her they hoped to see her tonight. Busy with other customers, she quickly forgot the exchange.

At closing, Erica approached Georgia. "Could I use your car tonight? Please. I'm going to go to the Breckenridge Brewery for a little while. I promise not to drink alcohol and to be home early. I'll be ready to go to church with you in the morning."

Georgia hesitated. She had no reason not to trust Erica, but something niggled at the back of her mind. Finally she said, "As long as you keep your promise about the drinking, I guess it'll be all right."

As Georgia drove them home, Erica briefly remembered the two customers from the afternoon. She decided they were harmless enough, and she wouldn't let them stop her from going to the Breck Brew. But later, as she walked into the brewery, she was surprised to see Manuel materialize out of nowhere. "Hey! Come on. Let us buy you a drink." He lightly touched his hand to her back as a guide to where they sat. "We have a booth near the door. Thanks for recommending this place. It sure is rockin'."

Erica was hesitant but, against her better judgment, let them whisk her to their booth. What could happen in such a crowded place? Anyway, she could take care of herself in most situations. She ordered a Coke. She noticed Jose and Manuel had had a few beers already. She was used to this when she lived in New York. No need to worry. After a short time of small talk, Jose asked her what had brought her to Breckenridge.

"I came here to get some answers about my father. I started working at the tea shop and I'm living with the manager right now." She ordered a second Coke and then excused herself to use the restroom. When she got back to the table, she finished her Coke quickly. She glanced at her phone for the time and moved to get up. Her legs felt like rubber. Jose grabbed her arm so she wouldn't fall.

"I'm sorry, I'm not feeling good. I need to go." She reached for her coat and pulled it on clumsily. She jammed her phone into her pocket. Something was wrong. She only had Coke. Even in her fuzzy state of mind, she knew she was in a bad spot. She let Jose and Manuel escort her outside. Not until they had helped her to the car, opened the back door, shoved her in, and slammed the door did she foggily realize it was not her car. As both guys jumped into the front seat, she cried, "Wait. I want to go to *my* car. I don't know... what...you did—"

Jose said something as blackness took over her vision and she slumped against the door, unconscious.

🍃 🍃 🍃

"Mission accomplished!" said Jose. "Now to find the drop-off spot. Easy money!"

Unfamiliar with the area, it took them a while to find Boreas Pass Road. They only passed four widely spaced houses, then the road narrowed and turned to dirt. They saw only a few other cars on the dark road. As it wound up and up, they became convinced they were lost. The leaves on the aspens had all fallen, and the trees looked like skeletal ghosts reaching with bony arms to grab the car. Jose and Manuel were city boys used to street lights and close-together houses, not dark, dirt roads. Just as they decided the directions they were given must be wrong, they came to a summit. In the moonlight they made out an old log section house on the left. They stopped, got out of the car, and surveyed the area.

"Manny, look up!" Jose said, adding an expletive.

These boys were used to seeing a few, dim stars in the night sky from the bright streets of Denver, but had never seen so many stars, like diamonds thrown against a black cloth. They stood silent while seconds passed.

"Hurry up. This dark is creepin' me out!"

"Get that flashlight on and go round the back of this old house!"

Jose opened the back door of the car. Erica was still unconscious from the Rohypnol, commonly known as the date rape drug. Whatever their original plan was, the two men were becoming anxious to get away from this deserted mountaintop. Jose heaved Erica over his shoulder and followed Manuel around the back, Manuel's flashlight bobbing in the dark night.

"Hey, Manny, what are you doing?" Jose hissed, cursing at intervals. "You're only carrying a flashlight, I have a load here."

At the back they found the window broken just as they'd been told. The boss wanted no late, fall travelers on the Boreas Pass Road to notice a broken window or door on the front of the old building which the railroad employees had used to stay in as they cleared the tracks of snow in the winter, when the train still ran.

They tied up and gagged Erica, then climbed back out the broken window and ran to the car. The instructions said to keep going south, whichever direction that was, on the road through Como to Highway 285 to get back to Denver. More precaution. But they chose to go back the way they came. The darkness was way beyond comfortable.

When they reached the relative brightness of Breckenridge, with high fives and loud expletives they celebrated their accomplishment of a job in an unfamiliar place. They didn't notice the state patrol car flip a U-turn until he turned on his lights. Jose looked down at his speedometer and spewed some more choice words.

"OK man, stay cool." He glared at Manuel. "There's no way he can get us for anything but speeding." Fortunately for both Jose driving and Manuel in the passenger seat, the effects of the alcohol had long worn off.

They were also in luck since Officer Gammel's computer was down. Unfortunately for the two, the patrolman was alert enough to sense their fear, and when he shined his light into the backseat, he saw a woman's purse. He told Jose to get it for him and asked why it was there.

Jose and Manuel both started talking at once, but with two different stories.

"Which is it, your sister's purse or a friend's purse?" Seth Gammel asked. The officer opened up the bag and found the wallet. An ID was in there, with a New York address.

"Does your sister live in New York?" He shined his flashlight in the men's eyes.

They did the right thing and kept their mouths shut.

Since no crime had been reported yet, the officer had no reason to be overly suspicious. After copying down the ID information in front of Jose and Manuel, he handed back the purse but collected both driver's licenses and went to his patrol car to write up a speeding ticket for Jose.

Jose and Manuel looked at each other with relief. Manuel growled, "Why didn't you take her purse and dump it with her?"

"I had the girl. You couldn't grab the purse?"

The patrolman returned to the window, with their licenses, a speeding ticket, and advice.

"You have a long drive ahead. Keep the speed down."

The two men pulled away slowly heading north and got on I-70, back to Denver and familiarity.

20 🍃

When Georgia awoke in the morning, it took her several minutes to realize she didn't hear Erica preparing for church. *She promised me she'd go to church this morning.* Georgia went to the bedroom door and knocked. No reply. She opened the door a crack and peeked in. There was a smoothly-made bed...but no Erica.

Georgia sagged against the door frame, frowning. The girl was usually not this irresponsible. She hurried through the kitchen and opened the door to the garage. No car! She took out her phone and called Tatum.

"Hi, honey." Her voice came out a little breathless.

"Did Erica spend the night at your house last night?"

"No. Why?"

"I let her take my car last night to go out, and this morning it's not in the garage, and Erica isn't here." Georgia thought for a moment. "She told me she was going to the Breckenridge Brewery where all the locals go. She wasn't going to stay long. She said she'd come home early so she could get up and go to church with us."

"I'll come get you," said Tatum.

As Tatum drove to Georgia's, she considered that all she knew about Erica was facts. She didn't really know her character. What kind of character does the streets of New York produce? Probably not the same as the suburbs of Denver. And Erica had little or no spiritual background.

"Lord, I believed you brought Eric's daughter here for a reason. Now what's going on?" She didn't like all this drama.

As Georgia waited for Tatum, she also was praying. In her spirit, she felt she heard, "One step at a time."

Tatum was there within thirty minutes. Without a word they drove to downtown Breckenridge. They didn't know whether to be happy or angry or worried when they saw Georgia's car in the Brewery parking lot. They sat there for a moment stunned. Tatum tightened her grip on the steering wheel. Georgia, not a crier, had tears in her eyes.

"I thought I was a good judge of character. For crying out loud! I'm even letting her stay in my guest room. Granted, she's only eighteen. But she seemed mature for her years."

Tatum added her thoughts. "I can't believe she would be this careless. She could have at least called." There was silence. Tatum finally added, "Something must be wrong. She wouldn't just leave your car here in the lot. I think we should call the sheriff's department and report her missing." It felt good to be the one with a plan.

Georgia agreed, and the decision was made to go to the police station rather than call. When they walked in, Georgia's boldness took over.

"Do y'all have an officer we might could talk to about a missing person?" Her Southern accent always became more pronounced under stress.

They were told to have a seat in the waiting area. Within five minutes Rick came out and escorted them into his office.

"Good to see you again, ladies. What brings you in here on this Sunday morning?"

"We think Erica is missing. She didn't come home last night," said Georgia.

"Well, lots of times young adults have a lapse in judgment and don't make it home. That doesn't mean they're missing. When did you see her last? Did she say where she was going? Has she ever done this before?"

"Rick, she borrowed my car and said she was going to go to the Breckenridge Brewery for a short time and then come home. My car is still in the Breck Brew parking lot. She's never been irresponsible before."

He had more questions. "Could she have stayed at someone's house and forgot to call?"

Tatum answered that one. "Up until now, she's always done everything she said she was going to do."

"Tell me more about her."

Georgia replied, "Erica Reyes came to Breckenridge a short time after the funeral of her father, Eric Martin, to try to glean information about a father she never knew. She had found out she was named in his will—"

"The will!" Tatum interrupted, louder than she meant to. "That's it! I'll bet this has something to do with the will. At the funeral Eric's brother told me about it. He seemed happy that Eric's part of the trust fund set up by their grandfather would now be his. He seemed like a sleazy type who might go to any lengths to get that money. I'll bet Walker has something to do with this!"

"Hang on, Tatum," Rick said. "I want to hear about this brother, but let me get the ball rolling on the missing-person report."

He left his office and stepped to the front desk. "We have a missing person," he told the woman working there. "Hispanic female, eighteen years old, five-foot, eight-inches tall, one-hundred-thirty pounds, last seen yesterday evening at the Tea and Java Du Jour. Her car is in the parking lot at the Breck Brewery. Name: Erica Reyes."

An off-duty patrolman passing by the desk just then was heading for the door after his all-night shift. He stopped "Did I hear you say Erica Reyes?

"That's right, Officer Gammel."

"I did a traffic stop for speeding late last night. Two Hispanic males from Denver. My computer was down, so all I have on the two males is their names and addresses. They had a purse in the back of their car and couldn't agree on their story." Seth Gammel flipped through his notebook as he spoke.

"Yes?"

"The ID in the purse was for an Erica Reyes." He consulted his notes, then nodded. "From New York."

"Get me the report," Rick Santiago instructed Sherry Ladlow, front desk officer, then to patrolman Gammel he said, "Thanks, Seth. We'll contact Denver PD and have them pick these guys up."

Sherry handed him the report.

"Put out an Amber Alert—this girl's only eighteen." Then Rick returned to his office, closed the door and sat down. "We might have a break," he said.

The two worried faces watched him.

"Or at least a start. Last night one of my patrolmen had a traffic stop—two guys who couldn't get their story straight. Officer Gammel noticed a purse in the back-seat of the car, and checked the ID. Erica Reyes."

Georgia jumped on that statement. "How come those two weren't arrested after finding a purse belonging to someone else they couldn't explain? Makes no sense to me."

"They had no missing-person report yet and no evidence of a crime. It was a lucky break Officer Gammel wasn't out the door yet and overheard me mention the missing person's name—and before you say anything, Georgia, I'll say it for you. It's not just lucky coincidence; it's one of those God-incidences."

Miles away, Erica was waking up. As awareness came slowly, she first realized she was cold, very cold. Next came the feeling of panic. She was lying on a hard surface, on her side, but she couldn't move her arms or legs. Her heart was racing and she was struggling to breathe. Something was covering her mouth. She squeezed her eyes shut. Her nostrils flared, but she willed herself to breathe slowly. After a moment her heartbeat slowed back down.

Calmer now, she opened her eyes and looked around.

She was on the floor of a bedroom with two sets of bunk beds. She was not very far from a broken window. The window sill was low to the ground and broken glass was on the floor. The bedroom door was open, and through the door she could see a larger room.

Where am I? How did I get here? She tried to remember what had happened last night. She could only come up with going to the Breck Brew after work. *Wait.* Another fleeting memory. Drinking a Coke and chatting with two guys. More came back as she remembered feeling ill, but it hurt her head to think. *Oh, Jose and Manuel. They must've had something to do with this.* But what was this?

As the memory of last night cleared, she chided herself for letting her guard down. Just because she wasn't on the streets of New York, didn't mean there wasn't danger. "*Muy estupida, Senorita.*" She thought of the guys sharing a glance when she told them her name in the Tea and Java. Her radar had gone up. *Were they looking for me, not really there to have lunch? Ha! Relocation business. Very funny. Yeah. Not so funny.*

Her hands were bound in front of her. That was lucky. She pulled them up until she could touch her face and pull the tape off her mouth. "Ouch!"

Erica lay trying to remember what had happened after leaving the local gathering place. Her anger boiled toward those two good-looking guys with ulterior motives.

"What happened while I was unconscious?" Different scenarios played through her mind, none of them good. She used her teeth to try to loosen the rope around her wrists. She couldn't work the knot loose. Her hands felt cold. She awkwardly reached to undo the rope around her ankles, trying to work on the knot with frigid fingers. She was glad she had chosen her warmer coat and had struggled to get it on before she had left the bar. She remembered that much.

Another realization came to her. They drugged her Coke! Roofies, they called it on the street. She kept working at the knot.

She stopped. Was someone in this house waiting for her to wake up? If they weren't here now, would they come back? Her breath came in short gasps as she again tried to calm down. The rope finally fell from her ankles. She rubbed them and considered her next move. Her wrists were still tied, but she could at least get up and explore. The sun was rising higher; more light was coming through the windows. She could see more of the cabin. But where was this cabin located? Had Georgia yet realized she didn't come home last night?

She looked for anything sharp that would help get her wrists free. There was a wood-burning kitchen stove and next to it a wood box. An ax leaned against the wall behind the box.

"If Georgia's house was right out of a magazine, this cabin is right out of a Wild West movie. What would the victim in this situation do in the movies?" *Give me the slums of New York any time.*

Erica looked at the ax by the fireplace and hobbled towards it. She wedged the ax into a crack in the hearth and began to drag the ropes on her wrists across the sharp edge. Little by little the rope frayed and finally gave way as she leaned against the cold hearth rock, sweating and light-headed. She took a deep breath and stood upright.

"Now to get out of here. Fast." The front door wouldn't open. "Must be locked from the outside."

"The window in the bedroom! I must've come in that way. Then I can get out that way."

She hurried to the bedroom and crawled through the broken window to freedom.

"OK. Now I have a new dilemma. Which way should I go?" She didn't much care which was the right way; she just wanted to get away from this house as fast as she could. She began to run, startling a flock of birds that flew ahead of her. "I'm with you guys," she said to the birds. "Lead me home!"

Erica slowed to a walk down the dirt road toward what she hoped was Breckenridge. She stuck her cold hands into her coat pockets. Her cell phone! Hopefully there was enough battery. Yes! But no signal.

"Dang. A lot of good that does."

21 🍃

Rick Santiago finally got off the phone with the Denver police department. Now he'd have to wait for them to locate the two men that Officer Gammel had pulled over last night. He'd much rather be doing something. Both women still watched him expectantly.

"They'll be located and interrogated," he answered their questioning eyes. "It may take some time, but maybe not. It depends. For now, all we can do is wait. How well do you know Erica?"

"Erica came here in August looking for information about her father, Eric Martin," Georgia said. "No one knew he had a daughter until she showed up. She stopped at Tea and Java, not realizing we knew Eric."

"What can you tell me about her background?"

Tatum answered that one. "She was raised by her grandparents in New York City. She's eighteen but could pass for older. She seems kinda street smart."

"How long has she been in Breckenridge?"

"She's only been here two months," said Georgia. "We hired her to work the register in the shop."

Tatum couldn't help thinking, *What do you mean, Georgia? You hired her and told me about it.*

"Oh, that sweet girl needs Jesus!" Georgia added. "She's been staying in one of my spare rooms, paying a small amount of rent."

Rick had more questions. "Does she seem the type to leave a bar with people she just met?"

"I'm a pretty good judge of character, and no, that doesn't seem like something she would do," Georgia said.

Tatum agreed.

"Is there anything else you can think of that might give us a clue about why this could happen?" Rick's questions pressed them to think beyond the obvious.

"Well, the will! I remember Eric's brother saying something about it at the funeral. Erica also disclosed information about the will."

Georgia said, "Erica told us she was named beneficiary on the trust fund as well as the insurance. The trust fund is in the amount of one-and-a-half million dollars but I don't know anything about the insurance policy. She can't access the money until she's twenty five. If you think Erica sounds like a piece of work, you could multiply that by fifty and you'd have Walker."

Tatum shuddered at the memory. "Eric never told me about the trust fund. He never told me about a lot of things." The tears threatening to fall were tears of anger now, not sorrow.

Rick knew how to do police work, but he didn't know how to respond to Tatum's emotion. He scratched his chin. "I'm going to go into the other office and make some calls. You ladies make yourselves at home here in my office. Can I get you anything? Coffee, tea, a soft drink?"

They shook their heads.

He was gone twenty minutes. He came back and announced, "I have Walker on speaker phone. He wants to talk to you, Tatum."

She shrank back, but when she saw she had no choice, she spoke to Walker with more anger than she knew she had in her. "What did you do with her? I know this is all about the money, and you better come clean or, or, or—"

"Hey, Tate. What makes you think this is my fault? That really hurts my feelings. I have no idea why or how Eric's daughter is missing." He paused. "I may have been upset when I first heard about this girl Erica being named beneficiary of the trust fund, but I would never stoop so low as to kidnap her. Maybe I have a reputation that might make you think otherwise, but believe me, that's even below me." Silence again, then, "Maybe it's a lover's quarrel and she'll be home as soon as she gets it straightened out."

Tatum lashed out at that. "Walker, you know nothing about Erica or you wouldn't say that. Maybe that's how you behave, but not Erica."

"OK, maybe I don't know, but if your cop friend wants to make me take a lie detector test, I will. Then you'll see that I'm in the clear. Come to think of it, did Erica get the title to Eric's SUV yet? Father had it in his papers. Since it wasn't in Eric's name, it wasn't legally in the will."

"You knew about this and you're just now telling us? That's pretty suspicious. What else are you hiding?" Tatum felt livid.

"How was I supposed to know what dear old Dad did or didn't do? But I do know the vehicle is still in Denver, and I don't think he knows what to do with it. If I can get the title from him before I come, I'll drive the vehicle to Breckenridge. Will that show you I'm being straight with you? See you soon." He hung up.

"So he's on his way here," Rick said. "I don't know if he has anything to do with this, but it's best to have him close."

Oh, joy. Not again. But he is Erica's uncle. Thank God I'm not related to him.

"I'll go to the Breckenridge Brewery and talk to anyone who worked last night, since the car is in the parking lot. Do either of you have a picture of her?" asked Rick.

Tatum asked for his cell number. "I have one on my phone. Let me send it to you."

Rick nodded when the picture arrived. "Hopefully when I get back here I'll have a message from Denver concerning this Jose and Manuel. And know I'll be praying."

22 🍃

Erica had been walking for what seemed like hours. No cars had passed. This late in September, the aspen viewing was over. She had seen a fox, squirrels and chipmunks, deer, and scores of birds.

Her feet hurt. "When I bought these four-inch wedges I never planned to hike in them. They're killing me."

She longed for human contact. She looked around and scratched her head. "I don't even know if I'm going in the right direction. This road is going downhill, but down to where? Man, I hate these shoes. Right now I'd pay my last dime for a pair of totally-ugly hiking shoes.

"And water! Tatum said it's not safe to drink from streams. I need a car to come by, and preferably a car with a water bottle. Oh, great. I'm talking to myself. Lucky no one can hear me. Just wish I knew if I'm going the right way."

🍃 🍃 🍃

Tatum and Georgia, back at the police station, waited for Rick to return. When he did, the look on his face didn't bode for well. He set his notebook on his desk and took his coat off. The two women barely breathed.

"Since this time of year the bar is usually full of locals, new people are relatively memorable," he said, turning to the first page of his notebook. "One waiter remembers saying 'Hi' to Erica when she came in, and another waitress says she took care of her table. She was sitting with two Hispanic men."

"Did she see her leave?" Tatum asked.

"Erica only ordered a coke, but the men were drinking beer. Shortly after Erica's second coke, the trio left. Erica stumbled out between the two men. She had her coat on. The waitress didn't think anything of it until I asked her to recall what she could remember. Her impression was the men were waiting for her, and as soon as she walked in—"

"Wait!" said Tatum. "Two Hispanic guys came to the Tea and Java yesterday for a late lunch. They seemed out of their element. I heard Erica speaking to them in Spanish, only for a greeting and then they switched to English. I wondered at the time if Erica knew them. Did you see them, Georgia?"

Georgia shook her head. "You and Erica were waiting on the tables, and I was in the kitchen helping with the prep and clean up. What did the guys look like?"

"The only thing I remember is they were about the same height as Erica. Nothing else comes to mind."

"Would you recognize them if you saw them again?" asked Rick. "The computers have been down, so we're waiting for info from Denver. Then we'll have pictures."

The phone rang. Rick answered in the middle of the first ring. As he listened, he grabbed a pad of paper and scribbled some notes.

Tatum tried to read what he was writing but couldn't make it out. She waited impatiently.

He finally hung up the phone. "The two were apprehended and questioned. They claimed they didn't know an Erica Reyes but switched their story when they realized the purse in the backseat had been examined by the police officer. Turns out they both had priors and didn't show up for a recent court date for petty theft, so they were arrested on outstanding warrants." He took a breath and continued. "I'm going to Denver to interview them. I think you two should stay in Breckenridge on the off chance Erica shows up. You have my cell number. Call me immediately with any information you find."

Tatum and Georgia left the station and went back to Georgia's condo. She put on the inevitable kettle of water for tea, got out tea bags and mugs, and the two sat down at the kitchen table.

Erica needed a rest. She looked for a rock close to the road to sit on, where she could jump up if a car came. She couldn't believe it—no cars. Didn't anyone travel this road? Maybe she was walking in the wrong direction—not toward Breckenridge at all, but away from it. The sun had settled lower in the sky, and a slight breeze made her shiver.

"OK. I'm in a world of hurt if something doesn't—"
Was that a car?
She jumped up and hobbled to the middle of the

road. No way was she going to let a car just drive past! The approaching vehicle, coming from the same direction she had come, was a beat-up old Jeep pulling a small trailer full of fire wood—going too slow to have to slam on its brakes. It coasted to a stop.

The driver took his time winding down the window. He wore a hat, but his long ponytail hung down his back. He was dressed in a flannel shirt under his bib overalls, and a corduroy jacket. Bark chips clung to the coat, and the aroma of fresh-cut wood poured from the car.

"You look a little out of place on this deserted mountain road, Missy."

"Am I glad to see someone! I'm lost and don't even know if I'm headed to Breckenridge or not. Could you give me a ride? Even if you're not going to Breckenridge, I'll go wherever you're going. Where *are* you going, by the way? It doesn't matter. Just take me to the nearest town so I can call my friends who must be really worried about me. By the way, my name is Erica. What's yours? Oh, I'm rambling on and on and not even letting you get a word in edgewise. It's a bad habit of mine. OK, I'll be quiet and let you answer. I'm just so glad to see someone. You wouldn't believe all that's happened to me in the past twenty-four hours. OK, I'm done. No more talking. *Nada! Callete!*"

The Jeep's driver shook his head slowly. "You sure use a ton of words to say a little bit. Get in the car. I live over the hill a ways, in Como, but I'm on my way to Breckenridge to drop off this load of wood before dark.

You're welcome to ride with me and my dog as long as you don't mind there's no front seat. I don't get many ride-alongs with me to cut or deliver wood."

He wiped his hand across a bearded face and smiled. "Name's Mose. Truth be told, I don't usually go to Breckenridge using this road, but I felt impressed to drive this way instead of over Hoosier Pass today. Guess it's your lucky day!"

Erica grabbed the battered Jeep's door handle and pulled on it. There sat the biggest dog she'd ever seen.

"Will he bite? Looks like I'm disturbing him. Gosh, what kind of dog is he? He must be part horse! Will we both fit? Oh, no, here I go again. Quiet, Erica. Shut your mouth."

"Her name is Tiny. She's a mastiff. One hundred thirty pounds." Mose nodded toward the massive beast. "I've heard it said, what the lion is to the cat, the mastiff is to the dog. But don't worry. She's a gentle giant! Her biggest downside is—how do I say this delicately?—she sometimes has problems with gas! She just ate before we got in the Jeep, so if you smell something, it's the dog, not me!"

Erica laughed but still hesitated.

Mose handed her a bottle of water.

Tears came to her eyes. *Even a bottle of water.*

"Thanks, Mose." With a sigh, she settled into the place where a front seat would have been, next to the dog, who reluctantly shared her spot.

It felt good to finally get off her feet. She pulled off the shoes.

Mose continued down the road.

Erica provided the conversation. "You're probably wondering why I'm out here—in these shoes! Long story. Last night I met two guys at the Breckenridge Brewery. They must have slipped something in my drink. I passed out and woke up in that cabin back there, tied up, duct tape over my mouth. They tied my hands in front of me, luckily. Not too smart. I could reach to pull the tape off my mouth. Didn't feel too good, let me tell you. I could also untie the ropes around my ankles. But the ropes on my wrists were a little more difficult! When I finally got out of the cabin, in a hurry to get away, but no clue where I was, I decided to turn right. So that's why I was walking down this road. I began to wonder if anyone ever drives on this road."

"That's quite a story, young lady. Glad I was coming this way today."

They had finally reached pavement. "Yeah. So am I. My friend Georgia calls them God things or something. Oh, now I know where I am. Turn right at the next road. Georgia's condo is the third on the left."

23 🍃

Georgia and Tatum had just finished praying for Erica and the whole situation when they heard a knock on the door. They glanced at each other, then Georgia jumped to answer it. There in the porch light stood the answer to their prayers: a bedraggled Erica with a huge grin on her face, holding her shoes in one hand. A large man in work clothes stood behind her.

Georgia squealed. "You're here! Our girl is home!" She threw her arms around Erica in a huge hug. When she finally let go, Tatum did the same.

"Come in, come in." Georgia pulled Erica through the doorway. "Girl, you gave us quite a scare. But you're safe. And who is this fine-looking gentleman? If you've helped find our Erica, you're welcome in this house any time."

He followed Erica inside.

"This is Mose. He and his giant dog, Tiny, found me on a road because he felt impressed to go the longer way to get to Breckenridge! Georgia, it was one of your God coincidences, for sure!"

Erica threw down her shoes and pulled off her coat. "Can you make both of us a cup of coffee and a sandwich? And we'll tell you all about it. I'm hungry and tired, but you have to hear the story."

Tatum was already dialing Rick's number. She told

him Erica was safe. Then she listened, nodded, and hung up.

"The sheriff is on his way," she reported. "Why don't you go ahead and eat, then tell your story as soon as Rick gets here, so you don't have to repeat anything. Mose, you have to stay. Let me take your coat."

Georgia went into her Southern hospitality mode and had coffee, sandwiches, fruit and scones on the table in short order. Georgia had finished saying a blessing over the food when Rick knocked.

They waited while Rick gave hugs all around, was introduced to Mose, and found a seat at the table. The banter was lighthearted.

Mose only smiled and let everyone else talk. He gave his attention to the simple but tasty spread before him, as Georgia paid close attention to his plate and never let it get empty. She asked him questions, which he answered with as few words as possible.

The sandwiches disappeared fast, with most on Mose's and Erica's plates. The scones and fruit didn't last long either. Georgia got up to make a second pot of coffee. When everyone had finished with small talk and food, Rick took charge, notebook in hand.

"Erica, can you tell us what happened?" he asked gently. "Start at the beginning when you went to the Breck Brew after work."

Erica started with the facts, leaving out nothing. When she got to the part about waking up and feeling scared, though, she hesitated. She turned to Tatum and Georgia with tears in her eyes.

"So many coincidences. Like Mose here. But the biggest of all was the bottle of water he handed me without me even asking. I tell you, I was thirsty by that time." She recounted her misadventure, covering every detail, answering Rick's questions carefully. Then she had a few questions of her own.

"I can't imagine why I can be safe on the streets of New York and get kidnapped in a small mountain town. What's our next move? How can we even figure out who did this? Hey, what's that smile on your face, Rick? You know something I don't know?"

Rick explained last night's traffic stop and finding her purse in the backseat. He told her Walker would be here the next day with her father's SUV and the title.

"You mean I'll now have a car of my own? Really? Awesome. What kind is it?"

"It's a black Cadillac Escalade," said Tatum. "A large SUV. Only the best for Eric Martin, and now for you."

Mose decided it was time to leave, since Tiny was still in the Jeep. Erica gave him a big hug which he returned. Georgia gave him a hug too, which surprised Tatum. Mose turned with a wink to all and left.

Erica leaned back with a sigh and closed her eyes. "You know, I thought this little mountain town was kinda on the boring side. I'll never say that again. Thanks, Georgia and Tatum. It's nice to know someone has my back. Now I'm going to bed. Good night."

Tatum rose to leave. "My grandma always said 'All's well that ends well.' Sure fits in this case. See you tomorrow, Georgia."

BLOG:

October 2

Relevant Ramblings—Home Safe

Never a dull moment with Erica around! This was pretty scary, though. She was kidnapped! But fortunately, the kidnappers were bumbling idiots. She is safe, and they're in jail. I have no idea what will happen to them, but I know Erica will be more alert when it comes to new people. I think she saw God in some of the things that happened to her, which is a good thing. But my guess is she still thinks she can handle anything that comes her way by herself. I certainly hope and pray that when she gets to the end of her rope, she knows where to turn. It's really not hard to give up control of something you have no control of anyway. Mose and Georgia sure hit it off! They seemed to be cut from the same cloth, only she's Southern cloth and he's mountain cloth. Hmmm. I'll keep you updated! #safelyhome #southernmeetsmountain

Heather: *I thought you said your life was boring. I think not! I'm glad everything turned out OK!*

Next day brought the first meeting with Erica and her Uncle Walker. Tatum could have gone without seeing

him again, but for Erica's sake she endured the meeting.

"Erica!" Walker greeted her. "I'd know those eyes anywhere. Just like Eric's."

"Hi, Walker. Do I have to call you Uncle?"

"Naw, that's too formal. First off, here are the keys to Eric's car. And here is the title." With a bow, he made a big display of offering both things to her. He seemed his usual, cocky self, but there was an immediate connection between the two New Yorkers. Erica's accent came out stronger as she responded to Walker's questions and comments. His accent seemed to do the same.

"Father is relieved to finally have the SUV off his mind." Walker rolled his eyes. "I can tell you he was a little shocked to know he had a granddaughter. His perfect, do-no-wrong Eric was finally flawed. I wouldn't expect much grandfatherly support from him."

"You mean he won't want to meet me?"

"He doesn't like surprises in his neat and tidy life, but maybe he'll warm up to the idea." Walker shrugged. "Mother, on the other hand was, in her words, 'pleased as punch,' whatever that means. Oh well, you can expect some relationship with her in the future, if you want it. Hey, maybe she'll pour her energy into you and leave me alone. Now that would be good."

He turned to Tatum. "Hey, Tate. Good to see you again. How are things?" She reluctantly accepted his hug and then shrank back. Undaunted, Walker focused on Erica again.

Erica was talking. "Thanks, Walker. You can give your mom my cell phone number. Then it's on her. Sorry we accused you of having a part in the kidnapping. It was all circumstantial evidence. I'm glad you didn't have anything to do with it."

"That really hurt my feelings." Walker's pretense didn't come off very well, and this time he seemed to notice. "Anyway, Erica, I'm glad you're OK."

She grinned. "It's nice to have another relative. Could we go out to dinner? I'll buy if you'll tell me more about my father."

"Sure, but I won't let my niece buy me dinner. How about tonight?... Tate, you can come too."

"Uh, thanks, but Erica won't want to share you.... Some other time."

BLOG:

October 3

Relevant Ramblings: Excitement

Our lives are back to normal—whatever that is. Walker got here with Eric's SUV and gave it to Erica with the title as his way of giving her a peace offering. (I can't say I was glad to see him.) Erica met her uncle for the first time. I don't want this kind of excitement again, but I'm wondering what I'm missing by always playing it safe. I think it's time to tear down the walls I've put around myself to protect me from risk. Those walls really didn't keep me from it anyway. I've been at the mercy of random, unexpected events. Time to be proactive and take steps of faith. First step—a new haircut. Notice I didn't say "a leap of faith"! I'm not ready for that! But I'm ready to get out of my comfort zone—I just don't know how. Lord, give me some direction in such a way that I know it can only be from you. #comfortzonenomore #smallstepsnoleaps

Heather: *That's a start. Blessings!*

Nicole: *Send a picture!*

24 🍃

A week later, as Erica and Tatum finished up with the lunch crowd, Rick Santiago came into the Tea and Java.

"How is our favorite sheriff?"

There she goes again! thought Tatum. *Erica never hesitates to speak her mind.* But Tatum just smiled and let Erica speak for her one more time.

"I thought you'd want to hear about my interview with the two kidnappers. I've uncovered some further information, Erica." Rick leaned against the counter.

Erica watched him eagerly.

"And before I go, I have a question for you, Tatum. So don't let me forget."

What in the world would Rick want to ask me?

"By the way, I like the new haircut, Tate."

Her mind on other things, she was slow in responding to his compliment. "Oh, thanks, Rick."

"Did I come at a good time?" he asked. "I was hoping not to interrupt your work."

Georgia came out of the kitchen and, when she saw Rick, she hurried over.

"You're a sight for sore eyes, Rick Santiago!" she gushed, wiping her hands on her apron. "Tatum's hairstyle is surprising, huh? So short and chic! Might we have a new Tatum here?"

"Yes, I figured I needed a reminder every time I looked in the mirror that the old Tate was gone." She pulled her fingers through her now short, almost edgy medium-brown hair.

"What brings you to the Tea and Java du Jour today, Rick?" asked Georgia. "Can you sit down? I'll be right back with some coffee for all of us. Don't say anything important till I get back!"

Rick laughed congenially. "I'll wait for you since you're bearing coffee. But I don't have a lot of time today. I'll ask Tatum my question while you're gone, Georgia."

Georgia was already through the door and dishes were clattering in the kitchen.

Tatum didn't have to wait long.

Rick said, "Tatum, I have two tickets to the Broncos game on Sunday, the first of November. Would you like to go with me?" Rick looked expectantly for her reaction. "I thought of you when a friend gave these to me because he and his wife can't go that weekend. What do you say?"

Before Tatum could open her mouth, Erica said, "Yes, she'll go! And if she takes too much time deciding, I'll go with you instead! I've never been to a professional football game, ever!" She grinned at Tatum.

"He didn't ask you, he asked me! And, yes, I'd love to go!" *Oops. Did I sound too eager?*

"Great. I'll talk to you before then to firm up details."

Georgia returned with a pot of coffee in one hand and cups in the other.

"You didn't miss a thing, Georgia!"

"I see those smiles. I missed something, and y'all don't get any coffee until I know what it is!"

"There was almost a fight over the Broncos tickets I have," Rick explained. "But Tatum spoke up quickly enough, so she's going with me this time. I'll let you know, Erica, next time I get tickets, and I promise I'll take you!"

"Erica, we'll watch the game at my house," Georgia said. "And we'll invite that good looking man, Mose, to join us. We'll have such great food that Rick and Tate will be jealous! Let them go to the game and fight the crowds. Now, Rick. What did you have to tell us about the investigation?"

"The two men are in jail on outstanding warrants, so we know where they are if we need to question them again."

"Did they tell you why they would want to kidnap me?" Erica asked, indignant.

"Not yet, but they might if we offer them a plea bargain."

"Come on! Can't you use scare tactics to get the info out of them? Or a little muscle? Like they do on TV."

"Erica, you watch too much TV! In real life we do it differently." Rick filled them in on the few details he was able to glean about the suspects. There was no way to trace back from the two young men to the origin of the idea. It seemed like a dead end.

BLOG:

October 8
Relevant Ramblings—Go Broncos!

On the first Sunday of November, I'll be in the stands cheering for my favorite football team. I'm a Broncos fanatic! Mild mannered Tatum in any other scenario is quiet and a little boring, but not when it comes to my Broncos! I will be sporting orange and blue, but I think I'll forgo the orange hair only because Rick has never seen the Bronco Fanatic Tatum. When it's my team, whether at Sports Authority Field or in front of a TV, I'm the ultimate fan. GO BRONCOS!!!

BTW, Rick noticed my new hairstyle. I'm glad I cut it short. Maybe next haircut will be even edgier! #milehighorangeandbluefever

Nicole: *You are so lucky! I've always wanted to go to a Broncos game.*

25 🍃

On the morning of the Broncos game, Rick met Tatum at nine thirty at the Tea and Java du Jour, where she left her car.

"Rick Santiago! Orange hair! And I thought I'd be conservative and forego orange in mine. Guess it wouldn't have mattered!"

"I should have warned you. But, I must say, it was priceless seeing your expression! Let's go."

This November Sunday was perfect football weather; cool air, warm sunshine, and only a slight breeze. As they pulled onto I-70 for the trip through the tunnel and on to Denver, Rick broached a subject.

"Tate, I know you've just basically been existing since all the tragedy entered your life. It's great you can work at the tea shop, but Georgia seems to have things under control. So you don't really have to make many decisions, right?"

"Well, yes," Tatum said. "But I'm not sure what else to do with my time and energy. I don't have to work; but I don't want to sit around doing nothing, either."

"I've been thinking about this for a while. And I thought I'd at least mention it to you."

"OK, you've got me curious." Tatum cleared her throat, wondering what would come next.

"Because of my position with Search and Rescue

in Summit County, I'm very familiar with Mountain Rescue Team that serves Clear Creek, Gilpin, and Jefferson Counties."

"That's the team that got us off the mountain in July."

"Yes! They're looking for volunteers for their upcoming training that starts in January. I think your situation lends itself beautifully to what they're looking for. And you could honor Eric's memory by becoming part of the team that rescued him on Mount Bierstadt." Rick looked at her out of the corner of his eye. "Would you consider joining the team?"

"I don't know anything about rescuing people!"

"As long as you have the physical capability, they'd train you to do the rest. And I think you're physically capable of performing any of the tasks they require."

Rick sounded so positive that Tatum couldn't just say no. She felt her heart beat faster. "Sounds intriguing. I'd have to think about it."

"If you decided to pursue it, you might have to move to Evergreen. Which, of course, isn't far away." He glanced at her again.

"But what about my house in Alma?"

"One solution is to rent it out. Now that Erica has a car, maybe she would like to be more independent."

"What about the Tea and Java du Jour?" Tatum tried to come up with an excuse to throw the idea out.

"Seems to me Georgia is more than capable with the day-to-day decisions and can run everything."

"But what about—"

"No more excuses! At least promise to think about it."

Tatum was silent, considering the possibilities. Then she said, "If Erica lived in my Alma house, she could take care of Spartacus. That would be the terms of the lease, whether she likes cats or not."

"See? You're already thinking in the right direction."

"And I would have a place to stay when I go to Breckenridge." Tatum's excitement grew, but she'd have to think about it much more.

"There you go! 'Nuff said." They were almost to the stadium.

"By the way, Rick. The mild-mannered Tatum disappears during Broncos games. I become someone completely different. Just warning you!"

"Bring it on!"

BLOG:

November 2

Relevant Ramblings—Like Minds & Out of My Comfort Zone

I was only a little intimidated at Sports Authority Field to find our seats were in a luxury box. But now I've found a kindred spirit in Rick. He's as fanatical a Broncos fan as I am. He even had the orange hair! The best part, of course, was the win. Go, Peyton Manning!

On a more serious note, I have to process what he discussed with me a little longer before I make any decision. Rick brought up a subject I haven't been able to stop thinking about. He had no idea that I had just voiced my desire to stop over-avoiding risk, but God knew! He was just waiting until I recognized my discomfort in my comfortable, boring life. Rick thinks I should volunteer with Mountain Rescue Team. I have been wavering between "Absolutely Not" to "Maybe" to "Yes, I Can Do That," back to "Never!"

Mountain rescue seems like a big risk. But I think with the risk would come huge satisfaction.

What to do, what to do? Lord, I need a very clear answer from you in order to get out of my rut. I'm beginning to realize this rut isn't fun. Like Rick said, I'm only existing. Show me, beyond a shadow of a doubt, my next step.

Maybe God wants me to take a leap of faith and not the little step I would feel more comfortable with. #whatcomesnext

Heather: *I think you should do it! I'll be praying.*

November 6
Relevant Ramblings—That Was Quick!

I decided to go to the orientation for the next training for the Mountain Rescue Team. I realized I want to do this thing! It was definitely a big leap for me just going to the meeting alone. I sat next to a girl and during a break we found we have a bit in common. Christiana was there to see if this was something she would be interested in, and so was I. Her life situation is such that she could drop everything if she was on the team and got called out for a mission. She lives near Evergreen and even knows about a condo nearby that's 'For Sale by Owner' if I decide to move to Evergreen. It seems that every one of my excuses for not joining was answered.

OK, Lord. I'll proceed until I come to a closed door. They may not even want me! But I'm going to do the very best I can and not worry about the rest, because that's out of my hands anyway. That doesn't mean I'm not a little scared! Faith is the key! #onestepatatime

Nicole: *You go, girl! I'm behind you 100%!*

December 12
Relevant Ramblings—My New Condo

Wow! It's been a little more than a month since I felt a need to change the direction of my life and what a whirlwind! I made an appointment to see the condo and fell in love with it. I brought Georgia to see it after discussing it with her. Obviously, you can assume by now that I've decided to try my hand at mountain rescue. The next class for new recruits is in January.

Georgia thought my decision to join MRT and move to Evergreen was sound. I value her opinion greatly, and if for some reason I'm not Mountain Rescue Team material, I can always rent out the condo for another source of income. She loved the condo as much as I did and agreed with me that it's a great value.

The elderly couple can't live at this altitude any more because of health reasons. When I met them and looked at the place, we all knew God had brought us together. They wanted so much to live near their kids and grandkids in Evergreen, but they will find a townhouse down the hill where neither will struggle so much with breathing. Since I have cash to purchase it, and we only have to wait for a lawyer to help with the contract and not for a bank loan, they discounted the price a little more. What a blessing! And they kept telling me I was a blessing to them! That is so like God! I used to think when my grandma would say, "God dovetails the details!" it was only a cliché. But He certainly did that here! I can move in two weeks! The discount in price lets me buy furniture. I think I'll go to the consignment stores and also look on Craigslist. No use wasting money! Thank you, Lord! #allcomestogetherfast #yikes

Heather: *When can Nicole and I come see your new condo? We have a house warming present for you!*

January 3

Relevant Ramblings—I Haven't Forgotten You

Dear Computer and Friends following my posts,

Sorry I've neglected you for so long! My life has been crazy since I last posted, but not because I don't love you! Christmas came and went. I bought a house and moved during that time. I've traveled back and forth from Evergreen to Breckenridge quite a few times and even worked at the Tea and Java when they needed extra help.

I know, I know. You're going to remind me about using my laptop. To tell you the truth, it was hard to post about mundane things.

Actually, it's nice that, although I've been busy, nothing too exciting has been happening in my life.

Now I'm back. #pleasedontdisownme

26 🍃

Tatum sat at a table in the meeting room waiting for the first training to start. Her heretofore play-it-safe life was about to change, though she could hardly call her recent life boring. She had begun to wonder what might happen each day, considering all the unexpected events lately.

The petite, extremely fit girl she had met at the orientation came in and joined her at the table. Her super-short hair fit her to a T. She proudly displayed her tattoos and piercings. "Hey, I'm Christiana. We met at the last meeting."

"Hi. Yes, I remember. I'm Tatum."

"Hi, Tate. Oh, I shouldn't presume. Do you go by Tate? What do you think of our options so far?"

"Yes, I answer to Tate!" Tatum smiled then shrugged. "I don't know. The training sounds pretty intense. It may be a stretch physically and psychologically. But you— you're already so fit! I'm just a little jealous!"

Christiana took a long drink of her bottled water then came up for air. "There's a good reason for that!" She snapped the top back on the bottle.

Spunky and outgoing.

"I've been training to do my second ultra marathon. The training hikes will be a stroll in the woods!"

"Wow!" *Try not to be quite so wide-eyed, Tatum.*

"Tell me about an ultra marathon. Is it bigger than a regular marathon?"

"Anything longer than a marathon. Could be 50K or fifty miles or, in my case, one-hundred miles," said Christiana.

"No! Who in their right mind would want to run one-hundred miles? That just sounds wrong!"

"I know!" She laughed. "It does sound crazy, doesn't it? But I've been extreme all my life, so for me it's just another challenge." Christiana ran fingers through her short hair. "My first ultra was fifty miles. I've learned a lot about long distance running through the mistakes I made in that race, so now I'm training for the Leadville 100. But it's actually a combination of running and walking and there are aid stations along the way, even though those are usually only a two to three minute stop each time. But enough about me. What made you decide to join MRT?"

"It's a long story, too long for now." Tatum had an idea. "What about having dinner at my place sometime? That would give us time to talk."

"I'd love that, as long as you let me bring something. Oh, they're starting. Let's talk more. OK?"

After the meeting, as the two girls walked to the door together, Tatum took up the conversation again. "Let's get together soon. My condo. We can both add to the meal. How about Saturday? I'll make chicken. Do you want to bring a salad?"

"That works for me. Hey, ten classroom trainings and the six field trainings before we can participate in a real rescue. Think we'll be ready by then?"

"Probably. But as they said, even when we have all the skills down, our attitudes play a part in whether we're accepted or not. I guess they want team players, not lone rangers."

"I have no problem being a team player. I'm excited. See you Saturday."

As Tatum drove the short way home, she realized the opportunity she had. Her story may not seem exciting, but woven through it was her dependence on God, and she couldn't leave that part out. "Lord, put the words in my mouth you would like me to say. My story is a journey of faith, doubt, and faith again. Help me to share my struggles in a way that will glorify you. Thanks ahead of time."

🍃 🍃 🍃

The dinner had to be postponed for two weeks, but the Saturday finally arrived.

"Welcome, Christiana. By the way, can I call you Chris or do you like people to use your full name? I know they call us by our last names during training, but I don't think you want to be called Parker. I certainly don't want to be known as Kessler."

"Chris is fine." She put the salad fixings into Tatum's hands. "My friend Madison gave me the recipe for this dressing. I made a copy for you. The chicken smells great!"

"It'll be done in ten minutes. Looks like Caesar salad! My favorite. You even thought to bring bread.

And chocolate for dessert? Mmmm. You're my hero!"

After enjoying the meal and cleaning up, the girls settled in the living room. Christiana surveyed the room with an appreciative eye. "I like your decorating. Everything fits and feels comfortable. I envy you. My condo is still 'early attic'—my parents' attic."

"This is all from consignment stores," Tatum admitted. "I love nice things but don't like paying full price." She settled deeper into the chair. "Can I ask you a question? You said you have a flexible schedule. What type of work do you do?"

Christiana made herself comfortable, resting her feet on the ottoman as she responded.

"I work on a computer from home, and I have work that has to be done each week, but it can be done at my convenience. It's a great job. Fits well with my training for the ultra and responding to pages for mountain rescue. Now let me ask you, Tate, what brought you to Evergreen? And volunteering for MRT? You don't work, do you?"

"Not right now, but I own a business in Breckenridge that someone else manages. It's a long story." She told Christiana about the Tea and Java du Jour. "I now own the tea shop because my parents were killed in a car accident a year and a half ago." She proceeded to fill in the details of that hard time in her life.

Christiana's eyes glistened. "That would be awful, being an only child and having to bury your parents! I don't think I could handle it. But you seem well adjusted."

Tatum breathed a quick prayer then explained, "I couldn't have survived without God in my life. He held me up through that terrible time, even though sometimes I was mad at Him."

"You can say that out loud, that you were mad at God? Isn't that a bad thing?" Christiana looked skeptical.

"He wouldn't turn His back on me for saying what I think. Georgia, my tea shop manager, says nothing can touch a child of God that doesn't first go through His hand. You look confused. Now, what are you thinking? You can be honest, too."

"Well, I believe there's a God, but isn't He way too busy running the universe or whatever to be interested in what goes on down here?" Chris shook her head. "You sound like he's a personal friend with His arm around you. That's just crazy."

"He is a personal friend." Tatum warmed to the discussion, reminiscent of the questions Erica had asked.

"The physical arms around me were Georgia's arms. She was Jesus with skin on. The emotional comfort came from God. Oh, oh. Another confused look on your face. Go ahead and ask. We have all night."

"You talked about God and Jesus. That's two people, and I've heard about the Holy Spirit or Holy Ghost—whatever. I've always wanted to ask this question and never knew anyone who could answer it. Does that mean you have three gods?"

"That's a great question. The trinity is very hard to understand, but here's a very simplified answer for now."

Tatum stopped for a moment to consider her words. "The sun in the sky is one entity but it does three things for us. We get light from the sun, but we also get heat from it. Then there's power—you know, like charging photocells. We know there are not three suns up there doing one thing each; one sun is doing all three things for us. That's kind of like the trinity: God the Father, God the Son, and God the Holy Spirit. Does that help a little?"

"I've never heard it explained that way. It's confusing. But yes, that helps. Now back to your story." Chris sat forward, waiting.

"There is more. But I think that's enough for tonight. To be continued!"

BLOG:

March 6

Relevant Ramblings—Christiana

My new friend, Christiana, is everything I'm not. I think you could put *extreme* before each of her qualities—in a good way. In a group she has a ready comeback to almost every comment. The guys seem to gravitate toward her. Her style of clothing is fun. Her hairstyle makes her look pixie cute.

She runs ultra marathons. But (are you sitting down?) she does the extreme of the extreme: 100 miles. Is that even possible? I guess so. That won't be rubbing off on me any time soon, but I would like some of her out-going-ness.

But the introvert I am will never be the extrovert she is.

She challenges me in all the training sessions, whether classroom or in the field, but she isn't pushy about it. Thanks, Christiana. #extremeandlovingit

Nicole: *Your new friend sounds awesome. I'd love to meet her!*

March 20
Relevant Ramblings—Caesar Salad

I know. A strange title for this post. But you'll love this recipe.

Madison's Caesar Salad Dressing

1 c. mayo, 1 T lemon juice, 1 t Worcestershire sauce, 1 clove garlic minced, ¼ t salt, ¼ t pepper, 1 T half & half. Combine all, then ½ cup shredded Parmesan. Cheese croutons on top. Enjoy!

#yumyumyum

27 🍃

Evergreen, Colorado. Tatum was glad she lived there now. The tranquil mountain community in the foothills was thirty-five minutes west of downtown Denver. Surrounded by mountain vistas, pine forests, aspen stands, abundant wildlife, and its crown jewel, sparkling-blue Evergreen Lake, Evergreen provided a beautiful backdrop for activities in every season: attending rainy-spring events at the lake house; skating on the lake in the winter. It was a great place to live—in the mountains but near the city.

Tatum's journey to this stage of her life was far different from what she had planned. She was glad to have a friend in Christiana. Although they weren't best friends like she and Heather, Tatum looked forward to their get-togethers—like today. Dinner at Christiana's place.

"Sorry we had to postpone this, but we're here now," said Christiana, welcoming Tatum. "I asked you to bring rice because we're having chicken lettuce wraps for an appetizer and beef satay with peanut sauce for the main course. Dessert is crispy bananas with ice cream."

"Sounds delicious. I'm starving!"

Indeed, the whole dinner was amazing. And the dessert! Banana slices sautéed in olive oil, covered with a honey-water mix and sprinkled with cinnamon. That would make any ice cream taste delicious; but with Blue Bell French vanilla ice cream, it was superb.

After the clean-up they settled on the couch.

"You said you had more to your story. I'm curious to hear the rest," Christiana prompted.

Tatum told her about meeting Eric online and their courtship and engagement. When she explained in detail his death after being hit by lightning on Mount Bierstadt, Christiana looked awe struck.

"Wait! You met Eric right after your parents passed away, you were just engaged, and then he was killed. Now I know you're super human, to have gone through that and be able to sit here and matter-of-factly tell me all this. I know I asked this before, but what's your secret?"

"I said this before too: God is the only reason I can sit here and tell you about all this and not be totally devastated." Her voice waivered slightly. "I'm not super-human, but He is! At the time, I wanted to give up, but again I had Georgia to physically walk me through the pain, and I knew that Jesus had his arms around me guiding me each step when I didn't think I could put one foot in front of the other. I've had a boatload of loss, but I've gained a lot too."

Chris shook her head. "I think that would be too much for me."

"It would be for me, too, without God!" Tatum had to give credit where credit was due. "But there's more, and this is not sad stuff." She smiled.

Tatum told Christiana about Eric's daughter Erica

who, receiving his trust fund and insurance as her inheritance, came to Breckenridge to learn about the father she had never known.

Chris laughed at Tatum's description of the street-smart girl from New York who decided to stay in Breckenridge.

"My kind of girl. I can't wait to meet her!"

Happily, they finished the evening on a light note.

Tatum and Christiana, and the rest of the newbies, fulfilled the training requirements. The field sessions gave them a look at what might be required of them, from lost hikers, to scree evacs, to medical emergencies. The written test covered all the information they had learned and included tasks such as tying a myriad of knots. That was the fun part for Tatum. Then came the practical test, the bivy—staying overnight, outside, in the mountains, in the open air, prepared to be out for forty-eight hour periods, whatever the weather. It was a culmination of all they had learned. Fortunately, the weather wasn't bad.

This final test was probably the most physically challenging event Tatum had ever endured. Her confidence was shaken, but she overcame even the psychological aspects. The others who were testing with her were there to give moral support and cheer her on. She passed with room to spare. So did Christiana. As they walked out of the meeting room side by side, they had reason to be proud.

"Congratulations on being accepted by the team, Tatum."

"Thanks. You, too." Tatum took the offering of Christiana's hug.

"All our hard work paid off! I guess, though, that means now the difficult work begins! We can officially respond to pages now, but we still have to prove we're not flaky or weird."

They laughed together.

BLOG:

March 28
Relevant Ramblings: I Did It!

I was notified today that I am now a probationary member in good standing of the Mountain Rescue Team. Not a trainee anymore. I'm excited to be a part of this great organization and I'm a little proud—well, a lot proud—of myself. I worked hard—to prove both to myself and the team—that I could do it. I know there'll be more to learn as we go. But I can be a vital part of a great team. There's still a little fear but not the paralyzing kind of the past.

Thank you, Lord, for helping me to realize this goal. Give me strength to perform well and help save lives of those who are lost or hurt. Help me also to be bold enough to see the spiritual needs of the lost and hurting and speak truth when I can.

I think I'll call Georgia and let her gush over me! I haven't heard a 'y'all' in a while! #proudofmyself

April 2

Relevant Ramblings: Gush. She. Did.

Actually, Georgia did more than gush (a funny word). She told me to come to Breckenridge and threw a party to celebrate my success. She pulled out all the stops—Southern style! She invited:

- Erica, of course.
- Mose (I think she looks for any reason to invite him over).
- Sheriff Rick.
- Heather and Nicole (a fun surprise!).
- and a few friends from the Breckenridge church.

The spectacular, southern menu included:

- fried chicken
- crayfish
- fried okra
- black-eyed peas
- green beans with bacon and salt pork
- shrimp and cheddar grits
- sweet potato casserole
- homemade biscuits
- blackberry cobbler
- sweet tea

Thanks, Georgia, for making me feel special. You're the best! #southernstylecookinyum

And by the way, I'm so proud of Erica for taking the children's tea-party idea and running with it. I haven't forgotten about the tea shop, but it has been lower on my priority list lately. I'm going to have to make a point to let Erica know how much I appreciate her. Everyone loves to hear that!

Heather: *Nicole and I loved surprising you! Your Georgia is amazing! No wonder there's never a dull moment when she and Erica are around!*

April 10
Relevant Ramblings: What's Going On?

Ever since I started the field training with MRT, one man (not Jerry—he's been encouraging) seems to criticize everything I do. I don't think I'm imagining this. It's such an insult when he thinks I can't do something. The very worst is when he says, "Speed it up." Does he think I'm just going at my own pace? Is this his attempt to help me prepare for a real situation? Isn't there a better way to do that?

Let me give you an example. On Saturday when we were practicing with ropes, he kept telling me I was too slow. I don't see him riding any of the other newbies. What's up with that? I'm glad he's not the only field trainer. Maybe I should just go on the trainings he's not leading.

That said, I'm learning a lot. Soon I'll feel ready for a real mission. Hard work physically? Yes! Some danger? Am I still afraid of heights? A little. I realize that as far as we can control the risk, MRT does. But we never know what the mountains will throw at us. #pickonsomeoneelse #overlookingbullying

Nicole: *You need to stand up for yourself! Want me to come and give him a piece of my mind!?!*

Heather: *I'm proud of you!*

28 🍃

Tatum's first mission was a lost hiker, who, while hiking with friends decided to explore by himself. When he didn't return, the group called 9-1-1. Emergency contacted Mountain Rescue Team. It was almost dark when the team got to the trailhead at the Jones Pass Road trail near the Henderson mine above Empire on Highway 40.

"Make sure your headlamps have extra batteries." The mission leader prepped the team and they started out. "And have your whistles out. We need to use a lot of attraction."

Being familiar with the general area the hiker was thought to be in, they soon heard an answering yell. The victim promised to never go off by himself and to be more prepared for night in the mountains with a warmer jacket.

Home by eleven o'clock p.m., Tatum considered her first mission a success.

What a thrill to reach the point in her training when she was allowed to go on rescues. In another six months the recruiting officer would say yes or no to her being a full member, a decision based on attitude and team work, as well as ability and availability.

Tatum's pager went off. Her heart pounded from the suddenness of coming out of a deep sleep. The clock said 4:20. She turned on the light and looked at her pager. Code 3. Serious enough to use lights and siren. She dressed and got in her car. She would probably beat other team members to the base, lovingly dubbed the cabin, because she lived so close. On late spring calls like this, the mission was likely a lost or injured hiker. She'd hear all the details soon.

When everyone had assembled, Tatum groaned inwardly. *Wouldn't you know, the team leader for this mission is Alex Witt. I thought Tom Ewing was scheduled next. They must have traded.* He'd probably give her the jobs most physically demanding then keep telling her to "speed it up!" *I try so hard to be liked by everyone. Why can't Alex Witt like me, or at least ignore me? What am I missing?*

However, she put aside her annoyance and concentrated on the job at hand. Rescue Vehicle 2, the newer of the two vehicles was chosen for the task. It had interior space for a command center with maps and the communication equipment. The vehicle for the others to travel in had been taken out of the shed, the garage where all the MRT's vehicles were kept.

A quick briefing took place before everyone would load into the vehicles.

"We have a hiker who has activated his satellite personal tracker. SPOT has acquired the exact coordinates from the GPS network, so our job is easy in that regard," Alex briefed the team. "But it will transmit a signal to the emergency response center every five minutes until canceled, so speed is of the essence. We don't know what we'll be dealing with, so keep up the pace." Alex glanced around the group, and during that last comment Tatum thought his eyes stayed longer on her than necessary. "You all know the drill at the trailhead staging area. Let's go."

Tatum hesitated a second to see what vehicle Alex boarded, then she hurried to the other one. It was a half-hour drive to the staging area. She sat back, thinking how life had led her to serve in a way that took calculated risk to a whole new level. Then her thoughts returned to the team leader. She had worked hard to become qualified and she never expected special treatment. But what had caused Alex's grudge? How could she win his respect?

The team arrived at the staging point. All was put aside but the task at hand. A lost or hurt hiker needed help.

"As always, we're assuming worse-case scenario until we know differently. We go top speed. Keep up!" Alex shot a look at Tatum again, and she felt her face redden. Was he sending her a message?

After a two and a half hour hike, adrenaline pushing them toward what could be a life or death emergency, they found their "victim." As it turned out, he had accidentally activated his SPOT and was very embarrassed when MRT arrived at his coordinates.

The upside was they got to see the sunrise when the

forest came alive with morning sounds and movement. Turning back down the trail, the team trekked leisurely to the trailhead and their vehicles.

"This is what I live for." Greg spoke the words they were all thinking. "A hike in the mountains with ten of my best friends!"

Everyone laughed, agreeing. All the way back to the parked vehicles, the mood was jovial, tension relieved.

Though physically tired after five hours in the mountains, Tatum felt mentally exhilarated—the feeling that came whenever she did something with such passion. Her heart rose in thankfulness for the insurance money that allowed her to volunteer for this worthwhile organization, and the income from the Tea and Java that covered her monthly expenses. *If someone had told me two years ago that my life would look like this today, I would have laughed in their face. Why, Risk and I have become downright friendly.*

She stayed at home the rest of the afternoon, happily doing nothing of importance. Late afternoon her phone rang.

"Hey, Tate, how are things? I'm on my way back to Breck from Denver and thought I'd see if you could meet me for dinner," came Erica's energetic voice over the line. "I want to tell you about my successful shopping trip!"

"I'm tired from a mission early this morning. Why don't you come to my house and we'll throw something together to eat?"

Erica agreed. "I'll stop for salad fixings."

Tatum was already in her favorite pajamas and snuggly robe. *Erica won't mind. Hmmm. Erica. The girl adversity put in my life. Things would be so different if The Accident hadn't happened.*

The door bell rang. Tatum pulled out of her reverie and opened the door to a smiling Erica.

Erica put her things on the table and gave Tatum a hug. "You look perfectly cozy in your pj's. I hope this isn't too much for you. You must be tired."

"I'm always glad to see you." Tatum headed into the kitchen, adding over her shoulder, "And this is way better than the junk food I would have probably eaten if you hadn't called!"

Tatum set out plates while Erica threw the salad together.

"I was thinking how my life has taken such a dramatic turn from my carefully laid plans of two years ago. Because of circumstances beyond my control, my life has become much richer."

"Things certainly have been out of your control." Erica chuckled.

"I would never have chosen any of this, but I must say I like my life much more now."

"Tate, you're my hero!"

"Come on, I'm no hero. But thanks for saying so."

"Well, you are. You're a member of a team that changes people's lives when they're in life-and-death situations in the mountains. Not everyone could or would do that."

"The mission today could have been life or death. We

didn't have any idea what we were dealing with when we set out. We hiked in two-and-one-half hours to find out the hiker had accidentally set off his SPOT."

"English, please."

"Oh, sorry! Satellite personal tracker. It's a GPS that is monitored by a central agency that can be used if you're in trouble. This hiker set it off accidentally, without realizing it. He was really embarrassed when we showed up. So we had a fast hike up and a leisurely hike down."

"Tatum, I never tire of hearing the story of my dad's rescue off Mt. Bierstadt. Would you tell me again?"

Tatum realized again that Erica had only the stories she had heard as her memories of her father, Eric.

"OK, but first tell me about your shopping trip."

Erica began the story with relish. "I found some more really great tea service sets for little girls. Actually I found two different kinds. Our little girls' teas have been successful, but now we'll have more variety, with child-size cups and plates." Erica became more animated as she continued. "I found some to use for tea parties, and others to sell. I know those darling little girls will beg their moms to buy them their very own tea sets."

"I can't wait to see them when I come up to Breckenridge...next week."

"I also found small hats and gloves to sell, and I even found some sets that have a boys' theme to them. I'm pretty sure the boys will not want to have tea parties at home, so I bought sets for the tea shop. But the pirate accessories will be a big hit with the boys."

"I'd never think of those things. I'm so glad you're part of the Tea and Java du Jour. Now, let's eat."

The chicken Caesar salad was perfect. During dessert of almond lace cookies, Tatum added to her previous narrative of the Bierstadt day.

"Don't know if I told you this part before. It was early—still dark except for the sun causing a glow behind Mount Bierstadt. We'd just gone up the trail a little ways when I realized I had forgotten my water bottle on the hood of the car. Eric had me wait on the side of the trail while he ran back to retrieve it. I've always wondered. If I hadn't forgotten the water bottle, would the day have turned out differently?" Her voice caught.

Erica reached her arm around Tatum. "You've told me that before. I said then and I'll say now, no 'what-ifs.' It is what it is."

Tatum received that with a smile, still unable to speak.

"Well, I need to go now," Erica said. "Thanks so much for everything."

BLOG:

April 29

Relevant Ramblings: The Tea and Java du Jour

Now I'm thinking of ways to increase sales. What if we served breakfast? And what if the breakfast included grits—a different flavor each day? Georgia could easily come up with five or six grits recipes. Of course we could have eggs, different breakfast styles, as an accompaniment—or for those not brave enough to order grits. We'd need a catchy name for our Southern breakfast fare. We'd only serve from six to ten, then re-open for lunch at eleven like we do now. What do you think? I'm pretty proud of myself for coming up with this idea. Now to see if Georgia and Erica like it.

For some reason, I was reticent about sharing my idea with Georgia. But what was her response? She said, "I think it's a terrific idea and I can't believe I haven't thought of it!"

Georgia says she already has eight or ten different grits recipes! Start thinking of good names and leave a comment. #goodideawhatnext?

Nicole: *The name needs to be catchy. You could serve breakfast six days a week, since you're not open on Sundays, and offer only one type of grits each day, and that would cut down on the work and the waste. And customers would know exactly what to expect.*

Heather: *I like the idea, too. In your town with all the people transplanted from somewhere else, not to mention the tourists, this would be a big hit!*

Tatum: *Thanks, friends. I'm excited to get started! We'll get Erica in on the planning, too. I'll bet Georgia will get Mose in on it too! A man's opinion would be helpful. Now,*

198

how do we present a mountain theme with a Southern twist? There's nothing else like that in town. Again, feel free to leave a comment with names you think of.

Heather: *How about 'True Grits'? or 'Grits and Gravy'?*

Nicole: *You could advertise by saying you may have to imagine the Spanish moss and the humidity, but the taste is authentic Southern grits.*

Tatum: *I like those, Heather. And, Nicole, we'll make that our tag line.*

29 🍃

B^{LOG:}

June 2
Relevant Ramblings: I'm Different

What has shaped my life until now? It wasn't what I expected. The life I imagined included a husband, two kids, going to Grandpa and Grandma's house for Sunday dinner after church, a house in the suburbs, and being a stay-at-home mom involved in some kind of charity work.

The life I have now is a far cry from my perfect dream of the past. But the truth is, this life is both satisfying and productive. My self esteem has increased tenfold. I've inherited a business that is profitable, and a mountain house in Alma I've rented to Erica. I've bought a condo in Evergreen, and I volunteer for an amazing organization, Mountain Rescue Team.

All the crises I've endured have helped mold me into the Tatum I see in the mirror. Would I have chosen this journey if I had known? No! Am I glad I'm not the same Tatum I was? Yes! Do I still have the tendency to want to play it safe in all my decisions? Sometimes, but not as much as I used to.

This Tatum is becoming comfortable in her own skin and I realize she doesn't need as much approval from others in every decision as before. My life now has excitement in it every time my pager goes off. But my training gives me the confidence that I can be a vital part of saving lives when people are in trouble in the high country.

Oops, there goes my pager! I'm off for more adventure! #differentandlovingit

Heather: *I'm a little jealous. Now my life seems boring.*

August 5
Relevant Ramblings: Anniversary

Today is the anniversary of The Accident. Some days I don't think about it at all, and other days I wish I could stop thinking about it.

I still miss Eric. He'll always be a part of me. Tall, blue-eyed men still give me a lump-in-the-throat, but I now have something of him—Erica. The hole in my heart that can't be filled with anything but my parents will always be there also. But that lack doesn't take my breath away anymore. The sadness will always be there. But the reality is, I have to live with it. Life as I know it is different but good.

I've heard it said about courage that you sometimes have to fake it until you feel it. I think I faked it a lot at the beginning, but not so much anymore. Would Eric be proud of me? I like to think so. My walk with the Lord? Well, I'm not mad at Him anymore. The tapestry called "Tatum's Life" looks like a jumbled, knotted mess from my side, but I have faith that God, the Creator of the universe, is designing something beautiful.

And, BTW, thanks for all your great ideas for a name for the breakfast portion of the Tea and Java. We decided to call it Authentic Southern Grits. We'll be up and running soon and will advertise at the hotels and resorts by offering a Buy One, Get One for a short period of time. Everyone likes a deal! #whatsmoreauthenticsouthernthangrits?

Nicole: *Has it really been a year since you lost Eric? BTW, love the new name for the breakfasts!*

Heather: *Praying for you!*

Tatum was spending the weekend in Breckenridge. She decided to stay with Erica in the Alma house rather than at Georgia's. She wanted to see if Spartacus had disowned her.

She and Erica sat in the great room looking at the view that never failed to inspire.

"Every time we're together I can't help remembering how we met and how different my life is since I moved to Colorado," Erica said. "Totally different from life in New York. It still amazes me. It's been almost a year since I got the call from my father's lawyer then came to Breckenridge. Remember?" She sipped her sweet tea.

"It's forever etched in my mind." Tatum's sarcasm dripped from every word. She knew Erica would catch the joke. Tatum crossed her arms and looked the younger girl in the eye. "But tell me, what are you up to? When your New York accent gets stronger, I know something's up!"

Erica grinned. "Tate, you know me too well. But, seriously, I'm glad you and Georgia suggested I go to school."

"Ha! It's not easy 'making suggestions' to some people!"

"Yea, I remember thinking at the time I didn't want adults telling me what I should or shouldn't do."

"You had definite opinions!"

"What!? You're saying I'm opinionated?"

They both laughed.

"Anyway, after I stopped being a brat, I decided to check out colleges." She paused for effect as if listening to a drum roll. "I'm going to go to Colorado Mountain College."

"That's fantastic. What will you study?"

"It was hard to decide. My dead-end life in New York didn't include going to school, and I hadn't even considered it before. But I've decided to get a degree in business. I've only begun taking the prerequisites so far, but I've found I can do this college stuff when I put my mind to it. My goal is to start my own business."

"I'm so proud of you, Erica. I'm sure Georgia is too. And I bet your father would be proud."

"Thanks, Tate. That means a lot. But I want to know

what's happening with you. Are you still enjoying the missions with MRT?"

"Oh yes! It's even more fulfilling than I expected."

"What sort of rescues have you had recently?"

"Well, one recent call came because a young woman (her identity is confidential, of course) failed to return home after a day hike. People from various rescue teams helped in the search, with very limited clues. Even the scent-finding dogs had difficulty picking up a scent in the rough terrain."

"Sounds just like the movies. Did the dogs find her?"

"It took a while. The sheriff's department even made reverse 9-1-1 calls to the neighboring vicinity in case anyone had seen anything."

"Is that typical?" Erica was on the edge of her seat.

"We use every available option when someone's life is at stake. We even used Verizon Wireless to help us locate her cell phone. They got a ping from a cell tower, but when searchers reached the GPS coordinates, there was no hiker."

"For real? Just like in the movies. Next you'll probably tell me an airplane helped you search!"

"No, it was a helicopter!" Tatum laughed at the look on Erica's face. "A Denver man had rented a helicopter to propose to his girlfriend, and en route they searched from the sky, but didn't see anything. The first night the searchers had to quit by one o'clock a.m."

"Were you there the whole time?" Erica's eyes grew larger.

"No. Since other agencies were involved also, we

took turns. We were about to give up for another night when a call came saying they found the lost hiker. I'll call her Vic. One of the dogs had shown great reluctance to leave the area, so it turned out to be a dog-man effort."

"Then you all could go home?" Erica sat back.

"Not yet. The searchers still had to bundle up Vic for warmth then put her into a litter. Then with ropes and belay devices, we got her up the steep slope. That took two hours."

"Have all your missions turned out so good, so far?"

"Unfortunately, no." Tatum shook her head. "Sometimes we go in for body recovery, especially in avalanche situations." Tatum considered how to say it delicately. "Even when hikers or skiers wear beacons, we can't always get to them in time. That's probably the most difficult part for me. But I have to deal with it."

"And I used to think this high country had no excitement compared to the streets of New York!" She raised her eyebrows. "But what is the beacon thing you mentioned?"

Tatum didn't mind the questions. She loved talking about mountain rescue.

"It's an avalanche beacon—a transceiver used for finding people or equipment buried under snow." She hesitated to add more detail, but Erica's eager eyes encouraged her to continue.

"It's not to prevent one from being buried by an avalanche. It's a way to reduce the amount of time buried. All the people in a group who are skiing or snowboarding in the back country should have a beacon and make sure it's set on 'transmit.' The rescuers set their beacons to receive mode."

Erica couldn't seem to get enough. "Can't skiers just avoid the slopes that are prone to avalanches?"

"You could take every precaution possible and still trigger an avalanche. I think the statistics say ninety-five percent of all avalanches are triggered by the victim or someone in the victim's party." Tatum stopped to recall her reading. "Most victims are males in their twenties."

"Can't they just ski faster to get out of the avalanche's way?"

"Erica, you are definitely testing my avalanche knowledge!" Tatum laughed. "If I remember right, the average avalanche travels eighty miles an hour or more. No time to react. No way to out-ski it."

"Isn't it just white, fluffy snow that comes down the mountain?"

"No. Sometimes, with wind, rain, and new snow, the layers of snow change rapidly, causing the avalanche. When it stops, the snow freezes solid and cocoons the victim beneath, so they're unable to move. Basically, it's white cement. A victim statistically has a much better chance of survival if they're uncovered within fifteen to twenty minutes. That's why all the skiers in the party should have the beacons, shovels, and probes. That's also why, by the time we're able to reach them, it's usually body recovery."

"That's horrible! Have you had to do that?" Erica's eyes darkened.

"So far, I've only gone on avalanche training missions. I don't think I'm ready for an real avalanche rescue yet. I'll let the experts respond to those calls. But as soon as I think I've had enough practice, I will respond."

"Oh, Tatum. Coming thousands of miles from New York to Colorado is nothing compared to being on MRT. And to think, you got started doing this because of my dad on Mount Bierstadt."

BLOG:

August 13
Relevant Ramblings: Thankfulness

I'm thankful for:

- The beautiful sunrise colors of pink, orange, blue.
- Sunsets that are the same colors but look different.
- Eric's daughter, Erica.
- The Alma house with its unbelievable views.
- My condo in Evergreen.
- The Tea and Java du Jour.

The first two on this list happen daily. Sometimes I notice them and sometimes I take them for granted. But the last four have only happened because of adversity. I would have never met Erica if not for The Accident, because she would not have known she was the beneficiary of her father's will. The Alma house is only mine because my parents provided for me in their will.

The condo in Evergreen is paid for because of my parents also. The tea shop is mine for the same reason.

These things are all evidence of Romans 8:28 in my life. I've heard it said, soil that contains manure produces more fruit than soil that contains only lifeless sand. There's been plenty of 'manure' in my life as of late. I wonder what kind of fruit it will produce. #thankfulformanureIthink

Nicole: *You crack me up! Can I steal the statement about the manure?*

Tatum: *Go for it!*

30 🍃

When her pager went off that morning, Tatum responded to the mission, arriving at the cabin before most of the others. In fact, she arrived before the mission leader, Alex Witt. When he walked in, he stared hard at her.

OK, Tatum, put steel in your backbone.

Alex sidled over to her and spoke to her under his breath. "I don't think you should go on this one. You may do something hazardous to the team and the victim. It's on Bierstadt."

Bierstadt. Feelings came back like an avalanche, destructive and unstoppable. All Tatum could hope for was that those feelings wouldn't sweep her away. She squared her shoulders and put a tight smile on her face.

"I'm a professional and I am *so* going."

She walked away with a stiff gait, her head held high, but not before she had seen the look that crossed his face. Was it surprise? *If I had a door to walk through, I'd slam it! Oh, Lord, I'm really going to need your help on this one. I might have disqualified myself if Alex hadn't said that, but now I have something to prove. Keep me strong and focused, please.*

Could she do it? She had to. This was part of the life she now embraced. She didn't want to go back to what she was two years before. But could she keep her composure on Mount Bierstadt? *With your help, Lord, I will try.*

From his conversation with Clear Creek dispatch, Alex briefed the team on what to expect. "The reporting party said we have a nineteen year old male who thought it would be exciting to slide down the snowfield on his boots, with no way to stop when the snow ended and the rocks began. In mountaineering terms this is *glissading*. It's also the quickest way to the emergency room. All we know is the victim is unconscious."

This was a Code 3 with lights and sirens. The team reached the parking lot at the summit of Guanella Pass in record time. Then the work began.

The last time I was on Bierstadt.... Tatum shook her head, set her jaw, and put aside the memories.

Adrenaline kicked in. They all climbed with urgency. At the snowfield, if Tatum had been thinking of anything other than placing one foot in front of the other and keeping up, she would have noticed there was more snow this year in June than the last time she was here.

The team reached the fallen victim, sprawled awkwardly on the ground below the snowfield. He had multiple abrasions and one foot was pointed at an odd angle from his leg. She listened as the EMTs assessed his injuries.

"Let's stabilize his neck and get him on the litter. We think there are multiple broken bones. And the head injury warrants Flight for Life." The team members who were expert in landing zone preparation went back to the parking lot to await the helicopter. Now to get the victim down as quickly as possible. Tatum walked behind with the friend who had reported the emergency. She refused to let her thoughts go to the other time.

The victim's friend said, "I tried to talk him out of that stupid stunt. We couldn't even see the bottom of the snowfield. But do you think Shawn would listen?" The friend swallowed hard. "I was hoping he had somehow slowed his downward progress and he'd jump up and laugh when I reached him. That's the way he was. But, instead, I had to call 9-1-1." His voice caught.

"I know how you're feeling. I had to call 9-1-1 because of an emergency on this mountain. MRT helped us off the mountain a year ago. Your friend is in the best hands possible." They reached the parking lot in time to see Flight for Life take off.

As Tatum sank into the truck seat for the ride back to the cabin, her adrenaline had drained away. She couldn't help but compare this accident with The Accident. While she was on the mountain, she was a viable part of MRT, doing her assignment with strength and courage. Now she had no resistance to the thoughts that took her where she didn't want to go. Eric had done everything right, yet he had died. This victim had done everything wrong, yet he would probably live. This victim, although injured and unconscious, hadn't stopped breathing. Eric had.

With Eric's accident, Flight for Life couldn't land because of weather. With this accident there were no

211

weather issues to keep the helicopter from landing. She slumped farther into her seat and buried her face in her hands. Jerry reached over and gave her shoulder a pat, but no one else seemed to notice. By the time they got back, she was able to act as if nothing was wrong. But she knew she was back at the stage in the grief cycle she thought she'd already conquered—anger.

After the debriefing, she drove straight home, gripping the steering wheel hard. "Alex Witt, this would have been a good time to tell me that you were wrong," she found herself crying out. "I kept up. I was an integral part of the team. But no. What did you do? You ignored me!" Tatum pulled into the garage, let the door down behind her, and then it started. The tears flowed like they would never stop.

"Why?" she shouted through the sobs, hitting the steering wheel with her fist.

But the tears spent themselves. After a time, an unexpected peace washed over her.

Her phone rang. It was Georgia. She answered.

"Tatum, honey, are you all right?" She didn't wait for an answer, "I had this strange nudge that I had to stop everything and pray for y'all. I've been lifting you up to the throne of grace for quite a while now. When I finally felt at peace, I knew I had to call you. What's going on?"

"Oh, Georgia, thanks for praying. I could definitely feel it!" Tatum sniffed. "I'm fine now and wasn't really in any danger." *Should she tell her?...* "We had a mission on Mount Bierstadt."

BLOG:

August 17
Relevant Ramblings: Mount Bierstadt

I just got back from the mountain that conquered Eric. The mountain tried to conquer a foolish young man this time. Eric had done everything right, but the mountain won. This young guy made all the wrong choices, yet he will live. I'm having a hard time trying to reconcile that. If I didn't believe in a God of love, I think I'd be mad! I think maybe I'm really mad anyway. His ways are certainly not my ways. If I ran the universe... But I'm certainly glad I don't. For the record, it's confusing. #backtotheplaceithappened

Heather: *You really went on a rescue on Bierstadt? You're my hero!*

31 🍃

Tatum was working on her upper body strength with a personal trainer. Not only did she not want to hear, "Speed it up," she also liked that her thirty-pound pack was feeling lighter. During field practices she found she could keep up with long-time team members. Her love of the mountains now far exceded the "Oh, gosh, how beautiful" phase. Now when she was in the mountains she had a healthy respect along with the awe, and hardly any fear.

Tatum had come to realize there was an emotional challenge along with the physical one. The adrenaline was high as she went out on a mission full of unknowns. Questions coursed through Tatum's mind every time she responded to a page. Mountain accidents weren't limited to the over-confident, inexperienced newbie. For anyone, the more time spent in the mountains, the higher the chances of an accident. Some dangers couldn't be controlled, only avoided. Still, accidents happened. As in Eric's case, it could be a matter of being in the wrong place at the wrong time. Bad things just happen.

One afternoon, Tatum was driving back from Breckenridge when she got the page. She pulled over to read the text. A fallen snowboarder on St Mary's Glacier! She realized she was only miles from the correct exit to get off I-70 and able to drive directly there. She might even be the first rescuer to arrive. "Lord, help me make a difference in this victim's life today, physically or spiritually."

She took the Fall River Road exit and drove the ten miles from I-70 to the glacier as quickly as was safe. When she got there, she texted the team leader. Wouldn't you know. Alex Witt.

I'm in the parking lot, prepared to jog to the victim. Will let you know.

Her phone's signal was weak, so voice data was out of the question.

Alex texted back: *Dispatch says victim tumbled thirty feet and is conscious.*

The reporting person had called 9-1-1 and MRT was then notified. Leaving the parking lot with her pack, a surge of adrenaline helped her jog up the three-fourths-mile, rocky road to the bottom of the glacier. She found a group of people kneeling next to a prone figure. She joined them.

"Hi, I'm Tatum with Mountain Rescue Team," she said to the victim. "What's your name?"

The young man, dressed in snow gear even though it was August, answered softly. "Jonah."

Good. He's responsive.

Tatum removed her pack. Without jostling Jonah, she examined his left leg. A broken femur! The most dangerous break of all. This information would help the next responders to know what medical expertise was needed for the victim.

"I want you to stay very still. Others are on their way and should be here shortly. Besides the leg, what else hurts?"

"Everything," came the muffled reply.

"I can imagine. Did you somersault when you hit the rocks?"

"Yes. It was awesome until I landed."

"Oh my gosh, a sense of humor. It could have been worse; you could have continued right into the lake. Someone was watching over you!"

"Oh, didn't think of the lake. Lucky, I guess."

She knew if Jonah's leg was moved incorrectly, the bone splinters could cut the femoral artery which could cause the victim to bleed out in eight minutes. She was only trained in basic first aid. More extensive EMT knowledge was needed here. Meanwhile, she could at least keep him talking.

She texted Alex: *19 YOM, broken femur, victim immobile but alert, awaiting hasty team.*

Alex replied: *ETA 3 minutes.*

"They're almost here," she told Jonah. "Just relax."

"I'm not going anywhere."

When four rescuers, two with more medical knowledge than she, ran into view, Tatum breathed a sigh of relief.

After a thorough examination and mobilization, Jonah was placed on the litter.

Alex made the decision that a call to Flight for Life was necessary. It could land in the parking lot. Tatum stayed at the young man's side, telling him what was coming next, trying to keep him calm. Then she stepped back and let the experts handle everything from there.

As Alex walked past her, she heard a soft, "Thanks." *Was that my imagination? Mr. Disapproval said thanks? What do you know!*

§ § §

Next day, after getting to the cabin because of another page, Tatum went out with MRT: this time, a lost child. Christiana and Tatum sat together in the vehicle on the way to the staging area.

"This one has more urgency," Tatum said. "I can feel it."

"Yeah, I agree," Christiana said. Both women spoke in hushed tones. "Can you imagine how scared the parents are, not to mention the little, two-year old girl. The dog teams will cover four times as much area, and much quicker, than MRT alone."

The little girl had last been seen the night before in a campground located in the foothills. Fortunately, the weather was warm and unlike higher altitudes, the evening would not be cold, just cool. Dogs were brought in, all-air scent dogs, and each team was assigned a different grid.

The dog team Tatum followed took a road to the left that looked to her to have no visible prints. She told the handler, "I don't see anything."

"We trust Thor's nose," replied the dog handler.

At the next crossroad, the dog never hesitated but

turned right. Dog and handler moved fast. Tatum had to pick up her jogging pace to keep up. She moved next to the trainer again. "How does your dog know which way?"

"Dogs can follow a deposited scent as old as thirty hours, so Thor's doing what he's trained to do. Oh, look, he's off road now, nosing around that downed tree."

The dog stopped, raised his head and wagged his tail so hard that his tail hit his sides. Then he sat. This was the signal. Jennifer and Tatum ran to look. There, behind the downed tree trunk, sat a tiny girl with a tear-streaked face! When the child saw Tatum, she almost flew into her arms.

The news crackled over the walkie-talkie. Found!

They turned and hurried the one mile or so back the way they came, where two parents frantically waited to get their daughter into their arms again. As they hustled back down the road, Tatum asked the trainer what reward Thor would get for his success.

"He gets to play tug-of-war with a special toy. And see, he gets to carry it back to our vehicle. He'll search for hours just to play with this."

"You mean it's not a food reward?"

"No."

In the MRT vehicle back to the cabin, Tatum recalled some of the details to the interested Christiana. "It was so amazing to see the dog go a direction that had no visible prints. I wouldn't have searched there, but Thor never hesitated."

Christiana nodded. "Our handler said he works with

his dog continuously, even now that she's certified as an SAR dog. That's a lot of commitment."

The following day, Tatum's team received a page to an urban search for a missing Alzheimer patient. The seventy-two year old man had a tendency to wander, but this time his absence wasn't noticed until lunch time.

The director of the Alzheimer's Daycare Center briefed them. "This man is becoming our resident escape artist. He's wandered off before, but we've always found him quickly. This time he's really eluded us."

The rescuers were given a picture of the man and told what he was wearing. The team split into four groups, going four different directions. The patient was rather frail; he couldn't have gone too far. He could have wandered into someone's backyard. The search was slow and methodical.

Team two reported on the walkie-talkie: "We found his jacket. He must have gotten warm and just dropped it. He can't be too far away."

It turned out he accidentally found his way back to the facility on his own, which was more of a surprise to his caregivers than to himself. He insisted he had known where he was the whole time. All four teams had a good laugh, glad for a third successful outcome in three days.

BLOG:

August 22
Relevant Ramblings: Lost and Found

Three missions in three days is kind of unique, from what others on MRT tell me. The dogs we used in one of those searches were amazing. The dog and handler worked as a team and you could tell that the bond between them was profound. From what I understand, the training is at least three years long initially, but continues throughout the lifetime of the dog. Since I've never had a dog, I can't imagine what that would entail. The dog thinks it's a game, and the reward for finding what is lost is praise and a game of tug-of-war with a special toy. The dogs make a big difference in the timetable. I love seeing the dogs work, but I'm not getting a dog any time soon. Cats may be stuck up, but they're way easier! I heard this joke (pretty hokey but funny just the same): "Dogs have masters and cats have servants." Actually, it's not a joke—it's true.

I need to call Erica and see how Spartacus is doing. #taataafornow

Nicole: *Never thought MRT would be needed in an urban area.*

Heather: *Loved the cat joke! Don't let Spartacus master you.* :)

32 🍃

He looked at his phone and his heart did a little jump. His last job didn't go too well, and he should have known it would not go unchallenged. Caller ID still said *private caller*, but he knew. He knew. Again, the voice was low.

"Surprised to hear from me? It's been a while. Don't think the last debacle has been forgotten. Because I'm a fair person, I'm going to give you another chance, and if you can pull this one off correctly we'll wipe the slate. This will take planning and patience, but if you succeed in this last job, you will be compensated accordingly."

He swallowed the lump in his throat. He was being given another chance. The failure still ate at him, but he refused to take all the blame. This benefactor expected one-hundred percent success—nothing less was ever a consideration. He wanted to redeem himself. This time he would not fail, even if he had to do this job himself. Yes! That's exactly what he would do. The financial reward and the glory of success would be all his own.

"I'll make sure it's done this time, no mistakes. Count on it. Want me to come up with the plan?"

"No! Here is the plan, and I expect it to happen just as I say," the low, raspy voice said. "The only thing in your control is the timing." There was no hesitation in the directive. "I will be checking in with you to see how you're progressing. I will call once every two weeks at the set time. Be available at eight o'clock p.m. Sunday evening starting two weeks from today. You'd better answer—and give me an update, so I can assess your progress. Do you understand?"

He had no choice. "Just exactly as you say."

"Now here's the way it will go down."

He listened closely, scribbling notes. When the call ended, he released a loud breath he didn't know he'd been holding. The plan seemed feasible, but it wouldn't be a walk in the park. He chuckled to himself. No walk in the park, but definitely a hike in the mountains. He started packing to move to Breckenridge. Half the money would be waiting for him there.

His employer came through as promised. He still didn't know for sure if the voice belonged to a man or woman, but he had a guess. Two weeks later, at the exact time, Sunday at eight o'clock the phone call came—again short and to the point.

"I've made contact and I'm getting in good with the subject." He left out the part about having to go to church, or that he'd tried to seem interested by asking questions.

"Remember, the only thing that's in your control is the timing. I will call in two weeks." The phone call was terminated before he had a chance to respond.

"Well, OK, then." He swallowed an expletive.

Exactly two weeks later another call came.

"Yes, things are progressing better than I expected." As he spoke, Javier was sitting in his car outside Erica's house waiting to finish his report before he went in to watch the movie he and Erica had agreed on. He would prefer a movie rated differently from what she chose, but he had to play the game.

"She's beginning to trust me, so I can pretty much tell her what I want and it gets done. But she's feisty, I'll give you that. I think I can conclude this business in four more weeks."

His employer seemed impatient. "Four weeks? That's a long time. Can't it happen sooner?"

This was the part that he could control, and he was going to do just that. "I don't think it can happen any sooner." This time Javier/Marcus ended the call before his employer could hang up on him. That felt good.

Marcus knocked on Erica's door and greeted her with a big hug. "What do you have to eat while we watch this flick? I'm starved. Dinner was a long time ago." Truth was he had skipped dinner. Thoughts of another phone call made him lose his appetite. But it was over. For now.

"I doubt popcorn will be satisfactory for you, so come into the kitchen and choose. I have more than enough for you."

Marcus bit back an off-color retort. Now was not the time to get Erica upset. Four more weeks and he wouldn't have to walk on eggshells around her and especially that busybody, Georgia.

The movie was boring, but the evening went well.

Another two weeks passed and the third call was much the same. But this time he gave the date of his action. "I can get this done in the next two weeks. I'm aiming for the Saturday before your next call."

"See that you do as we agreed. Remember, only the timing is in your control."

When the fourth call came, he'd be collecting his money. He'd ask for a bonus, too. He now had a pretty good idea who his employer was. The bonus would be blackmail of sorts. It bothered him not at all to think of it that way, just as it bothered him not at all to do the deed. His heart had turned hard years ago. He, Javier, thought only about number one. He'd learned that early.

Marcus had suggested a day hike to Erica for Saturday, two weeks from now. Since she hadn't hiked much, she called Tatum and asked her if she would be interested in going out hiking with her and give her some pointers, so she would have some idea of what she had agreed to.

Tatum thought that was a good idea. "I'll text you this list when we're done. You've got to have the ten essentials any time you go into the mountains."

"But it's only a day hike. Do we still need all that?"

"Being on Mountain Rescue Team, we've seen all too many hikers who thought the same thing and ended up in a situation that they weren't prepared for. All the things on the list are easily carried in a backpack. Look at it this way. Have what you need for worst-case scenario and hope you never need it. It's all about preparation and peace of mind. Think of it as you do seat belts. You seldom need them; but in the emergency, you're glad you had them on."

"Do I need a GPS? I don't even know what to do with it."

"No, not a GPS unless you're going off trail in the backcountry. But a compass is good, and a map."

"But I don't even know how to read a compass. You don't need those things to get around New York City."

"I'll show you the basics. It's really not hard."

"OK, what else do I need?"

"I'll text you the list. Why don't I come up Friday night and stay with you? Then on Saturday we can get up bright and early. The sunrises are worth the effort to get on the trail while it's still dark. See you on Friday."

🍃 🍃 🍃

Friday night the girls had a good time catching up on their lives and activities. Tatum suggested they go to bed early, so they could leave by five a.m.

Erica stared in disbelief. "You were really serious about seeing the sunrise? That's awfully early."

"Too bad! Set your clock for five and we'll leave by five thirty. I know just the place where the sunrise is spectacular. Now let's check your backpack to make sure it has everything you need."

Erica laid everything out with a flourish, eager to show Tatum she had followed her instructions. "Since you were bringing the map and compass, I didn't get those. But I have sunglasses and sunscreen, an extra hat, vest and jacket, a mini LED flashlight, some Advil and band-aids, some matches, a Swiss Army knife and some breakfast bars. I had no idea what you meant by fire starter; but I have all the rest!"

Tatum was pleased.

"And Tatum, let me show you my hiking clothes. You know, this day hike sure cost me a pretty penny, but I have to look stylish, even if it's Colorado hiking fashion." Erica made an exaggerated face. "My old friends in New York would fall on the ground laughing at my clothes! This is light years away from what I used to be seen in. Let me get them."

Erica came back with an armful of clothes and dropped them on the chair. She held each piece up with her explanation.

"The boots were my first purchase. After my kidnapping adventure, and walking in fashion shoes, I've had these for a while, but haven't had much of a chance to wear them."

Tatum watched, amused. "Keep going."

"This synthetic, sleeveless wicking shirt will keep the moisture away from me. Then I have a long-sleeved shirt—but not cotton. Over that I have a fleece jacket. Like the color I chose? I thought magenta would look best with my black yoga pants."

Tatum laughed. "Erica, only you would turn this into a fashion show. What else do you have?"

"This rain/wind jacket has matching rain pants and they coordinate with the fleece jacket. No mismatched colors for this hiker! And last but not least, I have two pair of socks, same color: thin liners and thick hiking socks, which are not cotton. What do you think?"

Tatum nodded. "The sales girl at the sporting goods store gave you good advice. All this is perfect! Now let's get to sleep. Five o'clock will arrive before we know it!"

Next morning, while still dark, Tatum drove the few miles from the Alma house to the turnoff for McCullough Gulch after the top of Hoosier Pass. There were other cars already parked at the trailhead for Mount Quandary, but they drove two miles more and parked near the gate. The sun was just lighting the mountain tops to the east as they started out. They hiked up the rutted road about fifteen minutes to the trailhead.

Tatum swallowed hard. This was the first hike she had gone on with Eric.

Erica stopped to catch her breath. She stared at the house with its *Keep Out* signs. "Who would want to live here? Surely no one works the mines now?"

"No, not anymore. On our way down we'll take a slight detour to see one of those mines and some of the old mining equipment. This is the first hike I took with your father, so it holds a special place in my heart. I love the roar of the waterfall. As we get closer, it gets louder. But before we go, turn around and look at the sunrise."

Erica spun around. Her mouth dropped open. "You were right. This is worth getting up early. The blues and pinks and oranges are spectacular."

The trail through the forest was easy to follow. Then they reached the talus field. There they picked the easiest route to cross all the rocks. After about forty-five minutes total they came to the rushing cascades that stair stepped down the mountain through a narrow chute. They chose a flat rock to sit on and eat their breakfast bars. After five minutes of silence Erica spoke up.

"Now I understand why people go hiking. This is amazing. What is that mountain over there?" She pointed south.

"That's Mount Quandary, a fourteener. The parking lot we passed was near its trailhead. You have to start out early to get to the summit and back down before the afternoon rains. I've never climbed it, but your dad did. These kinds of views are why he chose to spend his leisure time in the mountains. And he loved the challenge."

"It's nice to imagine him watching sunrises just like we did this morning."

Tatum agreed. Somehow, up here in the mountains he loved, it was less painful to think of Eric.

They continued up to the lake that fed the torrent of water rushing down the chasm. After some exploring, they headed back down. Tatum remembered to take the detour to see the mine. She took Erica's picture next to the sign that said trespassers would be shot. They got back to the car three hours after they had parked. Both admitted they were starved. Once they reached the paved road, Breckenridge was only seven or eight miles away.

🍃 🍃 🍃

Javier did a practice hike to the place his employer insisted would be the place where he/she would finally be rid of Erica. Javier was a city boy but knew how to adapt to his surroundings. He had gotten new hiking boots but rubbed dirt on them so as not to attract attention. For the same reason, he washed his new hiking clothes several times. The GPS was a little tricky. But once he got the hang of it, he was able to navigate to the sheer rock face his employer told him about.

"I wonder how my employer knew about this place? Oh, well, now I know how to get here in another week." He didn't take much time to admire the beauty of his surroundings. Soon he would be done with this part of the country.

🍃 🍃 🍃

Erica was having trouble falling asleep. The plans for Saturday were circling through her mind. First there was the hike in an area of the mountains new to her. The drive to the trailhead would take more than two hours, and Marcus said not to tell anyone because he had a surprise for her. She got out of bed and sat down at her computer and googled Flat Tops Wilderness Area.

"Wow, this looks awesome," she said to herself. "Different from the mountains around Breckenridge."

She read out loud: "It was so named because the crests of the mountains run across a flat plateau capped with lava." She guessed that meant a volcano at some point in history, though that seemed out of place in a state known for its jagged peaks. "This should be interesting."

Erica wondered which entry point they would take. "I can't wait to see what his surprise is. He's not a romantic kind of guy, but you never know."

She shut off her computer and headed for bed but still had trouble falling asleep, thinking about Marcus. He had come into her life about eight weeks ago, and it had been a whirlwind. She didn't know a lot about him yet, but he was handsome, funny, attentive, rich, and was even willing to go to church with her—though she herself went mainly because of Georgia. He was even asking some spiritual questions—questions she was still asking Georgia and Tatum.

"I don't know why Georgia has reservations about him." Erica spoke her thoughts out loud. "I guess she's just being protective of me like she is with Tatum. Oh, well. That's Georgia."

Thoughts of Tatum took her mind to the preparation of her day pack. Marcus had said he'd carry the heavy bottles of water. But she kept thinking of Tatum's advice to plan for the worst, so she decided to throw in one bottle of water, after all.

She glanced at the clock. *Better get to sleep or I'll be tired and grumpy in the morning.*

The alarm went off at four o'clock a.m. She bounded out of bed, took her shower, got dressed in the layers, dried her hair, put on her makeup, and was ready by five when Marcus knocked on her door.

In another part of Breckenridge, Georgia was jarred out of a sound sleep. An uneasy feeling filled her being. "What is it, Lord? This is important, but why? I need to pray, but about what? Who? OK, Lord, I'm praying. You know who or what this is all about." Georgia went to her prayer chair, wrapped herself in a warm blanket, and started her prayer vigil, only knowing she had to pray, not knowing much else.

"Are you ready for your day of surprises?" Marcus asked.

"I talked to Georgia briefly last night and started to tell her, but then remembered your warning, so I only told her I was going to be with you all day but not where we were going. And I went hiking with Tatum last weekend but only told her we were going hiking today."

"Good! I don't want to share you with anyone else. Have everything? Let's go!" Marcus carried her pack as they went out to his truck.

33 🍃

Erica and Marcus arrived at the trailhead at seven thirty, after a stop for coffee, a breakfast snack, and the two hour drive. Since this was September, the dark seemed to linger longer before the sun finally chased it away.

Erica had never been in the central part of the mountains past the Vail Valley and closer to Glenwood Springs. She asked Marcus about Glenwood Canyon and got a noncommittal answer that it was amazing and maybe they could go there sometime. She paid close attention to every turn and landmark. Marcus was again a good listener as she chattered about inconsequential happenings in her week.

"I've started school again but the homework load isn't heavy yet. How was your week?"

As usual, he deflected Erica's questions with something like, "It was OK." Or he countered with a question of his own: "How has work been?" or "And how is Georgia?"

"Georgia is Georgia. You take the good with the bad." She didn't want to tell him Georgia's opinions about his character.

Finally they fell silent. She looked at him expectantly. But he seemed preoccupied, not wanting to engage.

🍃 🍃 🍃

The crisp air, in the process of being overcome by the warmth of the sun, poured over their right shoulders. Erica considered herself directionally challenged, but on this day she stayed focused and made certain she knew where they headed. They started north on the trail, and after forty-five minutes, they came to a large meadow. The mountain peaks on the far north of the high meadow were indeed flat, and the surface of the lake in the distance sparkled like diamonds, as the sun began its journey across the sky. Only a few wildflowers remained to color the meadow.

Marcus and Erica stopped their steady hiking pace for a moment, to shed their outer jackets and tie them around their waists. Erica planned to put hers into her backpack the next time they stopped.

Marcus took out his GPS, studied it for a short time, then put it back. "We're going to cut across this meadow and meet up with the trail on the other side." He sounded like he'd been doing this for years. "That should cut off a good twenty minutes from our hike. What do you think so far?"

"It's a gorgeous day!" Erica twirled in a circle. "The terrain is different from what I saw with Tatum on the Breckenridge trail. Do you think this was created just for us to enjoy?" She glanced at Marcus.

He winced. "Your amazement is amazing! You're like a little kid!" Marcus reached one arm to give her a quick sideways hug. "Thanks for coming with me today." Then he started up the trail again, walking fast.

Erica followed, thinking. *What's with all the half-hearted comments? He seems distracted. Why did he want to do this, anyway?*

They crossed the alpine meadow and found seats on the rocks to eat their breakfast bars. He offered to share one of his bars with her, and for some reason she did feel reluctant to pull the food out of her own pack, so she took his.

"Thanks."

Georgia couldn't shake the heavy, uneasy feeling that had awakened her this morning. She continued to pray silently between welcoming guests and helping them choose their tea. She was sensitive enough spiritually to know something was going on that she needed to pray about, but again didn't know about what or whom she was praying. During a lull, she went to her car. Here she could do some "Pound on the steering wheel, hear me, Lord" supplication and no one would wonder if she had lost her mind.

"Lord, this feeling is getting heavier. I lift this up to you, God of the universe, you who know all and are always loving, always working for our good. If you need me to continue praying, Lord, I will. Thank you for what you're going to do. Amen." Then Georgia went back to work.

In the Flat Tops Wilderness area, Marcus consulted his GPS, and he and Erica headed out again. They weren't on a trail anymore, which was a little disconcerting to Erica, but Marcus seemed to know exactly where they were going. She searched for some distinctive landmark, but as they hurried along everything looked the same.

Erica's feelings about Marcus became increasingly uneasy. When she asked him to slow down, he glanced back at her and glared. When she asked if they could stop and rest, he completely ignored her. So she just stopped, sat on a rock next to the trail, and waited until he noticed she wasn't following. When he did realize she wasn't even trying to keep up, Marcus sheepishly walked back to her.

"I'm sorry," he said, seating himself on a rock nearby. "I guess I just had the goal in mind and wasn't enjoying the walk, but I can't wait to show you this awesome view." He reached to give her a hug but she scrambled out of reach. Looking annoyed, Marcus said, "It's really only ten or fifteen minutes more. Can you wait until then for our water break? I promise it's worth the wait, and I'll slow down then."

"If you can have an attitude, I guess I can too!" Erica crossed her arms and looked away.

"Aw, come on Erica. I said I was sorry. Just fifteen minutes more. It will be worth it, I promise." Marcus looked at her expectantly.

"OK." She made a face at him. "But just so you know, you owe me!"

The grin on Marcus's handsome face drove away her annoyance. True to his word, about fifteen minutes later they stopped. And he was right. The view was incredible. They were on top of a flat ridge with a sheer drop off ahead of them. The flat mountain tops in the distance sported dustings of early snow against the backdrop of Colorado's deep-blue sky.

They sat on a rock side by side. Marcus took the lid off a water bottle and handed it to Erica. Then he took a bottle for himself and drank deeply. They sat for several minutes, enjoying the panorama.

Erica felt lightheaded. Could it be the altitude? She tried standing but swayed and sat back down quickly. She looked at Marcus.

"Oh, no!" Real anger boiled up inside her. "Not again. Why? There's something.... How dare you!" She tried unsuccessfully to keep her words from slurring.

Marcus's face grew dark and smirking.

"You won't survive this time. It's the inheritance money. Someone wants you dead, and this time it won't fail. Sorry, Erica, this isn't about you. Strictly for the money. No hard feelings."

"How could you befriend me and then do this, Marcus?" She sounded like her tongue was swelling.

"You mean Javier." He laughed.

She couldn't keep her thoughts together. Confusion blurred everything. She just managed to say, "Help me, Jesus!" Then she slumped over.

"Bye-bye, Erica. It's been great. Sorry, Jesus can't hear you." He looked at her limp form. "Kind of a waste, if you ask me. I think I could have had fun getting in tight with you. The only thing I didn't like about you was the Jesus stuff from your friends."

He lifted her motionless form, backpack and all, into his arms. He carried her to the edge of the cliff and released her body to thin air, letting it fall helplessly and hopelessly out of reach. He didn't even bother looking down to see how she landed. He just turned, wiped his hands on his pants, and trotted back the way he had come.

Javier was wrong, of course. Jesus was there, and his angels were attending Erica. Yes, she had fallen, unconscious, but not to the bottom of the canyon as he expected. She fell about fifteen feet, then a jutting ledge of rocky soil stopped her fall. Her head hit hard; her wrist snapped as she landed; two ribs cracked and her shoulder dislocated. But Erica was still alive.

In Javier's careless rush to get the job done and be out of there, his eyes were blinded to the two water bottles lying on the ground where they had been dropped. Not only would the drug be identified later, but both bottles had his finger prints on them and his bottle would provide a sample of saliva with DNA.

34 🍃

"Georgia, there's a phone call for you. He says it's important." It was Julia, recently hired at the tea shop to wait tables, who was interrupting Georgia's lunch preparations with what sounded like urgent news.

Georgia wiped her hands on her apron, thanked Julia, and reached for the phone.

"This is Georgia."

"This is Walker Martin and I'm trying to reach Tatum. I haven't been able to get ahold of her." He spoke in a rush of words, the New York accent heavy. "This is very important and the only phone number I know to try, besides hers, is the tea shop. Can you get a message to her? Really, I wouldn't bother you if this wasn't way, way important."

"I remember you, Walker. What's so important?" Georgia was hesitant to take the words of this man at face value.

"Do you remember the woman that came with me to Eric's funeral? It's been a long time now since she and I were a number." Walker took an audible breath then continued. "I just came from the hospital where she was in critical condition after a drive-by shooting. She asked the hospital to call me. I was wondering why she would want to contact me, since we haven't

238

even seen each other in over a year. That sure seemed strange...until she told me her death-bed confession. Now I urgently need to get ahold of Tatum. This is about Eric's daughter. Will you tell Tatum to call me immediately? It may be life or death for the girl. I know you're probably thinking, there he goes again. People think I'm a big talker. Maybe I am. But this is for real."

Georgia thought of the prayer burden she'd felt all day. She straightened her back and gripped the phone.

"Walker, tell me what this is about." Georgia felt a sudden urgency. "I'm not sure I can reach Tatum. She's sometimes out with Mountain Rescue, out of cell phone range."

"OK." Walker spoke through short breaths. "Do you remember when Erica was kidnapped a year ago and everybody thought I had something to do with it?" Walker stopped, as if recalling the previous accusations. "Anyway, it turns out Brandi did have something to do with it. She was trying to get Erica out of the way so I could get the trust fund money and then she was going to get back in good with me. It wasn't me she wanted all along, it was only the money." He spitted out the last few words, as if they tasted bitter.

"She had someone hire those two guys to kidnap Erica in hopes that she would die in the mountains and the money would go to me. I wouldn't have thought she was capable of something like that. Now she's hired the same guy—to finish the job. Do you know where Erica is right now?"

"Let me get this straight," Georgia interjected.

"Brandi told this to y'all out of the goodness of her heart? You said something about death bed confession. What was that about?"

"Brandi didn't make it. She knew she was dying and wanted to at least get something right before she met her Maker. This guy she hired is going to be surprised when he finishes this job and can't get the rest of his money. Another kidnapping was planned...more sinister this time. She said the person she hired is a ruthless s-----" He caught himself and added, "He'll do anything to get the job done."

"Are there any other details you can tell me that might be important?" Georgia hoped she was asking the right questions. Her alarm was building.

"The only other thing she said was she hired this guy about two months ago. She told me his name was Javier Garcia but he's known to use aliases." Walker stopped to take a breath and then let the words spill out again.

"He knows how to disappear. Have you been around Erica lately? Has anyone like that showed up?"

Georgia couldn't help thinking, *I was right to have reservations about that Marcus. I wonder what the jerk's real name is, anyway?* Then out loud she said, "Yes, unfortunately, he's been around for about two months. In fact, he and Erica are together as we speak. We need to call the police!"

"OK. And try calling Erica's cell phone! Tell her not to trust that guy!" Walker was now shouting. "Maybe you can call your policeman friend. She's in danger!"

"OK, I get it. But I'm sure she's out of reach. I'll call

Sheriff Santiago. Give me your cell number so I can call you back." Georgia wrote it down and hung up.

She grabbed Julia and told her, "I have to leave. An emergency has come up. You'll have to finish the closing after the lunch crowd is gone." Georgia was already heading toward the door.

"That's OK. We can get it all done. Where are you going?"

"I'm going to Erica's house after I call Sheriff Rick."

Julia's eyes grew large but before she could ask another question, Georgia pushed through the door.

In her car, Georgia dialed Tatum's number first. It went to voice mail and Georgia shouted into the phone. "Tatum, call me immediately! It's a matter of life and death." Then she dialed Rick's number. When he answered, her words tumbled out. "Hi Rick, this is Georgia. Erica's in danger and I don't know what to do."

"Whoa, slow down. What kind of danger and how do you know?"

"Oh, Rick, it's that terrible Marcus. He's going to hurt her."

"Are you with Erica and Marcus now?"

"No, they're out hiking, but he's going to finish what he started with the kidnapping a year ago." Georgia's Southern accent thickened as she almost shouted.

Rick spoke slowly and deliberately. "How do you know this, Georgia?"

"I just got off the phone with Walker Martin."

241

"Georgia, where are you right now? Will you give me Walker's phone number, so I can hear his story first-hand?"

After repeating the number, Georgia decided she couldn't just wait and worry. "Rick, I'm going over to Erica's house. I may not have cell phone service there but I'll call you back in an hour." She was already out of the parking lot. Driving over Hoosier Pass, she reached the house in record time.

As she let herself in with the spare key, Georgia barely noticed Spartacus staring at her funny as she rushed to Erica's computer.

Of course. It was password protected. How in the world could she find out the password? She opened drawers in the desk but that was too obvious. She spoke out loud. "Lord, you know the danger Erica is in. Help me figure out where her password is so we can look for a clue to her whereabouts."

She sat staring at the keyboard, hoping for inspiration. Minutes passed. Then a thought came. She remembered when she worked in an office, management told employees not to write down their passwords. But a co-worker had showed her where she kept her password, because she was so forgetful—on a sticky note under her keyboard.

Fearful she'd find nothing, she picked it up and peeked underneath. There, attached to the bottom of the keyboard, was a sticky note with letters and numbers written on it! Three different combinations of letters and numbers, in fact.

"Thank you, Lord!"

The first one didn't work, but the second one did. Now the computer was opened and she went to the browser to look up the history that showed what Erica had been researching on the web. On Friday there were numerous entries for the Flat Tops Wilderness Area.

"Eureka! I hope.... Now to get back to where I have cell service."

She left the computer on and ran out the door. She had a fleeting thought of the cat but decided Erica was more important at the moment. She could come back later.

Just as she crested Hoosier Pass she got a signal. She called Rick.

He answered on the first ring. "Georgia, what did you find out?"

"The Flat Tops Wilderness Area! Do you know where that is?"

"Yes. I'll meet you at your house. I'll tell you what I found out from Walker."

They both arrived at the same time.

"What do we do next?" Georgia's words gushed out. "Should someone try to find Erica? Oh, we need to call Tatum again, and—"

"We'll get to that, Georgia. Calm down." Rick placed a hand on her shoulder. "I'll make a call to Garfield County. I know the sheriff there. You try to call Tatum." He took his hand away and opened his notebook. "By the way, didn't Mose live in Meeker before he moved to Como? He might know the area and be able to give us some information. Why don't you call him and ask if he can come over. Also, can you describe Marcus to me and do you know what kind of vehicle he's driving?"

"He's probably in his mid-twenties, good looking, about six-feet tall. He has black hair, not too long, and one pierced ear with a diamond stud. He drives a black truck with very dark windows. It looks new, but I can't tell you what make it is. He's always evasive when asked questions about himself. I don't know anything else."

Rick went to the living room to make his call to the sheriff, while Georgia tried Tatum again and left another urgent message. She then dialed Mose, who answered on the second ring.

"How's my Southern belle?" Mose's voice was deep and calm. "I was thinking about you this morning. Is everything all right?"

"I'm all right, but I don't think Erica is." Georgia felt tears coming on. Her voice shook. "Could you come over? I think this would be better in person."

"I'll be there in two shakes of a lamb's tail! Is that 'Southern' enough for you?" There was laughter in his voice.

"One shake would be better, but if it takes two, y'all just hurry. I'll be here waiting!" There was no smile in Georgia's voice.

🍃 🍃 🍃

At Georgia's kitchen table, a coffee cup in hand, Georgia had just finished telling Mose what she knew and what she suspected.

Mose sat in silence for a while, turning every bit of information over in his head and analyzing it. "Let me see if I understand all this. First of all, you had a nudge from the Lord to pray, but you didn't know what about. Then you got the call from Walker that Erica might be in danger. That put words to your uneasy feelings. You know that Erica is with this Marcus person, who showed up in Breckenridge two months ago. But she didn't tell anyone where she was going today." Mose stopped, his thought process getting in the way of his words.

"You then went to her house, found out her password, got on her computer, and looked up the history of what she had been researching on the Internet. There you found that she looked up a lot about the Flat Tops Wilderness Area. Does that summarize what you've been saying?"

"Yes, bless your heart! That's it! What should we do now?"

"We don't really know Erica is in trouble, but that doesn't mean we can't start looking for her. I'm not sure what the sheriff can do, because we really don't know if there's been any foul play. Tell me all you know about Marcus."

She repeated what she had told Sheriff Rick. "He came here about eight weeks ago and took an interest in Erica right away. I had an uneasy feeling from the start, but just thought I was being overly protective of Erica. She's street smart, but she responded to his attention immediately. He must have been really smooth.

She only spoke of him in glowing terms. When I cautioned her, she just laughed, gave me a hug, and told me not to worry."

Georgia stopped to take a breath, then continued. "She invited him to go along with her when I invited her to church and she said he didn't even hesitate in agreeing to go. He seemed pretty attentive—but more to Erica than the church service." Georgia stopped to recall events. She had a far-away look as she continued.

"When I asked her where he was from and what brought him to Breck, she couldn't tell me. Whenever I talked to Marcus, he was very good at asking me questions, but as soon as I asked him anything personal, he quickly diverted the conversation to something else."

"Do you even know his last name?"

"No. And Walker said he was probably going by an alias, anyway, so a name wouldn't help." Georgia spread her hands before her in a gesture of helplessness.

"If we got in the car and tried to drive to the Flat Tops, it would take us two hours to get there. Since its two o'clock now, that would get us there by four." He frowned in concentration. "That wouldn't give us much daylight, and we have no idea where they entered the area or what trail they took. The Flat Tops are too big an area for us to just start out looking."

"But we have to do something."

"I have a friend in Meeker. If Marcus and Erica took the obvious road into the area through Yampa, I could have my friend start in Meeker right now and drive the byway that cuts through the heart of the Flat Tops. My friend could look in the parking areas of each obvious trailhead for Marcus's vehicle."

"Yes! Call your friend! Ask him to do that! Do you know him well enough to ask him to drop everything on a Saturday afternoon to do that?" Georgia's voice rose with her excitement.

"My friend is a her, not a him. Her name's Sheila." Mose ducked his head sheepishly. "In fact, she's my ex-wife. And yes, she would do that for me. We parted on good terms, we just couldn't live together peaceably. It's part of my past that I'm not proud of and usually don't talk about. Now is not the time to get into that, but later, when we have this situation resolved, I'll tell you all about it if you want to know. I'll call her right now and tell her the description of the truck she should look for and why." He pulled out his phone.

Sheila called back in a surprisingly short time to say that she had left her house immediately to look for the black truck. She had pulled her vehicle into each trail-head parking lot with no success until about the half-way point. She had turned into the Flat Top Mountain Trail parking lot when she was almost sideswiped by a black pickup. The driver offered a nasty hand signal before pulling out onto the road and heading toward Meeker. Sheila said she followed it until the vehicle turned to go south on Hwy 13 to Glenwood Springs.

"It did have a temporary sticker in the back window, but if your guy is as devious as you say, I'm sure he will stop and put a license plate on." Sheila was silent a moment. "I can tell you that the vehicle is a Ford F150, newer model, although I don't know the year. The only identifying item is that the back bumper on the passenger side is dinged. I hope that helps."

Mose got off the phone and sat silently for two full minutes. Georgia finally spoke up. "I don't want to interrupt your thoughts, but I sure would like to know what's going through your mind. Could you tell me what Sheila said?"

"The only added information we know is what trail-head they may have started out from." Mose repeated what Sheila had said. "We still don't know anything about Erica, except she wasn't in the truck with Marcus, or whatever his name is. It's almost dark now, but maybe it's time to call in reinforcements. How about you call Sheriff Rick and tell him what we suspect and ask him what we should do now."

Twenty minutes later Rick Santiago joined Georgia and Mose at Georgia's kitchen table. Georgia gave him a cup of coffee then told Rick all they had learned. He listened with interest, sitting forward a little more with each piece of information.

Rick asked for Sheila's phone number, which he called and got a firsthand account of what Sheila had witnessed. Though calls to Erica's cell phone went unanswered, it was still too soon to file a missing person report. Little could be done at this late hour anyway. Rick explained that at first light, if there was still no word from Erica, Garfield County would be called.

Georgia's phone rang. Caller ID: *Tatum*.

Georgia grabbed the phone. "Tatum, Erica's in danger. We need Mountain Rescue to help us find her!"

"What do you mean, 'danger'? I don't understand. And I can't call out MRT. Only the sheriff can do that."

"Let me talk to Tatum." Rick reached for the phone, ignoring the smoldering look from Georgia. "Tatum, we have reason to believe Erica is in danger. We know she's with Marcus, and we're pretty sure they're in the Flat Tops Wilderness area, which is in Garfield County—"

"Tell her what Walker said," interrupted Georgia. "Tell her—"

Rick put his hand over the phone, shot a look at Georgia, and walked into the living room to fill Tatum in, leaving Georgia with her mouth open.

Mose took her hand in his large one. "Rick will tell Tatum everything. We're doing all we can for the moment. Maybe you could pray right now."

Georgia seemed to shrivel a little, then she looked into his eyes. "You're right. Thank you." Then she closed her eyes and broke out in prayer. "Lord of the universe, we ask you to protect our Erica. You know where she is. Give us the wisdom to know what to do next. Give me peace, help me to trust you in this. Thank you, Father. Amen."

"Amen," Mose agreed.

Rick came back in and handed Georgia her phone.

"Tatum wanted to come here immediately, but I advised her to stay in Evergreen and we'll keep her informed. Garfield County has called MRT to assist in searches in the past, and if it comes to that, Tatum would be more useful on the team."

"What's next? I feel useless just sitting here."

"We can only wait until Garfield County calls their rescue team or calls MRT for assistance. I'm going back to the office and put Javier Garcia's name into the computer and see if it comes up with anything. We'll see if Brandi was truthful with the name. Mose, will you stay here with Georgia and make sure she doesn't do anything silly?"

Georgia heard a smile in his voice. But she just gave him a dirty look and turned her back, which made Mose chuckle.

35 🍃

Erica gradually awoke to darkness. She shivered. She was lying on her side on something hard and she hurt. She tried to sit up. Tears sprang to her eyes. Her head ached, her shoulder hurt, her right temple throbbed. She tried to reach up to feel it with her right hand, but her hand wouldn't move. Feeling starved for air, she drew a deep breath, *Ouch*! Excruciating pain. Nausea. *I'm not going to try that again.* Her ribs on her right side felt on fire. She held her breath as long as she could then only took shallow breaths. Finally the pain faded. Very gingerly, she adjusted her position. *My backpack is still on.*

Where am I—and why? Oh, déjà vu! Slowly, painfully, awkwardly, she pulled herself to a sitting position. Her left foot seemed to hang off into space. She felt with her left hand. *I'm on a ledge! What the—* She scooted back carefully, her shoulder gripped with stabbing pain, until she was leaning against the cliff face.

Marcus! How could I have been so wrong about him? She thought back to the last two months. Man, my street smarts really failed me this time! She had foolishly followed his lead and not told anyone where they were going. The pain of betrayal and regret were almost as bad as the physical pain. It even hurt to think. But first things first.

"My shoulder must be dislocated or broken or whatever happens to shoulders when you fall. My head aches something fierce and since I can't take a deep breath without awful pain, I must have broken ribs. Probably my right wrist is broken too."

"Oh, Lord. I'm in a world of hurt and no one knows but you." Between shallow breaths, Erica cried, "You have my attention, Lord. All this time I've listened to Georgia and Tatum talk about you. I thought it was nice, but didn't think I needed that. I've heard them talk about God letting people come to the end of their rope so they feel their need for God. OK, I'm there. I know you're real, God. And I need you."

She stopped as she tried to control her sobs. "I'm afraid, Lord. No one knows where I am. And I'm angry, not only with Marcus but with myself for being in this situation. Couldn't you have gotten my attention in some other way?" She released a shuddering sigh then sat in silence.

The silence didn't last long, though. "I know I've been stubborn. I know I need you in my life to direct me, because I'm doing a lousy job of it myself. Would you come into my life? I'm tired of doing this all on my own. You have a lot of stuff to forgive, but you're God and Georgia and Tatum say forgiving is what you do."

A gentle peace came over her and she rested in His Presence for a time.

Her circumstances didn't change, but somehow her attitude did. The all-encompassing pain didn't hinder her from applying her mind to solving what problems she could. "How do I get this backpack off without moving my right side? At least no one can hear me talking to myself. Well, maybe an elk or a deer.

"OK, Erica, use your head. There has to be a way to get into this backpack. Oh, there are adjustment straps on each side. I'll bet I can pull the right side open!"

She took her time because every movement sent extra pain to her injuries. Trying to reach the opposite side of the backpack with her left hand was agony. She took short gulps of breath. She would have to undo both straps of her backpack.

The straps finally came apart. She eased the pack awkwardly onto her lap.

What did I put in there that I could use? In the dark, she felt into the pockets of the pack. Her jacket she had taken that off when it got warm. She set that aside until she could figure out how to get it on. Hopefully there was a way, because her teeth had started to chatter. Then her hat. But how could she put it on with one hand? After a few awkward attempts, it was somewhat in place. Next the scarf. She wrapped it around her neck twice. That was a little warmer. She found her gloves and set them aside.

Next, the water bottle. Good thing she added that at the last minute. She held the bottle between her legs and with her left hand twisted off the cap. After a long, careful swig, she remembered: it was her only source of water. How long would one bottle of water last? She'd have to ration it. She wished she could find the Advil in her pack, to dull the pain. Her hand found her cell phone. She grabbed it and turned on the power. No signal. But she could use the phone's flashlight.

The ledge looked to be about six-feet square—two feet by three feet. She pointed the light upward but couldn't make out how far she'd fallen. The time said 2:45. A long time till daylight. She wanted to keep the phone on for the small comfort of the light, but didn't want to run out of power. She turned it off.

She put everything back in the pack, fearing she might accidentally knock them off the edge. Her hand found the ace bandage. Could she somehow wrap it around her wrist? Now that she had a mental list of things to do, she could think a little more clearly. The pain, now less excruciating, was nevertheless unrelenting. Her fingers latched onto a Vitamin C drop. She unwrapped it using her teeth and popped it into her mouth. A little bit of sugar couldn't hurt.

She found the extra pair of socks but there was no way to get her shoes off, those on, and shoes tied again. So she sat on them; the rock was cold. She winced as she shifted to push the socks underneath her.

Next she found the breakfast bar. She'd save it for later. She bit back another sob, thinking of all the things she should have done to prepare for this hike. *Why didn't I at least tell someone where I was going?*

"Lord, I remember how real you were during my other ordeal. Georgia and Tatum are thinking this is another kidnapping. They wouldn't know Marcus tried to kill me. And they wouldn't know where I am. But you know." Erica didn't know how to pray. *I guess it's all right to just talk to God?* "I know you're here. I don't know if anyone even knows I'm missing yet, but I'm going to thank you ahead of time, just like Georgia always does, for the good you're doing."

She stopped, overwhelming feelings coming over her like a flood, encasing her in fear and dread.

"Could you make that help come and find me fast? I hurt bad and I'm scared. *Gracias, Dios Precioso.*"

She sobbed quietly but felt oddly comforted.

BLOG:

August 28
Relevant Ramblings: Erica's Missing

I need to get these feelings down on paper.

Erica is missing—again. Foul play is suspected. Georgia wanted me to call Mountain Rescue Team immediately, but of course that's not possible. I feel helpless sitting here in Evergreen waiting for a call from Georgia or MRT.

I think of her as the little sister I didn't have when in reality she was almost my stepdaughter. Lord, you know where she is and what is happening to her. Keep her safe and help us find her. Help her feel your presence. #feelinghelplessbuttrusting

Nicole: *Praying! Keep us informed.*

Heather: *Praying too. And trusting.*

36 🍃

Early Sunday morning, true to his word, Rick Santiago confirmed that Erica had not come home, so he filed the missing person report. He also put a call into the Garfield County Sheriff, Michael Handel.

"Hi, Michael. Rick Santiago here."

"Rick! What's up? Is this a friendly call or business?"

"Hey, man. I do want to know how you're doing, but it'll have to wait. I have a missing person, and we think she's in your jurisdiction."

Sheriff Handel was all business now. "Can you tell me more?"

"The missing person is a twenty year old female, five-foot eight, dark hair, blue eyes and we think she's been kidnapped. We have reason to believe she's in the Flat Tops because of what we found on her computer."

"I'll call Garfield Search and Rescue immediately. Can you get me a picture?"

"I'll send it right away. Keep me informed."

🍃 🍃 🍃

Tatum's pager went off. Garfield Search and Rescue (SAR) was requesting MRT's help.

Yes! She threw her clothes on and drove as fast as she could to the cabin. As she arrived, her phone rang.

"Hi Georgia. I can't talk long. MRT just got called and I'm on my way. Any news on your end?"

"Nothing! What can you tell me?"

"I'll know something after our briefing. Gotta go."

Alex Witt was team leader. He explained, "This is a missing female, age twenty. Her name is Erica Reyes. We're headed to the Flat Tops area."

Did Tatum imagine that Alex glared at her briefly? She kept her eyes down.

The MRT vehicles used lights to take some time off the two hour trip, and Tatum called Georgia back.

"Georgia, we're headed to the Flat Tops to assist in the search. That's all I know right now. Just pray! I need to go. Bye."

🌿 🌿 🌿

MRT arrived at the staging area only a little behind Garfield SAR. Their team leader, Aaron Gretski, explained they weren't exactly sure this was the Place Last Seen (PLS), but were going to go on that assumption.

As they left the trailhead at a fast clip, Tatum noticed the Garfield County SAR team leader's excellent tracking skills. To Tatum's dismay, though, Alex fell into place beside her, scowling.

"Since this is your former fiancé's daughter we're looking for, what do you know about this?" He spoke in a low tone but she heard disapproval in his voice. His face had a hard expression.

Tatum's throat constricted. She tried not to verbalize the unkind thoughts that tried to invade her answer.

"I don't know any more than you do," she responded. Then she pressed her lips together. She wasn't going to volunteer anything.

Alex shot a hostile glance at her. "I'll be watching you closely. You better not let emotion get in the way of doing a professional job. Don't disappoint me. And keep up." His posture was stiff and his jaw clenched.

Tatum nodded curtly then fell back behind him on the trail. *Disappoint? I'm always trying not to disappoint someone. Well, I'm going to start making decisions so I don't disappoint Tatum. At night when I lay my head on my pillow, that is the real issue.* She squared her shoulders and almost marched up the trail.

The Garfield County SAR leader was on point, looking for any unusual signs. This popular trail had a lot of evidence of foot traffic. Every now and then he would stop, bend down, and point out a pebble with moist dirt facing upward. He said this suggested it was recently overturned. When they came to the large meadow, they stopped as he pointed out the shine, explaining the bruising of the grass, and the two tracks cutting across the meadow. He showed how he could see the direction the two traveled by the way the grass was flagged. Even in twenty-four hours, the grass hadn't completely recovered.

"We have no healing of the vegetation yet, so these tracks have been made recently." Aaron sounded like he loved to teach. "Since this trail is well known to us, I'm sending a few around the trail, and the rest can follow me across the meadow to meet up with the trail. You three," pointing to three of his own people. "Go quickly along the trail and look for any littering but remember this is a well-traveled route for hikers. Meet up with us." Twenty minutes later Aaron stopped again to show those following him what he was looking at.

"The scuff mark coming out of the meadow and meeting with the trail again shows me they're still headed up." He stopped and chuckled. "If this was a wise kidnapper, versed in tracking, he might have headed down the trail and cut back across another rocky spot, for counter tracking. Or we might see backing—walking backward to disguise the direction of travel—but I don't think we have that here. We'll head up this trail and look for anything out of the ordinary."

The team continued as the sun rose higher. They could see much more clearly now. The three team members sent around, met up with them.

The SAR leader pointed out footprints and tamped-down grass next to the rock just off the trail. "See, here they sat on a rock for a short time. So far, it's textbook tracking."

"Well, wouldn't you know it!" he remarked a short time later with a disgusted look. "Just as I say that, the footprints go off trail. We'll have to watch closely for overturned rocks and any heel marks in the dirt areas. Everyone, keep your eyes open."

Another rock was spotted where it looked like someone had been sitting, but only one pair of footprints led up to it. They called the team leader over. He looked around and saw a set of prints leading away, coming back and then two pair resuming in the direction of the large cliff face they knew was about fifteen minutes farther ahead.

Then fifteen minutes later, near the cliff, they spotted two discarded water bottles by another large rock. Since this was also a criminal investigation, as Jerry with MRT picked up the two water bottles, he was careful not to leave his own fingerprints on them. He was the one with a police background and knew how to approach a crime scene. The rock would have made a great viewing spot to look out over the grand panorama, and apparently it had been used that way. Footprints could be seen all over it. There seemed to be one set that went toward the edge, as the smaller rocks had been moved in a shuffling pattern. The SAR leader approached the edge. He looked down.

"We've found her!" he shouted. "Someone's down there—on a ledge about fifteen feet down."

Tatum ran to the edge. "That's Erica! I know her well! Let me rappel down to her! I can assess her injuries." Tatum was near panic. She shouted down to Erica, "Don't worry, we've found you!"

Alex Witt grabbed her elbow and spun her around. "This is not our rescue. We are here for mutual aid. I knew this would happen. You are out of line. Let Garfield County SAR make the decisions."

Aaron had been listening to this exchange and, much to Tatum's surprise, asked if she would go down to Erica. Tatum turned her back on Alex. "I'll be glad to go down." She opened her backpack and retrieved her harness for rappeling.

The ropes were readied for her to descend as she buckled on her harness. She began the rappel down.

Erica heard the voices but couldn't draw a breath deep enough to shout. *That sounds like Tatum's voice. I didn't think MRT came this far.*

"I'm here!" she tried to shout, though the words came out in little more than a whisper. Oh, the fire in her ribs that even a shallow breath caused. When she realized they were coming down to her, she closed her eyes and waited. *Thank you, Lord.* She repeated the words over and over as she faded in and out of consciousness. When she opened her eyes there was Tatum! "How in the world?"

"Another God thing," said Tatum.

"Oh, Tate, you found me. I was so scared and I prayed and—"

"Shhhh, it's all right. You're safe now, and we're going to get you up from this ledge. Tell me what hurts while we wait for the litter to come down. Then I'll go up and let the medical team come down and prepare you for evac."

"I think my right wrist is broken, my right shoulder hurts and I can't take a breath without my ribs feeling on fire. Other than that, I'm good."

Tatum laughed. "You're good; that's funny."

Erica tried to laugh, but it ended in a whimper.

"Seriously, Erica, the team will stabilize your injuries, put you in the litter and raise you up. They're pros at this, so they'll do it with the least amount of pain possible. See you on top."

Erica nodded. "How did you know where to find me?"

"I'll tell you all about it later. Right now, know that your dad's brother even had a hand in the rescue!"

Tatum went back up to allow room on the ledge for the EMTs and briefed them so Erica could receive the medical attention she needed to get her safely in the basket and lifted.

Once Erica was on flat ground at the top of the cliff, the six men chosen to carry the litter first started off at a fast clip. Tatum carried the ropes back to the vehicles. She remembered following another litter a year ago.

How different life is this time.

BLOG:

August 30

Relevant Ramblings: Erica's Rescue

I love being on Mountain Rescue Team but it's pretty harrowing to go out on a rescue of someone you love. We didn't even know if we were going the right way and especially didn't know what we'd find.

From the little knowledge we had, Marcus (or whatever his name is) planned to finish the job the first kidnapping failed to do—getting rid of Erica. So now it is called attempted murder.

We'll let the authorities track him down, but there is a certain satisfaction that Marcus is going to be very surprised when he finds out he won't be able to collect the last of his payment because his 'employer' has died.

I'll have to rethink my opinion of Walker. After all, he is Erica's uncle, and he had a big part in helping us find her.

We'll wait and see how this crisis has changed Erica—if at all. Lord, help her to see her need for you. Thanks ahead of time. #servingaGodofmiracles

Heather: *You could write a book, your life has become so exciting! So glad Erica is OK!*

Nicole: *I agree with Heather. Rescues, kidnappings, crime scenes, SAR dogs. Where has our timid Tatum gone!*

37 🍃

Tatum's phone vibrated. When she took it out and looked, she gasped.

Why would Alex Witt text her? And why would he want to see her at the MRT headquarters cabin, at her convenience? With this guy, everything was at his convenience, it seemed. Now what had she done wrong? Was he going to tell her she couldn't be on the team anymore?

OK, Lord. I did my best and only had a bad attitude once in a while, and now he's going to tell me he wants me off the team. Help me accept his decision with your grace, because I don't think I have much grace on my own toward that man.

She spoke out loud. "OK, stick up for yourself, Tatum, even though you'd like to avoid this at all costs. I know you, but this time you're going to be bold. This isn't the worst thing in the world. It only feels like it." She half chuckled, half groaned.

By the time Tatum arrived at the cabin, Alex was already there. She took a deep breath and climbed the stairs to the second floor meeting room, not hurrying. Her knees felt weak and her heart was racing. It was one thing to tell herself to stand up to Alex in the safety of her car and another thing completely, now that she was here.

When she entered, he looked up and gave her something like a smile.

Tatum looked around the room. As usual, the chairs were set up as a classroom with tables to the far side; but today it felt like there was hidden danger. She sat down at the table across from Alex.

"Thanks for coming, Tatum." He hesitated only an instant. "I'm not going to beat around the bush. I want to apologize to you."

Her mouth dropped open and she stared. *This is not what I expected. What's going on?* "You want to apologize to me?" Had she heard him right?

"Let me get this over with. I'm not very good at apologies. I want to tell you why I've been so hard on you." Alex had his head down, not making eye contact.

What? "You want to apologize for being so hard on me?" She had prepared herself for a dismissal not an apology.

"Yes. Just let me continue. I was a friend of Eric's and—"

"You were a friend of Eric's?" Understanding still eluded her. "What does that have to do with MRT? Could you get to the point?"

"I was going to be his best man and—"

"You're the Alex that was going to be Eric's best man? You're the Alex he was always on the phone with?" Tatum had raised her voice. All the pent-up emotion was pushing against her self control, and now the conversation was including her former fiancé?

"Are you going to repeat everything I say? If you can just sit there and keep your mouth shut, we can get this done with quickly."

Tatum stared at Alex as if he had two heads. She was stunned into silence. *You called this meeting, you carry the conversation, buddy.* She waited.

Alex looked up. "Sorry. That sounded rude. Can you let me finish? Then I'll let you talk."

She pressed her lips together and nodded, uncomfortable with the eye contact.

In a shaky voice Alex said, "Eric was my best friend and my climbing partner. I didn't know what to do with the void in my life after he died."

Tatum could only guess he stopped to gather his thoughts and get more in control of his emotions. Shaky voices and apologies were foreign to him.

"I didn't know how to grieve his death. When you started training to be on Mountain Rescue Team, I knew who you were, but you didn't seem to remember me from the funeral."

"That time in my life is pretty much a blur. And with Eric's father dictating all the funeral arrangements, I felt like an outsider. Sorry I didn't remember you." *That didn't sound sincere at all. Oh well, I don't care. Let's just get this over with.*

"I was the one who dared him to go on the dating website. I put a lot of energy into trying to make your life miserable because... I guess I wanted to blame someone for his death."

"Why would it be my fault that lightning killed

Eric? That makes no sense at all." Tatum wasn't willing to give him much grace yet.

"It wasn't very logical to blame you for a lightning bolt. The feelings of loss and disappointment felt so strange to me. When I finally realized what I was doing, I didn't want to stop."

Alex seemed to remember something. "What brought me to my senses was the way you stood up for yourself and didn't quit like I thought you would. My tactics weren't working and my actions weren't professional. Actually they were downright rude."

Tatum sat there unable to say a word, not even realizing her mouth was open. Did Alex Witt just apologize to her? *There has to be a catch. He has to know how awkward this is. What in the world is happening, Lord?*

In the uncomfortable silence, Alex watched her face. His developed a small smile. "You can say something now if you want."

"Yes, you were rude! I'm speechless! I've been trying to figure out why you hated me this whole time. I dreaded going out on a mission with you as the team leader." She let out a sigh of relief. "I could tell by the look on your face every time you walked into the cabin."

Alex was grinning.

"So when you told me to pick up the pace, I was really doing OK?"

"Yes, you were probably doing OK."

"And when you had me carry the heavy equipment back down, it wasn't because I messed something up?"

"No, it wasn't because you messed something up."

"One more question. When we went to Garfield County to assist, you knew I'd put my personal feelings aside and act professional, but you still had to warn me. Tell me: Did I act professional?"

"Yes, you were professional."

"I guess I understand now. But *you* weren't acting very professional."

"That's what I'm apologizing for. This is killing me, Tatum, dragging it out like this."

Tatum laughed out loud. "OK, I accept your apology. I thought for sure you were going to tell me I couldn't be part of MRT anymore, and I was prepared to throw a very 'un-Tatumly' fit and tell you all the reasons why I should still be on the team." She chuckled. "I should still give you the little speech I had all prepared to put you in your place. But you've taken the wind out of my sails!"

He waited.

In a quieter voice she said, "Thank you for telling me. Talking about Eric makes me realize how much I miss him. I'd like to hear more about your friendship."

"Besides being the best mountain climber I've ever known, he helped lead me to faith in Christ."

Tatum started to repeat his statement, then with one hand over her mouth, she waved her other hand for him to continue. "I promise not to repeat everything you say."

They sat in the meeting room forty five minutes longer as Alex told Tatum story after story about their climbing adventures.

"But the best thing about Eric was he not only led me to the Lord, he discipled me and challenged me to live my faith out loud."

Tears were stinging Tatum's eyes.

"Thank you so much, Alex. I will treasure the memories you've shared of Eric. As you know, his daughter has come into my life, and all she has of her father is other people's memories. I know she'll laugh at the story about him doing a triple somersault down the scree field, landing on his feet and continuing down, unscathed."

Then Tatum met his gaze pointedly. "Does this mean I'm still on the team and you won't give me a hard time anymore?"

Alex chuckled. "Yes, Tatum. You're still on the team. I think you're a valuable member, and I've seen you work hard to prove yourself." He smiled. "Maybe now you won't cringe when you see me as your team leader. I may still get on your case now and then, but if I do, know it's because I want to help you improve your skills. Now, as a peace offering, will you go out to dinner with me tonight? I think I owe you something more tangible, not just an apology."

"You don't owe me anything more, but if it will soothe your conscience, I'll let you buy me dinner." Tatum actually felt flattered. "I can meet you at Tuscany Tavern at seven o'clock tonight. That's my favorite restaurant here in Evergreen. Deal?"

"Deal! But I can pick you up. I know where you live."

"No. That's all right. See you there at seven. I'm not letting you off the hook too easily! Appetizer, entree, dessert, virgin Margarita—what else can I think of?" Tatum laughed.

There was a genuine smile on Alex's face.

As Tatum got in her car for the short ride home, she breathed a prayer of thanksgiving. "Thank you, Lord, for letting this turn out all right, and it's nice to know there's another believer on the team. And thanks, Lord, for helping me hold my tongue when I wanted to lash out. Alex is not as bad a guy as I thought!"

38 🍃

Erica rested in Georgia's comfy guest room. Her ordeal seemed like a bad dream—or a bad movie. Tatum was on her way over. Mose was already here. Rick Santiago was invited to this meal, too, so all the key players in her adventure could finally tell her the whole story. She had talked to Walker on the phone to hear his part in all this. It was almost too much to believe. An inheritance had caused her all this trouble!

The doorbell rang. Georgia answered the door. Tatum came in and took off her coat. She gave Erica a gentle hug, careful of her cast and sling, then they all convened in the kitchen to wait for Rick.

"Tatum," Erica said. "I'd really like to hear your perspective."

"Maybe we should wait until Sheriff Rick gets here." Tatum smiled, noting the big wink from Mose.

"You can start telling me all the pieces you were involved in, even before Rick gets here, can't you? Please! I can't wait!"

"Bless her heart, she's impatient! But she still has to wait!" Georgia laughed.

"Don't talk about me like I'm not even here," Erica grumbled. "This isn't fair."

The doorbell rang. Erica rose, but Georgia reached the door first and welcomed a smiling Sheriff Rick.

"Get in here Rick," Erica said. "They won't say a word until you get here." With everyone seated around the table, she ordered, "Now start talking, all of you!"

Georgia laughed. She set the pot on the table, said grace, then began her side of the story, while everyone helped themselves to the fragrant chili and cornbread.

"You gave me quite a fright because of the phone call from Walker. I realized you were with that Marcus person but none of us knew where you had gone."

"Yea, that was pretty dumb of me," Erica said.

"I decided to go to the Alma house and see if I could find anything on your computer. That was pretty dumb of me, because I don't know anything about passwords and the like. But God brought to my memory an office I had worked in years before. We weren't supposed to write our passwords down but a girl in the office, who was rather ditzy, showed me where she kept her password because she was always forgetting it."

Mose laughed. "Are you calling Erica ditzy?"

"No, no, no! Sorry, Erica. I didn't mean you were like that." Georgia waved her hand at Mose in a dismissive gesture. "Shush, and let me continue my—"

"I was glad to get the call from Georgia about what you had been researching on the computer," Rick said. "We didn't have much, but at least we had a 'where.'"

"It was hard for me to stay in Evergreen when I heard about Walker's call. I wanted to come to Breck right away," Tatum added.

Georgia said, "I'm so glad Mose knew a little about the Flat Tops. That helped you out, didn't it, Rick?"

"Yes. But at the time we still couldn't call her a missing person. We had to wait till the next day."

"A long twenty four hours," Georgia said dramatically, and everyone around the table agreed.

During a break in the conversation, Georgia, always reading people, asked Erica, "Hey girl, what's going through your mind? Talk to us!"

Erica's eyes glazed over a little, remembering. "It's hard to wrap my mind around it all. Everything was out of my control. Someone was moving all the puzzle pieces." She shook her head. "I'm used to taking things at face value. But as things were unfolding here, someone in New York suddenly had a conscience and told my uncle a part of the story that was super important in finding me. Which reminds me; Marcus told me his real name was Javier. Maybe that helps." She forgot and took too deep a breath and immediately regretted it. Her ribs were better but still hurt.

"I need to tell you what I was thinking about that night on the ledge," Erica added.

They all leaned forward slightly. They hadn't heard this part.

"I was scared and in pain but I remembered, Tatum, what you and Georgia talked about all the time, that God sees us even when no one else does." Tears welled in her eyes. "I have to tell you, Georgia, everything I remembered about God began to make sense. I prayed and asked Jesus to help me, not only on that ledge but from now on in my life."

All those around the table were smiling and nodding

and enrapt as they listened, even Mose. Georgia grabbed Erica's hand across the table and squeezed it.

Tatum reached and grasped both of their hands. "That's a decision you'll never regret, dear friend."

Rick, eyes glowing, kept quiet.

"And..." Erica gave Georgia a hard but playful stare. "I may have to change where I hide my passwords!"

General laughter resounded.

Tatum spoke up. "My team leader knew I knew you, Erica, and wanted to make me stay at the base and not be included in this mission. And if Alex Witt had his way, it wouldn't have been me coming down to you on that ledge."

"I'm so glad it was you, Tatum. After feeling so hopeless, I can't tell you how comforting it was to see my big sister, Tatum!"

Rick added a thought. "If that scumbag, Marcus, or Javier, as we now know, had walked six feet in either direction before he dumped you over the edge, we would not be here discussing this wonderful outcome. That was the only ledge on the whole cliff face."

"Thank you, Jesus!" Mose spoke the words the whole group was thinking. Georgia gave him a quick but appreciative look.

"The last thing I remember before waking up in pain on the ledge is saying, "Help me, Jesus." And he did. He was right there! I don't even want to think of what could have happened." Erica shuddered, then ducked her head. "I won't be forgiving Marcus, or Javier, or whatever his name is, any time soon, though. When he's found, he'll deserve everything he has coming to him."

Georgia jumped in quickly. "Yes, Marcus/Javier does deserve the consequences for his actions, but eventually you'll need to forgive him."

Erica frowned. "What? That not only doesn't make sense, I don't even want to do that."

"It may not make sense, but your peace will depend on it," Tatum spoke softly. "Believe me, I know. I had to forgive the drunk driver who killed my parents. The nice thing is that you don't have to feel forgiving in order to begin to forgive. You just have to be willing to be willing. The feelings will come later."

"That hurts my head even trying to figure out what you just said, Tatum. Can we talk about that another time?" Her voice sounded uncharacteristically tired.

Tatum nodded and hoped she had planted a seed that would be watered and grow as Erica let God work in her life. Then she remembered something and sat up straight.

"I almost forgot! I had dinner with Alex Witt last night!"

"What? Do you mean that team leader who's always giving you a hard time? Well, bless his heart!"

Everyone laughed at Georgia's incongruous statements.

"Yes, that team leader. No one is more surprised than me. He apologized for the way he kept coming down on me so hard. It turns out he and Eric were mountain climbing partners and he unjustly and illogically—those were his words—blamed me for Eric's death. He even shared that he had come to Christ because of Eric's testimony."

"Does that mean you're still on the rescue team? I know you were worried about that," said Erica.

"I'm still on the team." It was such a relief to say that.

"Alex is a pretty nice guy, actually, without the chip on his shoulder. As Georgia would say—let me try my best Southern accent here—'Thank you, Jesus!'"

Heartfelt laughter followed.

BLOG

September 10

Relevant Ramblings: Guest post by Erica

Hi! This is Erica.

The only thing I knew about my father as I was growing up was I had his blue eyes. I didn't even know his name. Then he was killed by a lightning strike on a mountain. I was named beneficiary of his trust fund and insurance and I came to Colorado to learn more about a man who must have at least loved me a little.

I thought my life was exciting in New York City. But since I've come here I've been a cashier (that was familiar), a waitress (that was new), a house guest of a Southern lady (what a trip!), made a new friend (Tatum, like a big sister to me now), gone on buying

trips to Denver with Tatum to expand the Tea and
Java du Jour (right up my alley), been kidnapped twice
(crimes still unresolved), and accepted Jesus as my
Savior (which will take me a lifetime to understand)!

If I'm asked to write a guest post again, I'll tell
you about the kidnappings. But for now, suffice it to
say that in spite of all the bad things, good things
happened also. When I get my head wrapped around it
all, I'll let you know! Thanks for listening! #badturned-
togood #alliswellbodyandsoul

Heather: *Hey, Erica, glad you're OK!*

Nicole: *Sending hugs!*

39 🍃

Four days after her dinner with Alex at Tuscany Tavern, Tatum received a text message. She dug her phone out of her purse. It was Alex again. Her insides did a little, unbidden flip. She scolded herself for reacting.

She opened the text and read:

Thanks for the forgiveness! Could we go out again? I want to enjoy dinner without having to soothe my conscience with grovelling. What do you say, dinner on Friday night?

Tatum texted back immediately. If she waited and thought very long, she might talk herself out of it.

Sure, I'd like that.

She hoped she wasn't coming across as too eager. But she had to admit, now that the air had cleared, she wouldn't mind getting to know him better.

Friday night Alex picked her up at her house. He'd made reservations at Capital Grille, down the hill. She had never been there but had heard the food was good. Alex put her at ease as soon as she got in the car.

Since Tatum only saw Alex when both were volunteering for MRT, she was taken aback at how nice he looked with casual khakis, a button-down, collared shirt, a leather coat and leather slip-on shoes.

"Hey, you clean up nice!"

Alex laughed. "You look pretty good yourself. Aren't we quite the pair in our black-leather jackets? Have you ever eaten at the Capital Grille? It's one of my favorite downtown restaurants."

"No, I haven't. I hope you can help me choose from the menu."

"How about letting me order for you? Everything there is good, but some of the selections are outstanding. What do you say?"

"Sure, why not. Just don't get too exotic." Tatum grinned.

They traded small talk until the valet came to park the car. Inside, the hostess knew Alex's name. When their waiter came for their order, Alex took over.

"We're going to share the pan-fried calamari with hot cherry peppers, and we'll each have the spinach salad with warm bacon dressing. Tatum will have the filet mignon with the cipollini onions and wild mushrooms, and I'll have the seared tenderloin with butter-poached lobster tails. We'll decide on dessert later." The waiter nodded and left.

Tatum was impressed that he handled himself as well in a fancy restaurant as in the wilderness.

As they waited for their appetizer, Alex posed a question. "Will you promise not to bring up my childish behavior again?" He looked down at the table as he said it. "I just want us to have a nice time getting to know each other better." He looked up hopefully. "Deal?"

Tatum smiled sweetly. "I won't bring up the past—unless it becomes relevant and I have need to remind you of your unreasonable behavior that lasted for months and months!"

"That's not much of a promise, but I'll accept it for now." Alex took a drink of his water. "So why did you decide to move to Evergreen and join MRT? I know bits and pieces but not the whole story."

Where to start? "The girl you see now is not the girl I was for most of my life." She sighed. "After the death of my parents and then the tragedy with Eric, I came to the realization that playing it safe, as I had always done, had gotten me nowhere. So I decided to change." She continued to describe the metamorphosis and her reasons. "I was never much of a risk taker."

Alex leaned forward, appearing interested in her every word. "I would never have believed that about you. You certainly take calculated risks with MRT."

"I know. I'd seen my parents take a risk by buying the Tea and Java du Jour, and then it suddenly became mine." She shook her head at the memory.

"You obviously don't have to work there all the time. Does someone run it for you?"

"The manager who my parents hired does a great job with the day-to-day operation. I help Georgia with the decisions and once in a while I go up for a weekend to work." She smiled as she described the Southern woman who was such a big influence in her life.

The calamari came, halting conversation. Tatum took a bite. "Whoa, that's hot!" She blew gently and fanned her mouth.

Alex laughed. "I should have warned you. It seems to

calm down as you eat more with the marinara sauce."

They concentrated on the food. As they waited for the salad to come, Alex asked her to continue.

"Well, Eric took risk to a whole other level. And I saw how fulfilled he was when he climbed mountains."

"That's a great observation. Mountain climbing really is exhilarating...and fulfilling."

"He got me out on a few practice hikes, and then finally I agreed to climb Mount Bierstadt with him. You know how that turned out. But after I got through some of the grief, I decided I wanted to do something different with the rest of my life. On the recommendation of a friend of mine in Breckenridge, I started training for MRT. That's when I moved to Evergreen." She grinned. "More information than you needed."

The salad and then the entrée came and conversation was again suspended for a time. She continued as they waited to order dessert.

"So, tell me about you. I don't know much except in connection with MRT."

"I'm thirty. I was born in Colorado."

"I'm a native too! An exclusive club."

"I stayed in Colorado for college so I could climb on the weekends. Got my degree in finance from CSU.

"And you own your own insurance business?" That was the little she knew about Alex.

"Yes, I have an insurance company, and the girls in my office can handle almost everything without me. That's why I can go on most calls with MRT." Alex seemed to be considering what to say next when someone close by cleared their throat.

They hadn't noticed the tall, shapely blonde come up to their table. She stood there with her hand on her hip.

"Hi Alex." the woman said, showing all her perfectly white teeth in an expression that was more of a glare than a smile.

Tatum's defense antenna shot up.

"It's been ages. Where have you been keeping yourself?"

Alex stuttered. "Oh, ah, hi, Cheryl."

"Are you going to introduce me to your date?" Cheryl gave the stunned Alex a nudge and he forced a smile at Tatum.

"Tatum, this is Cheryl. Cheryl, Tatum."

Both women waited for Alex to say more. As nothing was forth coming, Cheryl's cold eyes focused on Tatum.

"Alex and I were engaged at one time." She spat out the words. "Fairly recently at that. His explanation is an interesting one. Want to explain, Alex, or shall I tell her?" Cheryl crossed her arms and gave him a mocking sneer.

Alex mumbled something under his breath then looked directly into her eyes. Tatum physically shrank back. This could get ugly. She held her breath.

"We were just getting to that," Alex said. He rose from the table. "Would you care to join us? We're about to order dessert. No? That's too bad. Nice to see you again, Cheryl.... Tatum, I'm suddenly not hungry for dessert. What do you say we leave now?"

Cheryl rolled her eyes and addressed Tatum. "Honey, if you want to know about the real Alex Witt, call me any time." She reached in a pocket, threw a business card on the table and stalked away.

"That went well." Alex let out a loud sigh as they waited for the check. "She is seriously capable of causing a big scene. I'm not being sarcastic."

Tatum nodded but pressed her lips together as she reached for her jacket. Confrontation was not her strong suit. She kept her head down as Alex paid the bill. He took her elbow and they walked out together, silent until they were in the car.

"I wanted to tell you the good things about myself before we got into the not so good." He laughed half-heartedly, trying unsuccessfully to lighten the mood. "This is not how I envisioned the evening. I was going to tell you about my engagement. Fortunately, we hadn't set a wedding date." He drew a deep, loud breath and gazed out the window.

"Alex, you don't owe me an explanation. I thought you handled the situation well. When you're ready to tell me more, I'll listen."

"You and Cheryl are polar opposites." He started the car, still not looking at Tatum. "She loves confrontation, as you could tell." Now he glanced briefly her way. "I don't think she knows how to really connect except in a good fight." He heaved a sigh that sounded like relief. "She moved out of Evergreen when we broke up, and I can tell you this for sure, my life is so much more peaceful. This is the first time I've seen her in over eight months."

"You really don't have to explain."

"I want to. I'll tell you the story. But I have a question for you. Will you go to church with me on Sunday, and then to lunch? I'd like you to meet my family. I usually go to their house after church for a home-cooked meal once a week. My parents love a large crowd around the dining room table for the Sunday meal."

"Um, sure. I have no plans except if I get paged out by MRT—and then you'd get paged out, too, so it wouldn't be a problem anyway. And, Alex, I'm not upset about tonight. I saw how you handle adversity. You did great."

They drove home in relative silence, each in their own thoughts. Neither one knew what to say.

BLOG: September 14
Relevant Ramblings: Meeting the Family

I went to church with Alex on Sunday and enjoyed it immensely. After church we went to his parents' house. There were nine of us around the table. His mom's a wonderful cook. His family aren't believers but seem like good people. They only teased Alex a little about bringing a girl home to meet them. They don't seem to disapprove of his choice. What fun it was being included in a large family. #withthefam

Heather: *Ooohhhh!!!!*

Nicole: *Tell us more!*

BLOG: September 15
Relevant Ramblings: MRT

How does news travel so fast? Thursday night was the bi-weekly training at the cabin, and even though Alex and I didn't walk in together, after our hello the teasing started. It was all good-natured. As soon as the program for the evening started, everyone, including Alex, was a professional. I was certainly off base if I thought it would be different. We haven't talked about it, but from his behavior this evening, I know if we're on a mission I won't get any preferential treatment. I wouldn't want it any other way, really.

We're going out on Friday again, this time here in Evergreen. Might he be trying to avoid running into any more ex-girlfriends? #notsobadbeingteased

40 🍃

On the evening of their dinner date, just as Tatum was opening the door to Alex, both of their pagers went off.

"This was inevitable!" Alex said. "Both being on MRT may put a crimp in our style. I have to respond because I'm team leader for this one, but what about you, Tatum?"

"I'm in. Let me get my keys and coat and I'll meet you at the cabin."

Three hours later, after a short but exciting rescue of an injured hiker in a park in the foothills, they were seated in the Tuscany Tavern for a late dinner of cioppino with garlic toast.

"Tell me about your insurance business," Tatum said between bites.

"I sell all kinds of insurance. Unless I'm with a client, when my pager goes off, I can leave everything with my administrative assistants to handle. Since my office is here in north Evergreen, I can get to the cabin pretty quickly—almost as quickly as you can from your house." He winked at her good-naturedly. "My condo off Louis Ridge Road is convenient too. Since I know when I'm team leader, I schedule appointments around that; then I decide whether I can respond to pages when I'm not team leader."

"Isn't it nice having such a great boss! I have one like that too!"

Again they laughed together.

"I have something else I want to ask," said Tatum. "You told me Eric helped bring you to faith. I'd like to hear about that."

"It's not dramatic, except for maybe the location." He seemed eager to share his story. "I told you Eric and I were in a mountaineering club together. It was loosely formed and just consisted of guys who loved to climb, and we challenged each other to take calculated risks and become better."

When he paused to gather his thoughts, Tatum interjected, "Eric told me a little about it, but not very much."

"In the car on the way to wherever we were going to climb, we would all talk about our interests and somehow Eric always managed to bring the conversation around to God. Some of the guys would roll their eyes and tune out, but I started asking questions. His question to us was always, 'If the unthinkable happened and the mountain conquered us, do you know where you would spend eternity?' Even though expert mountaineers control their risks and know their limits, sometimes accidents happen (as you know). I hadn't lived a bad life; but I knew that the spiritual side was rather neglected."

"So what was so dramatic about the location? Were you on top of a fourteener?"

"Eric and I were climbing in the Mount of the Holy

Cross Wilderness Area alone that day." He stared across the room at nothing. "For some reason something had come up for everyone else that day, and they had canceled."

"Georgia would call that a God incidence."

Alex nodded. "We had stopped for lunch and were looking at the cross in the rocks across the valley and he was explaining again why Jesus died on the cross for me and how I could never be good enough to get into heaven on my own. My soul really responded. I wanted to know where I would spend eternity. He led me in a prayer to ask forgiveness of my sins and for Jesus to be Lord of my life and I've been trying to grow in my faith since then. I have to apologize again for my unchristian-like behavior toward you for so many months."

"I understand more now, and you're forgiven! You know, you don't have to keep apologizing." She smiled. "I'm glad to hear about your spiritual journey, though. Let's order dessert and then how about coming to my house and watch a chick flick with me! It's a Friday night and too early to call it quits." Tatum's hand flew to her mouth. "Oh, my," she giggled, "I'm usually not this forward. If you hate chick flicks, we can watch something else."

"Your house it is and a chick flick it is, only if you agree that the next movie will be a macho kind that I pick out!"

"It's a deal!"

BLOG: September 18
Relevant Ramblings: Movie Night

I haven't had that much fun watching a movie in a long time, if ever! Alex kept up a running dialog making fun of Legally Blonde, the girly movie I picked out. I'm going to have to sharpen my skills to keep up a running dialog when we watch his macho movie. #whatcomesnext

Nicole: *You're not good at sarcasm—let me come along for the next movie and I'll show you how it's done!*

Tatum: *Not on your life!*

41 🍃

The page went out for mutual aid from Park County Search and Rescue. Five teams responded, providing over forty rescuers, Tatum among them, to help a stranded pair on thirteen-thousand foot Mount Rosalie. The rapidly accumulating snow was fierce and the storm was moving in faster than expected, so the rescue teams rallied to ascend the five miles up the mountain. This rescue required survival gear for both the victims and the rescue team members. The snowmobiles couldn't make it more than a mile, and the stranded hikers were above timberline where the snow was coming down even heavier.

Tatum was in the second wave behind the hasty team, and the white-out blizzard conditions with the wind and snow made it slow going. Fortunately, the victims had been able to relay their GPS coordinates, or it would have been like trying to find a white glove in a sea of white snow.

"You know, this is one of those times the victim truly had an accident." The team leader, Jerry, briefed the group as they started their climb. "She fell, and we know there are broken bones. They knew weather was coming in, but all the safety precautions go out the window when there's a fall." The wind took away the rest of his words, but at least Tatum caught that much.

Other snatches of conversation came with each short lull in the storm, when it seemed to catch its breath to blow even harder.

"Hope they have survival gear and training," said one team member. "This blizzard's gaining in strength. I can't imagine how hard the wind's blowing above timberline," said another.

Tatum redoubled her efforts to climb through the intensifying blizzard.

Four-and-a-half hours later, the hasty team reached the victim. Christiana was with them. Then Tatum's group arrived carrying the litter. Already Christiana was engaging the victim in conversation—she'd discovered the victim's interest in ultra marathons. Her name was Sierra.

"Oh, and do you have extra clothes for my friend and hero?" Sierra asked softly, indicating Sierra's friend Jesse. "She gave me almost all her outer layers to keep me warm. She must be freezing."

Tatum was touched that someone in great pain would think of another.

They strapped Sierra into the litter and readied themselves for the enormous task of descending the mountain with their load. The wind had increased to fifty miles per hour. Carrying a loaded litter down a mountain was hard enough without the extra concern of keeping it from being caught by the wind and flying out of their hands. Even more difficult for Tatum was hearing Sierra's cries of pain. She sidled over and jogged beside the litter.

"Sierra, I'm Tatum. Keep breathing—in, out, in, out."

As Sierra breathed the way Tatum directed, slowly in and out, she seemed to calm.

"I heard you talking about running the Leadville 100," said Tatum. "I can't imagine running for twenty-four hours straight. How did you do it? I'm sure you had to walk some of it."

She answered weakly. "It took me twenty-nine hours. I hope to improve my time next year."

Tatum could barely hear her but kept asking questions to engage Sierra.

"Thank you for coming." Sierra's voice became even quieter. She was now relaxing more into the stretcher.

"We love what we do," Tatum said with feeling. "Thank you for being such a good patient. And don't worry. I'm planning to stay by your side."

A few rescuers went ahead of the rest to break a trail through the deep snow. This gave the litter handlers an easier path to follow. Tatum was off trail, though, staying at the victim's side. She knew the encouragement to breathe through the pain was helping the brave girl, so she kept up as much as possible.

But she was sinking thigh deep in the snow. She had to do what hikers call post-holing, which was agonizing. To take her mind off the pain of lifting each leg high, over and over, Tatum whispered a cadence to herself. "Lift high, step down, lift high, step down." *Is there a graceful way to do this? Nope; sinking a fence post into a deep hole isn't a graceful exercise, at least not when the post is your leg. Especially when you have to lift the post straight out again then sink it down into another hole. First one, then the other, over and over. I have no choice but to continue, no matter how awkward it is or how much it hurts.* "Lift high, step down, lift high, step down."

After some time of moving slowly through the snow this way, Tatum began to feel that she couldn't go on. The litter carriers switched places with the rescuers who were ahead breaking the trail, but no one relieved Tatum. She gritted her teeth and somehow, between encouraging Sierra and her self talk, even with burning thigh muscles, she endured.

After an hour, taking care not to spill their human cargo, they made it below timberline. The combination of wind at their back and steep terrain made it difficult going. In the relative safety of the trees, they stopped to transfer Sierra to a more stable litter for quicker transport. Tatum stayed by her side trying, between her muffled cries, and as the rescuers did their job, to calm her.

"Good job, Sierra. You're handling this like a trooper." The wind was less fierce in the trees, but she still had to yell to make herself heard.

Tatum could only imagine the effort the other rescuers had to exert to get Sierra from the first litter to the more stable one without causing too much extra pain. Park County SAR had taken the lead in the transfer with minimal fanfare. After cocooning her for stabilization, six people lifted her from one litter to the other.

After a half hour in the trees, which felt like hours to Tatum, they reached the road. There they attached the

litter to a snowmobile for quicker transport to the waiting ambulance. Tatum watched as the snowmobile has-
tened the litter carrying Sierra to the ambulance a mile
away. Tatum still had that mile to walk; but walking in
the snowmobile's track and at a much slower pace, she
finally made it to the vehicles. All in all, the rescue had
taken twelve hours.

Connecting with Sierra, and helping her through
her ordeal, brought Tatum a deep sense of satisfaction.
More than ever she understood the sentiments heard so
often from her fellow team members: "This is what we
live for."

Now to get warm. And home to bed...exhausted.

BLOG: October 20
Relevant Ramblings: Blizzard Rescue

The rescue yesterday on Mount Rosalie was as harrowing a rescue as I've yet experienced. We responded
to a request for mutual aid from Park County Search
and Rescue in blizzard conditions.

Two people were on Mount Rosalie above twelve
thousand feet. One of them had fallen and had broken
bones. But the conditions were so bad with such strong
winds that, if they hadn't sent the GPS coordinates, we
could have got close to them and never known.

If I never again have to post-hole to get through

deep snow, that will be too soon. And I hope I never again have to spend that long in blizzard conditions or shiver so hard my teeth chatter.

But I can't describe how rewarding it is to help in this way to make a difference in people's lives. #outofthecomfortzoneandlovingit

Heather: *I understand people wanting to go into the mountains. But why would they go if they knew it would be bad weather?*

Tatum: *If one of them hadn't fallen, they would have gotten off the mountain before the snow. The storm just moved in too quickly.*

Nicole: *Tatum, that's amazing.*

42 🍃

The day in Evergreen dawned clear and cold. It would be even colder in the high country, but with the bright sun it wouldn't stay that way. Three adventurous, twenty-something men set out early with their snowboards, setting their sights on the ridge top, hoping to make the first tracks in the pristine snow.

By noon the weather had warmed. Conditions became exactly right for a perfect storm, the kind that can cause avalanches. Snow, wind, sun and snowboarders: a potentially deadly combination. The exuberant guys ignored the signs posted that warned of danger. They shouted and laughed as they high fived each other at the top of the ridge. They owned their little world, they were doing what they loved, and nothing would deter them. They'd hiked a long ways up, and they weren't going to give up the bragging rights they knew would be theirs for boarding from this particular ridge to the bottom of the bowl.

Each of the three started separately down the untouched snowfield. The first boarder carved his way down with perfect precision then rode to the edge of the field to watch his friend. The second one stayed in the same track, and when he joined his friend and looked back up the slope, it appeared to be only one track. They high fived, then turned to watch their friend.

They had agreed to travel the same path down into the bowl, but this third man, usually the renegade, decided to take a different route. When he got about halfway down, the slope gave way. The two friends stared in disbelief as the snow billowed into a white cloud and swallowed up their friend. Their feelings of invincibility melted. The snow raced past them with the force of a tsunami. No one—not the strongest, extreme athlete—could out run the avalanche.

The mountains' rules always hold precedence, but these snowboarders chose to defy the rules, and the last man took it a step farther. He set off the wall of white that broke loose and completely engulfed him. The first two reported later they didn't hear the avalanche release, and it only sounded like a whoosh of air as it passed them, carrying their friend.

The page came at about twelve noon on a Saturday, reporting a party of three boarders, two accounted for, one missing. Clear Creek County dispatch called MRT immediately. This was definitely a Code 3.

Tatum now felt confident enough to respond to this call. She had done numerous field trainings and had just completed a mock mission for avalanche response.

What would it be, a rescue or a recovery? Tatum was one of the first to arrive at the cabin. Alex would be the scene commander. Even before they got in the vehicles, their bodies were pumping adrenaline.

As many as could fit in the main vehicle clambered in. With lights and siren, it took off. Others followed with lights flashing. A second rescue vehicle pulling two snowmobiles in a trailer joined the caravan. As soon as they reached the trailhead, the hasty team set out on the snowmobiles toward the slide area.

The early spring sky couldn't have been more blue. The sun had warmed the top layer of snow, a potential hazard. A secondary avalanche was a definite possibility. Alex directed each MRT responder to their locations. They knew the procedures. The reporting party had last seen their boarding buddy downhill from there. The two friends had started a systematic search with their probes. But the debris field was two hundred feet wide and three hundred feet long, and they hadn't gotten very far.

"All beacons to transmit for beacon check," Alex directed.

Tatum and the others turned their avalanche beacons to transmit. As each one was checked, the rescuer would raise their hand until all hands were raised. All beacons were working correctly.

Reassured, Alex gave the order. "All beacons to receive." As soon as the victim was found, all beacons would be turned back to transmit, to be prepared in case another avalanche broke loose.

Fortunately, the three snowboarders all carried beacons. However, because they had mismatched beacon manufacturers, their beacons kept giving false signals. Alex speculated that the beacons were transmitting and sending at different rates, confusing the snow boarders. They might as well not have had them.

Alex laid out the pattern for the probe line they would use below the place the two boarders thought they'd seen their friend go down. Looking for something solid under the snow, they all punched their probes into the snow, each hoping their probe would find something near the surface. Tatum was assigned an area near the northwest edge of the snowfield.

She probed, hoping with every plunge to hit resistance. Then she heard a soft *whumpf* farther up and to her left. Before she had time to understand what she had heard, another, smaller avalanche let loose with the speed of a racehorse in the final stretch of the race. The powder cloud gained speed, swept her up, and carried her downward.

MRT now had two victims! They rushed to the second avalanche. This was one of their own! Suddenly the search became personal. Of course Tatum had her beacon activated—but set for receive, not send!

Alex chose to do something unorthodox. He shouted for everyone to turn their beacons to send, hoping against hope they could hear Tatum's beacon receiving their signals.

Near the bottom of the second slide area, Christiana spotted a single glove. She shouted to Alex and then took off, sliding down the snow in her haste. She started probing as fast as she safely could. In everyone's mind loomed the possibility of setting off a third avalanche.

Only three minutes had passed since Alex realized Tatum was the victim, but it felt like an eternity. He prayed out loud as he probed.

"Oh, Lord. Please, Lord, please." He continued his litany over and over under his breath. He didn't care who heard him.

Christiana felt a resistance against her probe, lifted it, then probed again.

"I've found something! I've found something!" she screamed. Jerry arrived first, then Alex. All three carried shovels and began to dig furiously. Within ten seconds they uncovered what had resisted their probes: Tatum, head downward, feet upward, one foot at an unnatural angle against her back.

Alex knelt and dug with his hands around her head to uncover her face. He kept up with his mantra of "Oh Lord, Oh Lord, Oh Lord."

Other rescuers arrived.

"She isn't breathing!" Alex said and immediately started mouth-to-mouth resuscitation.

Awareness came slowly to Tatum.

The sky is so blue.... What am I doing on my back in the snow? Brrrr! And why does my leg hurt so much?

She saw people, all intently staring at her. The one closest to her was Alex. He was asking her a question. She stared, uncomprehending.

"Tatum," Alex tried again, breathing hard, almost

panting. "Can you hear me? You gave us quite a scare! Are you all right?"

Realization of the situation gradually returned to Tatum.

Alex waited impatiently.

Panic rose inside her. "The avalanche! Did we find the boarder?" she cried as loud as she could.

Alex smiled. "That's what I love about you, always thinking of others!"

What? I must have imagined that. But it sounded nice. Then out loud, "Why does my leg hurt so much? Could you help me straighten it out? Can you help me up? My word, why all the fuss?"

The litter had arrived. Despite embarrassment, Tatum had to let the team package her and move her to the vehicles.

Then they continued probing for their first victim. Their "avy" beacons were back on receive mode, though they weren't very positive they did any good because of the report from the two friends. It was now almost ninety minutes since the call came in and the chances of finding him alive were remote. Finding an avalanche victim alive after an hours-long burial was rare but not unheard of. Rescuers never assume a victim is dead. They keep up the pace, hoping for a miracle.

And a miracle it was! A shout went up! They had found the snowboarder! They dug as fast as possible and got his face uncovered.

Amazingly, he was alive due in part to the Avalung he carried, a device to help him breathe under snow. It moved the carbon monoxide down, underneath him, rather than into the small air pocket around his face. Having the presence of mind to get the mouthpiece into his mouth as the avalanche carried him down the mountain faster than a roller coaster, saved his life.

The first order of business was always to make sure the victim was breathing, then address the hypothermia. He had been buried for over an hour and his cold tomb leached all heat from his body. His left tibia and fibula were broken. As they packaged him into the second litter, they stabilized his leg. Once his leg was wrapped in the "bean bag" that served to stabilize, they also wrapped him in sleeping bags to try to bring his temperature up. A successful outcome! And a great relief for all, including Tatum.

43 🍃

Hours later Tatum was home sitting on her sofa, her foot in a large boot. She had never broken a bone before, so this was all new. The crutches rested against the sofa next to her. Alex was in the kitchen preparing sandwiches. It was nice to have someone waiting on her, but she feared the prospect of boredom. She grabbed her cell phone and called Georgia, who answered on the first ring.

"Hi, Tatum. How's my girl?"

That beautiful Southern drawl filled Tatum with a sense of home. "Where do I begin?" She paused. "First of all, I have a question for you. May I come and stay in your guest room for an indefinite period of time?"

"What are you talking about? Spill it, girl! But wait. This sounds bad. Do I need to sit down first?" Georgia wasn't above using drama.

"I broke my ankle. Alex will drive me if—"

"Of course you can stay here! You know my answer, girl! Y'all just get here soon or my imagination will run away with me!"

"Thanks, Georgia, you're a peach! See you in two hours!"

On the drive from Evergreen to Breckenridge, in the comfortable silence Alex cleared his throat. "*Ahem.* Uh, Tatum, I'd like to talk to you about something."

She watched his face and waited for him to continue. It wasn't like Alex to be tongue tied.

He kept his eyes on the road but found his voice. "As we were looking for you after the second avalanche, I realized my life wouldn't be complete without you. More than anything I wanted to tell you...that I love you." He glanced at her then looked back at the road. "You don't have to respond. I just...want you to know."

Tatum looked out the window into the darkness. A pregnant silence hung between them. She answered slowly. "Alex, I enjoy our time together and I look forward to seeing you or hearing from you every day. I really like you. Is that sufficient for now?"

"Yes. I'll be satisfied with that...for now." He grinned slightly and his shoulders relaxed. "Now tell me more about Georgia, so I know what to expect."

🍃 🍃 🍃

By nine o'clock Georgia, Erica, Tatum, and Alex were sitting around Georgia's kitchen table with the inevitable coffee, soup, and snacks; fruit with dip, bread, and cookies. A knock sounded at the door, and without missing a beat, in walked Mose.

Georgia looked sheepish. "I want Mose hear this first hand, so I won't have to explain it all later." She glanced around as if looking for an escape from the ribbing that was coming. "Alex, this here is Mose, who brought our girl home after the first kidnapping."

Was Georgia blushing?

"Sit down, Mose, and let Tatum tell us her story.

And don't change the subject, Tatum. Tell us what happened."

"Hey, Mose." Tatum couldn't help it. "Has Georgia invited you over so much that now you just walk in?"

Georgia blushed.

Tatum and Erica laughed.

"Aw, our Southern girl is sweet on someone."

Georgia pretended to fan herself in a fluster but gave Mose a coy glance. He, enjoying the fun, gave Georgia an obvious and exaggerated wink.

Now Georgia waved her hands over her head. "Enough already!"

"This happens more than you know, Tatum!" Erica couldn't resist a small jab, too.

"I'm getting very aggravated with a few people around this table! Alex, since Tatum is being so difficult, would y'all please tell us what happened to her—"

"I'll tell you!" Tatum said through her laughter. Then she told her story, describing MRT's call to the avalanche earlier in the day and then the second avalanche. Alex filled in his part of the rescue.

BLOG:

November 8
Relevant Ramblings: Avalanche!

Yesterday I went on my first real avalanche rescue, and I ended up being rescued! All the attention made me feel a little foolish. We were there to rescue a snowboarder who was caught in a snow slide—who, by the way, is recovering from a broken leg and hypothermia. I, on the other hand, was only buried about five minutes when Christiana found me, but they tell me I wasn't breathing. I have no recollection of anything until I was on my back looking at the sky. Chris told me Alex gave me mouth to mouth to get me breathing again. Wish I could remember that! :)

I'm now a temporary resident of one of Georgia's guest rooms. I'm not going to mind being waited on by my own personal Southern Mother Hen. But I'm sure I'll get cabin fever. I did bring along a stack of books I've been meaning to read. After I'm off these crutches and out of this boot, they tell me I have to have physical therapy before my ankle is back to normal. I'll miss going out with MRT on rescues. But as soon as I can drive, I'll at least go to the trainings. I'm going to miss seeing Alex regularly, but he promised to call every day and said he'll come to Breck when he can.

I need a long talk with Georgia—maybe she can help me sort out my feelings for Alex Witt. I'm a little afraid to let myself love again. I seem to lose those I love the most. Would I lose him? Georgia will know what I should do.

More to come!

#rescuerturnedvictim #happyending

Heather: *Now I know an avalanche victim/survivor!*

Nicole: *Heather and I plan to visit you soon.*

EPILOGUE 🍃

BLOG: November 29
Relevant Ramblings: Hug-a-Tree

During my three weeks at Georgia's we had great talks—most importantly, about Alex. She asked me how I felt about him, which was easy to answer. He treats me like a precious treasure. Who wouldn't love that? Do I love him? I think I'm scared to. She said if God brought us together, He will guide and protect. I remember a long time ago when I complained about "not knowing," she said if we knew everything, then where would trust come in.

So, about the title of this post. It's the name of the program I've been teaching to scouting groups and grade school classes. It teaches kids that if they're lost, they should stay in one place: hug a tree! Since my ankle still needs rehabilitation, and I can't go out on missions, at least I can do something productive. And I'm actually enjoying it! Those kids are priceless!

OK, now back to Alex. Now I know how he feels about me. I need to trust God with my future—our future—and let him know how I feel about him. Trust. God helped me conquer mountain-sized fears. Surely I can trust Him with this. Sometimes I have to remind myself that God is interested in every area of my life. Stay tuned!

#relevantramblings #conqueringmountains

ACKNOWLEDGMENTS

This is a work of fiction. But my inspiration came from a real rescue team, Alpine Rescue Team, in Evergreen, Colorado. My idea of their rescue world, I'm sure, falls far short of reality. Thanks, ART, for doing what you do when someone is having a bad day in the mountains. Thank you, Paula, Vicky, and Shirley for all your help. And a huge thank-you to my publisher, Cathy, of Cladach Publishing. You made this possible.

BOOK CLUBS AND GROUPS

Discussion Questions by Paula Perkins

1. Tatum had a fear of taking chances. She wasn't willing to climb mountains with Eric because of that fear. How was she ultimately able to conquer that fear? What are some of the things you fear? How have you faced your fears?

2. Tatum thought about the loss of her parents every day. While it was hard for her, she was willing to share her thoughts with Eric's mom. If you had experienced a similar loss would you have been able to share with someone not close to you? Why or why not?

3. Tatum thought she knew Eric until Erica appeared. Why do you think Eric didn't tell Tatum about Erica? What would your reaction have been if someone you knew well kept that kind of secret from you?

4. Georgia kept Eric's secret by taking the envelope he gave her and not telling Tatum. Do you think she was doing the right thing by keeping the secret from Tatum? What would you have done if you were in Georgia's place?

5. Tatum had experienced so much "bad." But after meeting Erica she began to believe that good could come

out of a difficult situation. Have you experienced a difficult situation? What good thing came out of the experience?

6. Tatum was very excited about becoming part of Mountain Rescue and the changes it would bring to her life. What did you think of her decision? What is a decision that you have made that changed your life (for good or bad)?

7. Tatum thought Erica was very creative with her ideas for the tea shop. Did you like the ideas? Do you think the ideas will be successful or unsuccessful? Why or Why not? Do you consider yourself a creative person?

8. Alex's apology took Tatum by surprise, and it was clearly hard for Alex to make it. What are your thoughts about the way Alex treated Tatum? Have you ever been in a similar situation where you had to forgive someone you felt had mistreated you?

9. Erica did not seem to have suffered significantly from the trauma of being pushed over a cliff. Why do you think she was able to recover so quickly? How easy would it be for you to recover from that kind of an event?

10. Tatum was sharing with scouting groups and grade school classes what to do if they got lost. It is called Hug a Tree. Why is this such an important rule? Describe why this could be a hard rule to follow.

ABOUT THE AUTHOR

Jeanie Flierl lives and works (as a business owner) in Evergreen, Colorado. She loves people, the mountains, and good stories.

Born and raised in Milwaukee, Wisconsin, Jeanie moved to Colorado during her twenties because of her love of the mountains. After home-schooling her children, she devoted her energies to her retail store that sells quality chocolates, nuts, and candies.

Jeanie is married to Denis. Together, they have worked in marriage ministry for over twenty-five years, teaching communication skills. They have spoken at small conferences and MOPS (Moms of Preschoolers) groups on subjects related to marriage.

Jeanie's greatest joy is spending time with her seven grandchildren, three daughters and three sons-in-law.

To Conquer a Mountain is Jeanie's debut novel. She is currently writing a sequel.

Find and follow Jeanie online at:
http://www.facebook.com/JeanieFlierlAuthor/